DEATHTOLL

The Broslin Creek Series, a reader favorite, began with the story of Kate and Murph (an eye-witness running from a deadly assassin and the soldier who steps between her and a violent death). DEATHTOLL, the last book, features the same couple. Kate and Murph are back in Broslin Creek, thinking they're safe, their worst enemy dead. But soon people around Kate begin to die under suspicious circumstances, and she and Murph must face the terrible realization that Asael followed them home, and not only are their lives in danger, but also the lives of the townspeople who took Kate in years ago.

DEATHTOLL

Dana Marton

DEATHTOLL
Copyright © 2021 by Dana Marton.

All rights reserved. Published in the United States of America. No part of this book may be used or reproduced in any manner whatsoever without the written permission of the author.
http://www.danamarton.com

First Edition: 2021
ISBN-13: 9781940627458

This book is a work of fiction. Names, characters, places and incidents are products of the author's imagination or are used fictitiously. Any resemblance to actual events or locales or persons, living or dead, is entirely coincidental.

DEDICATION

My sincere gratitude to Sarah, Diane, Linda, and Toni for all of their brilliant help. And many thanks to my wonderful reader friends in the Dana Marton Book Club on Facebook. I don't know what I would do without you.

CHAPTER ONE

Kate

Don't ever *dance like nobody's watching.*

Because somebody will be watching. And they'll be smirking. And then you'll have to choose between dying of embarrassment or murdering them. And what kind of choices are those? Damn bad.

Kate Bridges was browsing the Broslin Farm Market, scrutinizing cookie labels and wiggling to the *90s Hits* soundtrack from the loudspeakers, when she looked up and saw Murph Dolan coming toward her.

Because life likes to ambush the shit out of you, just when you least expect it. She wasn't supposed to run into him for another hour yet, at Hope Hill, at work.

"Nice moves." His raspy voice went straight to her heart.

Every freaking time.

So did his eyes—the color of the finest dark chocolate—as they filled with feral hunger for a second before he shuttered his gaze. Then there were his muscles, flexing as he pushed his cart. Muscles she'd *licked*…

Kate's visceral reaction to him was a primal response to the man who'd kept her safe and made her body melt in bed. And in any number of other places: on the kitchen table, against the wall, backseat of the car, shower, bathtub, etc., etc.

Don't think about Murph naked!

Easier said than done when he was standing *this* close with that former soldier, ex-cop, still-in-excellent-shape body. He probably worked out just to torture her.

He'd been the last man she'd seen naked. And it'd been months ago, and—

"Here is a universal truth of life." She slammed the lid on thinking how much she missed...*things* she wasn't going to admit missing.

She aimed for an unfailingly neutral tone. "The second you find a product you like, stores will let you have it maybe twice before it's discontinued. They'll dangle it in front of your nose just enough so you fall in love and can really mourn the loss."

Should not have said "fall in love."

She winced.

Please respond with something light, then move along. Don't bring up anything that'll make my heart bleed in aisle three, dammit.

Disappointment flashed in his eyes, as if he was thinking *Is grocery store stock really what you want to talk about?* But then he played along. "So, you know you're gluten sensitive for sure?"

The acute sense of relief settled over Kate like her weighted blanket, which she had to use since she'd left Murph, so she could get at least *some* sleep without him.

To give her eyes something to do other than mournfully stare at him, she checked the list of ingredients on another box of cookies. "I don't know what else to try. I've already given up dairy."

"You could see a doctor."

"It's not that bad. My stomach is just off." She slid the box back on the shelf and picked another one, all-natural, organic, almond flour cookies that cost a fortune. Everything in the special-diet aisle did.

"I wouldn't recommend dietary restrictions for anyone." She used the box to gesture at the $7.99 price tag on the shelf. "Unless they win the lottery first."

Instead of agreeing with her on that, Murph slid his gaze to her torso. Lingered. "You lost a lot of weight."

"I'm starting to gain it back." She dropped the cookies into her cart, appreciating that at least they smelled like real vanilla, then pulled her phone from her pocket to check the time. "I need to go. I don't want to be late for work."

"Why are you grocery shopping in the morning?"

"Picking up a birthday treat for a patient. Might as well grab a few other things."

"You have your car back from the shop?"

"Tomorrow. Emma is driving me. She flew up from LA."

His eyebrows twitched as his eyes met hers again. "When?"

"Day before yesterday."

His mouth—that had done unspeakable things to the most sensitive parts of her body—tightened. "Were you going to tell me?"

Murph had always treated her family as his own. He'd gone to LA with Kate every time she visited. He and Emma had hit it off from their first meeting. Of course, he would want to see Emma. But just then, inviting Murph over was beyond Kate. She was still working up to it.

Silent reproach thickened the air between them for a second, then two.

And then, his expression closed, Murph moved past Kate. "Tell your sister I said hi."

She fought the urge to follow him as the tide followed the moon. *Habit.* They used to shop together, going down the aisles side by side. They used to do everything together.

Kate rocked on the balls of her feet. "See you at the office!"

He looked back. She should just have kept her mouth shut and let him go. She clenched her jaw.

Don't say anything. Please.

Because he knew her, he heard her silent plea. He simply nodded at her before he walked away.

And then she could finally breathe. *Sweet chocolate-covered cherries.*

She hurried in the opposite direction, toward Emma, who just turned the corner with a bag of carrots and avocadoes for her breakfast smoothies.

Her sister craned her neck. "Was that Murph?"

A twenty-something guy trailed behind her like a puppy. An almost comical look of disappointment crossed the guy's face when he realized Emma was with Kate. He'd probably been hoping to chat her up.

He moved on with a barely stifled, mournful sigh.

Kate sympathized. *No love to be found in aisle three today, buddy.*

Emma noticed none of that. She'd always been oblivious to the effect her long legs, enviable raven hair, and overall LA glamour had on men. She was…shiny. No, *radiant* was a better word. Then again, she did work out like a professional and took her smoothie boosters as seriously as a heart attack, which, obviously, she was never going to have.

"Is there anything more annoying than ridiculously beautiful women who don't realize they're beautiful?" Kate punctuated the question with a long-suffering sigh.

Emma looked around. "What? Why? I'm not beautiful."

Kate sent a pointed glance toward the admirer who just then walked into a shelf because he was still looking back.

"Is there anything more annoying than ridiculously beautiful women who don't realize they're beautiful *and* insist that they aren't?" Kate amended. "*And* they're good at math? You're my little sister and I love you, but if you discover a sudden special talent for art or music, I'm going to have to let you go."

Emma rolled her eyes. And, really, she was so good at it, it could almost be considered an art form. "Mind if I go and say hi to Murph?"

Now?

"Would you mind, not to?" Kate felt like an idiot for asking, but she did it for self-preservation. "Not right now? I'm just having a weird morning." A weird couple of days. "The lack of sleep is starting to get to me. I feel like…" She let out a frustrated groan.

"Like?" Emma stepped aside so they could move on to the next aisle.

"I don't know. This stupid insomnia is beginning to affect my mental state. I keep thinking I'm being watched. You know that weird feeling at the back of your neck?" Kate flashed an I'm-stupid-right smile. "I've spent so many years running and hiding. I have trouble fully settling into safe and normal."

Emma watched her with concern. "Being vigilant all the time, living your life on guard, is not a good way to live. You have to learn to relax."

"I'm not sure if I know how."

"It's literally your job. You make people relax for a living."

"And that's the irony of it." Kate forced a smile and stopped in front of the shelf that held an overwhelming variety of tea. She picked the nearest box and dropped it into her cart, then headed to the checkout. "Let's get out of here."

Emma kept up. "So, things are pretty bad between you and Murph?"

"No." He wasn't in any of the cashier lines, thank God. "Honestly, like I said, having an off morning." Kate pressed a hand to her stomach, then dropped it. Working with Murph was *not* giving her an ulcer. And if it was, then there was her answer.

"Fine," Emma said.

The hurt tone sliced through Kate. "Listen—"

"I guess we're not that close anymore, right? You no longer tell me things. I guess I just need to be grateful that you finally chose to tell us that you weren't *dead*."

"We've talked about this. I couldn't tell you any sooner." Kate reached for Emma's hand, but her fingertips brushed air as Emma pulled away. "I begged them to let me contact you and Mom and Dad."

Emma fixed her gaze on the shopping cart's wheels as they moved forward with the line, checkout scanners beeping around them. "I *grieved* you."

"I know. I'm sorry."

"For four and a half years, I thought you were dead," Emma said under her breath, low enough so the people around them wouldn't hear. "Mom and Dad thought you were dead."

God, were they going to have this conversation in the checkout line? Apparently. *Okay. Fine.* It had been brewing for a while. They'd spent way too much time tiptoeing around the topic since Kate had come back. They couldn't keep that up forever.

"Because I wanted you safe," she whispered.

"Because you didn't trust us to keep your secret."

"It wasn't up to me."

"The FBI couldn't have stopped you from sending a postcard!"

This last sentence was hissed, fractionally louder than the rest, loud enough so the woman in front of them in line—a frazzled mom with two toddlers who were trying to climb her legs—glanced back. So did the cashier guy.

When Kate refused to meet their eyes, eventually they returned to their own business again. The woman unloaded her cart, promising the kids candy as soon as they hit the car. The cashier dragged each item over the scanner.

Emma filled her lungs and opened her mouth, and Kate had to cut her off, say something, *anything*, because their current argument was so not grocery store checkout line material.

"Murph proposed."

A whiplash double take. "When?" Emma's eyelashes twitched she stared so hard. "What did you say?"

"Three months ago. I had a panic attack."

"Oh my God. You said *no*?"

"I ran off to my office to hyperventilate."

"What did Murph say to that?"

"Nothing. I asked him to give me some time and space. He's respecting my wishes."

"I can't believe you didn't tell me." Emma shook her head.

Probably not the best time to mention that Murph had proposed before, and Kate had said yes, and then she'd reneged, because she didn't want to get married in witness protection, with none of their family there.

They moved forward another few steps in line.

She tried for a lighter tone with "How long are you planning on being mad at me? Just so I know how to plan?"

They'd had fights before, shouting matches even, and then they would make up, be best friends again.

This time, Emma's face remained humorless. "He proposed

11

three months ago, and you didn't say a word all those times we talked on the phone. I guess while you were *dead*, you forgot that we were *sisters*."

"I'm sorry." Kate reached the conveyor belt and began unloading their cart. "I know you must have felt abandoned when I...left," she ended up saying instead of *faked my death*.

"You're the one with abandonment issues." Emma's response was quick with impatience. "I don't even remember anything before Mom and Dad."

Kate had been in middle school by the time they'd been adopted. She'd gone through several foster parent transfers. Emma had been a toddler. She'd been spared some of the trauma, at least, and Kate was glad for that.

The cashier, a previously bored-looking high school kid, rung up their purchases, openly listening. Openly checking out Emma too. Age gap or no, Emma looked like a comic book heroine with all that hair, piercing dark eyes, her body trim in the right places, curvy in others. She wore high boots, chunky heels, with her short skirt. Her current, stormy I-don't-take-shit-from-no-one expression made her into a Comic-Con Kick-Ass Babe, and apparently teen boy catnip.

"That's a lot of cookies," she told Kate, in a tone that made it clear the conversation was not over.

"Betty is coming over tonight for a cup of tea."

"Your neighbor?"

"She had me over a bunch of times when I was moving and didn't have the kitchen fully set up yet. My turn. She's sweet. I get her prescriptions filled, she signs for my deliveries, if I'm not home. We're both women living alone. We watch out for each other."

Resentment tightened Emma's eyes again.

Kate felt like a ten-thousand-pound elephant tiptoeing through a minefield. "What?"

"You're making friends here," Emma said with as much disgust as if Kate were kicking puppies.

"Give me a break. I have a long list of things I feel guilty about, but I refuse to feel guilty about putting down some roots for the first time in my life. I live here. I work here. I bought a house here. Broslin is my home now."

"Thousands of miles from your *family*." Emma's gaze hardened another notch. "I could see it when you were with Murph. You deserve love. I was happy for you. He's a great guy. But you aren't even with him anymore. Why can't you come back to LA?"

Kate paid the openly listening cashier. "I have responsibilities here. It doesn't mean I don't love you, or care about you, or miss you like crazy."

Emma flashed a cold look before she turned away to finish loading their bags into the cart.

"I'm so glad you came up to see me," Kate said to start their disastrous conversation over. "I don't want to fight the whole time you're here."

Emma marched forward, the lovelorn checkout boy casting a heartbroken look after her. "It hurts when you don't tell me things," she said when Kate caught up with her. "I don't like being treated like a stranger. We used to share everything."

"I didn't tell you about Murph because I feel like I've made a mess of things." The glass doors slid aside, and they walked out into the crisp fall air. "I'm still so unsure about so many things."

"Murph is in love with you. How obvious can a guy be?"

Kate stopped short to let a blue minivan go by. "I'm thinking about going back to therapy."

"You should."

"It's not all in my head. We do have real issues."

They loaded the groceries into Emma's white Honda Civic, an airport rental.

"Like what?"

Kate didn't respond until they were in the car, Emma driving.

"I was running for my life when we met, hiding in a stranger's house. Murph had no idea his brother rented out the place behind his back while he was overseas with the Reserves."

"Imagine that. Siblings keeping secrets from each other," Emma said in a loaded tone, then added, "When Murph came home, he took it all in stride because he's a good guy. He let you stay, and he protected you. He freaking *shot* the idiot who was after you. Here is a man who *killed* for you. He is movie hero material.

How are you having doubts about him? You lived like an engaged couple for three years in Ohio, in witness protection."

"Because we had to. How do I know what we felt was real and not some codependent bullshit due to forced proximity? Or Stockholm Syndrome."

"You do not have Stockholm Syndrome. Murph wasn't keeping you captive."

"Circumstances were."

Resentment hardened Emma's eyes all over again. "You have no idea how weird it is that you had this whole life I know almost nothing about, while we were all thinking you were dead in the cemetery. We freaking visited your grave. Brought flowers. I talked to you in heaven!"

"I explained why it had to happen that way. I was an eyewitness to murder. The only person who could identify the hitman. He tracked me down and fricking shot at me. I crashed my car."

"And you decided to let everyone think you died." Emma's tone held a chill that put the weather outside to shame.

"The FBI decided. Just until they caught Asael."

"You agreed."

"What if, next time, you were in the car with me? What if, next time, it was a firebomb at the house, with Mom and Dad inside?"

Emma said nothing, just stared at the road ahead.

Kate sighed. "Being on the run, hiding, was no fun. By the time I came to Broslin, I'd lived under half a dozen false identities, in all different places. Then the hitman's partner tracked me down anyway."

"That Mordocai guy? What I still don't get is, why didn't he tell Asael he found you?"

"The FBI said Mordocai wanted to make me a surprise gift." The thought sent a chill down Kate's spine, as if a ghost was tracing her vertebrae with an icicle.

"You should have told us you were alive. At least after Murph took out Mordocai."

"Asael was still out there. I had to keep on the run."

"Murph left everything to go with you, to protect you. You

realize he would have spent the rest of his life in hiding with you, keeping you safe?"

"But can't you see how unfair that would have been to him?"

"So now that Asael is finally gone, explosion, *bam*, pink mist, you just dump Murph because you don't need him anymore?"

"It's not like that."

"I really thought you two were in love."

"Me too, but …" Kate turned to look out the side window for a moment, at the houses that whooshed by. "I can't tell if what we have is a healthy relationship or some weird codependent mess. When we left Ohio, I didn't even consider going back to LA." *Ah, dammit.* She shouldn't have said that. She pressed on. "I came with Murph to his home, to Broslin. We started Hope Hill. At least in Ohio, I had a separate job. Here, we've been living together *and* working together, in each other's pockets twenty-four-seven. I need some distance. I need to at least have my own place. If we get married, it's forever. So, I want to make sure we're both really choosing it."

"You have some serious attachment issues, you know that, right? You doubt your feelings too much."

"That's what being bounced around in foster care does to kids. I'm working through it, all right?"

Emma drove in silence for several seconds. "I'm sorry you got such a bum deal. I feel like I skated off scot-free." She glanced at Kate before returning her attention to the road. "I wish I could remember more."

"Nothing there worth remembering." Just endless hunger and endless beatings. Kate pointed at the large silver-and-turquoise turtle on Emma's finger and asked, "Is that a new ring?" to change the subject.

"I went up to the Yurok Reservation a couple of weeks ago."

Kate's heart clenched as she waited for more.

"I didn't expect to find him," Emma said. "I guess I was looking for a part of myself." She flexed her finger, and the silver caught the morning sun. "Turtles represent protection because they have a shell. They represent a lot of things: Mother Earth, a long life, patience." She glanced at Kate for a second. "It was interesting to drive through that land, think about what it meant to have ancestors."

"Did you feel a connection?"

Emma shook her head. "Maybe because *he* would be my connection, so that link is missing in the chain."

When Emma had turned eighteen, she'd asked to see her adoption papers, curious about her biological father. The paperwork offered little help. *Identity: Unknown. Race: Native American (Yurok)/African American,* the only bit of information the woman who'd given them birth had provided to Social Services.

Kate had even less information in her paperwork, all the fields under *Father* left blank, but she remembered the woman referring to him a time or two as *That Irish Bastard* who wouldn't give her money for an abortion. Kate never cared, never wanted to find her father, but Emma did, so Kate felt bad for Emma that it wasn't likely to ever happen.

"It had to be difficult to go up there," she told her sister. Facing the past was never easy. Neither was facing oneself. "If you ever want to talk—"

"I'm not the one currently messing up the best thing in my life." Emma was back to flashing heat as she pulled into Hope Hill's parking lot. She stopped in front of the main entrance. "Okay, off you go to make other people feel better while you're an emotional wreck."

"I don't want to spend your visit fighting."

"This is the first chance I've had to tell you how I feel, all right? The first year you were back, I was just happy you were back. And Mom and Dad would have killed me if I looked at you sideways. The second year, I was working at the London office. I have a lot of pent-up emotions about this." Then her expression softened. "I still think you should have told me you weren't dead. But you came back. And here we are together. And I'm glad for that."

The words peeled a layer or two of tension off Kate. "You know I love you. You're the best sister ever. I've missed you so freaking much."

"Me too." Emma offered a semi-smile at last. "Wait until I tell

Mom and Dad that Murph proposed."

"Please don't. Not yet." Kate wasn't ready to bring even more people, and more opinions, into her mess.

Emma's lips snapped back into a tight line. "You're going to keep it a secret."

"Let's fight about this later?" Kate unfastened her seat belt and wiggled out of the car with her bag on her lap. "Thanks for the ride. Try not to get into too much trouble and terrorize the townsfolk with your LA, big-city ways."

Her sister accepted the attempt at ceasefire with "Does that mean I can't get a nipple piercing in the shop window of the tattoo parlor on Main Street?"

"There are no tattoo parlors on Main Street."

"Freaking small-town morals." Emma rolled her eyes as she drove away.

Kate smiled. The lighter mood was good. They would work through their issues. They loved each other too much to let anything stand between them.

The janitor was sweeping dead leaves off the steps. Behind him, potted evergreens bracketed the covered entry, topiary hemlocks flanking the double doors. WELCOME, the sign said in golden letters on the glass. While the doormat proclaimed, WE'RE GLAD YOU'RE HERE.

This was the dream that had brought Kate back to Broslin, the dream that she and Murph had planned endlessly in Ohio. Hope Hill was a state-of-the-art rehab facility for disabled vets, with the most comprehensive range of alternative therapies in the country.

Once, the building had been a sketch on a piece of paper towel, the design hatched over breakfast. Now the facility and its services were real, financed partially from the hundred grand Murph had received as reward for leading the police to a bank robbery gang right before he and Kate left Broslin. In addition to that, Kate had run a million fundraisers. Then they'd applied for government grants for the rest. They'd created something out of nothing, a place of healing that actually helped people.

She might have had doubts about Murph on the personal-relationship front, but she couldn't deny that professionally, they made a great team.

"Hey, Joe. How is Gracie?"

"All better." The fifty-something janitor paused his work. "Cast is coming off tomorrow. She says to thank you for the delicious lasagna. We appreciate it."

"Anytime."

Then Maria sailed through the front door, the new therapist.

"Forgot my phone in the car," she told Kate. "My brain is mush in the morning. This is why I schedule paperwork for the first hour instead of an appointment. I don't know how you do it."

"Therapeutic massage is not the same as talk therapy. Even if my brain is asleep, my fingers know what they're supposed to be doing." Kate's gaze dropped to the woman's enviable red pumps. "Hot date after work?"

And, *ooh*, the dress was nice too, now that she was paying closer attention. Deceptively simple, a subtly shimmering charcoal gray—but the cut hinted at a designer boutique.

Maria wiggled her eyebrows. "Keep your fingers crossed."

"Done." Kate entwined her fingers and held them up. "Do I know him?"

"Probably not. Clinical psychologist from Philly. We met at that conference last week."

"He didn't waste any time asking you out."

Maria's grin widened. "Second date."

Kate tried a wolf whistle. Failed. Maria started down the stairs, laughing.

"I want to hear all the details tomorrow!" Kate called after her.

Her own love life was a disaster, but she could still be happy for her friends. She would just focus on other people and not think of Murph.

Easier said than done.

She wasn't behind her desk five minutes when he popped into her office.

CHAPTER TWO

Asael

Figure out what you like doing, then find someone willing to pay for it, was the best advice Bobbie Brenton had ever received.

At age seventeen, he hadn't fully grasped the concept, paying scant attention to his guidance counselor, but as he'd gone on with his life, he thought of the words now and then. Eventually, he accepted the truth in them. Action followed epiphany, and by the time he was twenty-seven, he was a fully self-supporting assassin.

He'd found what he liked: killing. And he'd become a *pro*, meaning he earned his full income from assignments. They weren't a side gig or a hobby.

Bobbie Brenton died, for the first time, in a Pittsburgh house fire. Rauch Asael was born from the ashes, and, in a few more years, became one of the highest-rated killers for hire on the dark web.

Rauch meant smoke in German.

Asael was one of the names used for the devil.

He'd perished a few more times, as needed. He discarded any compromised aliases with the same ease as he discarded his targets. He enjoyed the freedom of starting a new life.

He dodged morning traffic in his Nissan Altima—one of the

most common cars in America—and drove to the outskirts of Broslin. The ancient silo that stood at the edge of the cemetery was the quietest place he'd found so far in town. He parked on the wilting fall grass and cut across the graves. Drew in a deep breath. He liked the scent of decay.

He was halfway to his destination when a chubby black cat jumped from a gravestone to follow him. "Hello there."

He stalked straight to the silo that was covered in ivy, then ducked under the rusty chain that held a rusty sign announcing private property, while claiming danger and telling him to go away, for his own safety.

"Morons." He climbed.

Even as a kid, he'd liked high places. He used to climb out his bedroom window and lie on the roof at night for a smoke and some drink—both stolen from his father. Later, he'd spent time on the stage, enjoyed being up there and looking down at the audience. He'd always had a flair for the dramatic. Theater had taught him makeup and costuming, how to turn himself into someone else. And for a while, prop knives and fake blood had been enough. Until they weren't.

Asael owned no property, could afford no permanent ties, but when he was in between assignments, he always stayed in the tallest high-rise of whatever city he was in, in the penthouse apartment. He liked feeling on top of the world.

As he stood on the rust-dotted silo and looked out over the stupid little town before him, he wished he was in Dubai instead, at the Gevora, the tallest hotel in the world.

Autumn frost had kissed the trees overnight, the leaves brown or already fallen. He turned up his collar. This time of year, he preferred taking jobs in the tropics.

"I could be standing on a private beach right now," he told the cat that'd managed to climb up after him, "with an icy drink."

Instead, he'd been in small-town purgatory for the past three days, and he still couldn't puzzle out why he had allowed a vague sense of unease to draw him to Broslin. A premonition prickled at the back of his neck, a sense of something unfinished, a miniscule piece of thread hanging. And he listened to it, because an assassin lived or died by his instincts.

He imagined ordinary people felt something similar when they left the house and suddenly thought *Did I shut off the stove?* And then, even if they were a mile or two down the road, they had to turn around. Because…

"You have to check," he told the cat.

He knew one thing: He had *not* come to avenge Mordocai.

A Broslin cop had shot the fellow assassin and ex-lover five years before, but revenge for revenge's sake had never been Asael's modus operandi. Hotheaded retaliation was a good way to get caught. He'd survived this long because he limited his exposure. He would not hazard everything he'd gained over the years on a sentimental gesture. When he acted, he expected compensation in proportion to the risk he was taking.

"And yet here I am." He said that to the town, as a warning.

Here he was, for certain. But why?

He wasn't following a trail. He was following a vague pull that stubbornly curled around him, like a gossamer wisp of smoke, like the black cat weaving between his legs.

If he'd come on assignment, he would have a packet of information from his client. He would know *exactly* what his next steps were.

"Wasting my time." He looked past the cemetery, watched the morning light glinting off windows of houses people thought would keep them safe. He didn't know any of them.

"Never even heard of Broslin until Mordocai's death," he told the cat, which was clean and had a collar, not a stray. Hanging around the cemetery for fun. Asael almost liked the damn thing. "I don't suppose you knew Mordocai or what he was doing here?"

Mordocai had moved to the self-proclaimed Mushroom Capital of the US under the alias of Fred Kazincky, retired mechanic. On an assignment he never completed. According to an online article, Fred Kazincky had kidnapped a woman, but was caught.

"Last time he called me, he said he found a gift."

Had to be something he'd seen here that reminded him of their time together. Something he thought would get him back into

Asael's good graces. But what? The shop windows on Main Street brimmed with mushroom-shaped mugs and mushroom-print shirts. What on earth had given Mordocai the idea that Asael would be interested in anything fungi related?

Didn't matter. Mordocai had never bought that gift. Never sent it.

"He was killed," Asael told the cat, then added the bit that nagged in the back of his mind. "The cop who killed him, Murph Dolan, disappeared immediately after, witness-protection style. Except, he wasn't a witness to anything."

The cat looked at him with slanted yellow eyes and an expression of *beats me.*

Beat Asael too, and he loathed not knowing, loathed that all he'd learned since he'd arrived in town could be summarized in two sentences. "Dolan's girlfriend, Katherine Concord, disappeared with him. Then, three years later, as if nothing happened, they returned."

Right after Asael had sacrificed another one of his identities and convinced the authorities that he'd died for real, at last.

Was he too paranoid to think there could be a connection?

The cat rubbed its head against his shin and purred.

"Has to be a coincidence, because the only other option is impossible: that those two left because they felt in danger here. Mordocai was dead and buried. They wouldn't have run from him."

"Did they expect revenge? Who did they think would be coming?" His fingers tightened on the railing, rust flakes digging into his skin. "Did they run from *me?*"

Except the theory presupposed that Mordocai had talked about him, *betrayed* him—an unthinkable breach.

"If he did…" Asael told the cat. "I'm going to burn this town to the ground just so I can dance in the ashes."

Then he added, "But first, Murph Dolan and his damn girlfriend."

He knew just where to find them.

CHAPTER THREE

Kate

Kate would have liked a little longer grace period before she had to face Murph again, but she wasn't going to get it, so she pasted on a smile while Murph dropped a distinctive pink bag from Sweet Beginnings on her desk.

"Assorted bonbons. Gluten free. In case you're running low on chocolate."

Her stomach turned. So weird and stupid. *Chocolate* used to be her favorite word. She pushed the bag a little farther away from her nose. "Thanks."

Swear to Saint Bean of Cocoa, if she was coming down with a chocolate allergy, she was going to sue the universe.

He watched her with that expression he often wore lately, as if he was at the end of his rope regarding what to do with her.

He took up a lot of room in her office. A LOT. In the small space, it was impossible to look away from him.

"I ran into an old friend the other day," he said. "Tommy used to work in construction, hurt his back a while ago, so he took a desk job, managing a granite shop in Wilmington. He could probably hook you up with some heavily discounted countertops. Let me know if you need his number."

"Kitchen's all done." Kate paused to adjust her tone. She sounded put out with him, which she wasn't. "Are you going to Finnegan's with the guys tonight?"

"Staying here. I'm applying for another grant."

All right, work talk she could handle. "For?"

"Zip-line course in the woods. More of an obstacle course, actually, with some zip line."

"That'd be great. Some people grow bored with the gym and yoga classes after a while." The men and women at Hope Hill were all military vets, used to a higher level of action. "And exercise out in fresh air, in the woods, will do a world of good for mental health too."

Kate didn't add, *Let me know if you need help.*

She didn't want to work late with Murph, then walk out together. She didn't want to feel that draw toward *his* apartment on the premises, a place that a short while ago used to be *theirs*.

The living room with its big masculine leather couch where they'd made love a dozen ways: lying down, sitting up, her bent over the soft round arm and Murph behind her, and…

Then the kitchen… She couldn't bear thinking about the table, the counter, or the fridge door cold against her back.

And, *God*, she could definitely never face the bathroom—the tub *or* the shower—ever again.

To say nothing of the bedroom and the bed. Or any horizontal surface in the apartment really. And also any vertical.

Heat spread through her.

Let's go back there, her body said.

Fortunately, her body didn't get to make decisions for her. She was a grown-ass woman. *At work.*

She cleared her throat.

"Good luck," she told Murph. "I hope we get the grant."

There. Everything all professional. And now they could be done.

Except, Murph rubbed a hand over his mouth as he watched her, and she knew he wasn't going to let it go.

He didn't. He dropped his hand and asked, "So, we're just

going to pretend everything's all right?"

Kate braced herself for what he was going to say next, but her first patient for the day appeared in the doorway, *thank God*, saving her from an uncomfortable conversation.

"Hey, Murph. Ma'am. Dan Washington." The former Navy SEAL—Kate had read his file already—glanced between her and Murph, not missing the tension in the room. "I have an appointment?"

"Hi, Dan. Please call me Kate." She stood to shake his hand, then gestured toward the open door that led to her treatment room. "Why don't you go in and get comfortable? Take off everything except your underwear, then slip between the sheets on the table. I'll be with you in a minute."

As Dan limped by them, Kate headed to the door behind her desk, the small private bathroom that opened from her office. "I'd better change."

She worked in scrubs to save her regular clothes from the massage oils.

For a second, Murph made no move to leave, and it was all there in his eyes, how she'd undressed in front of him a thousand times before.

She couldn't now. "We need to find our boundaries."

"Why?"

She needed to find out who they were without the sex, which they'd fallen into pretty fast at the beginning. The chemistry between them had been instant. It had distracted them from everything else in Ohio too. But she'd carried her own baggage into their relationship, and Murph had carried his. "Using sex to distract ourselves from our problems isn't healthy. If we want to move forward together, we'll need to build a better foundation first."

He shoved his hands into his pockets and rocked back on his heels. "What problems, exactly?"

"Our relationship has been completely unrealistic. We've never even had a fight. We couldn't. We were in an emergency situation. We had to stick together."

"You want to fight?"

"Don't make me sound like I'm crazy. Most couples break up

and make up all the time. I don't even know what you look like when you're mad at me."

"I'm not going to break up with you," he said. And then he strode away.

Kate changed in her bathroom, cursing the stupid tears that burned her eyes.

She was tugging up her pants when boots scuffed on the floor outside, somebody stepping into her office. Not Murph. She knew the sound the black sneakers he wore at work made.

"I'll be right out!"

She yanked on her shoes, but by the time she walked out of the bathroom, her office was empty. She looked out into the hallway. Nobody there either.

No big deal. If somebody needed her, they'd come back.

She crossed to the treatment room and knocked on the door. "Okay if I come in?"

"I'm ready."

Dan Washington waited on the table, covered to his neck. He was twenty-eight, an underwater demolition expert injured in an explosion. He still wore his black hair regulation short, his eyes darting away from Kate.

"Have you ever had a therapeutic massage before?" she asked.

He blushed. "No, ma'am."

"Ma'am is not necessary."

"Yes, ma'am."

She smiled. "So, this is the treatment room. This is where we'll have our sessions, once a week, for the next twelve weeks. I'm going to evaluate any issues while we work together today. You can ask me questions you might have, at any time. Any concerns before we start?"

"No, ma'am." He winced. "Sorry, ma'am." Cleared his throat. "Kate."

She lit a candle. "Lavender. It's nice, isn't it?" Then she folded the sheet down from Dan's back. "I won't go straight to the injury. We'll work around it at first."

As she poured the prewarmed massage oil into her hands, she noted the smattering of scars on her new patient's skin. Nothing out of the norm. She treated warriors. She was used to wounds, old and new.

"All you have to do is relax." She placed her hands on him and began to work his tense muscles, gently, then applying more pressure.

He sniffed the air. "The lotion smells good too."

"Scented with tea tree oil. Our ecotherapist has information on aromatherapy, if you're interested. Annie Murray. She's not in this week, but you'll be meeting her too, at one point."

She worked over Dan's wide muscular back, covered it up with the sheet again, then uncovered his left leg first and smoothed out the knots in his muscles. Only then, half an hour into the session, did she move on to his injured leg.

The second she touched the sheet on that side, Dan stiffened. He put a hand over the fabric to hold it in place. "You shouldn't have to look at all that ugliness."

"I'm not going to do anything you're not comfortable with, but I'd like to ask you to trust me. We have people here with all kinds of injuries: shrapnel wounds, burns, amputations, other stuff." She didn't say *torture*, ever, since the word itself could be triggering.

"I see about six patients a day," she told Dan. "So that's thirty just last week. I've seen every kind of scar there is. I have five more appointments after you today. One with a former pilot who has burn scars over almost seventy percent of her body from a helicopter crash. You don't need to worry about sparing my sensibilities. I see scars every day just from looking into the mirror."

She stepped into his line of sight and pulled the neckline of her scrubs away from the white lines on her shoulder, courtesy of the woman who'd given birth to her then beat her every day until Social Services had finally intervened.

Dan's eyes focused on the spot, and she let him have a long look before she tugged the shirt back into place. "What are you most worried about?"

He responded in a voice thick with embarrassment. "It's ugly."

"You healed. You're walking. That's as beautiful as it gets."

A second passed, two, then he moved his hand out of the way. "Okay."

Kate stepped back to his leg, then drew up the sheet with slow care. "Skin injuries improve a lot with time. There are excellent pharmaceutical creams now. Aloe gel does wonders too, if you'd like to try something natural."

She began to feel her way around the damage, and, little by little, Dan relaxed under her hands again.

He had scars that were two feet long, some from the original injury and some from repeated surgeries. His file said he had pins in his bones. Burn marks ran up the side of his leg, his skin bunched up and rough.

"Let me know if anything I do hurts." Kate worked every muscle, smoothed out every knot.

"Is this what you always wanted to do?" he asked, maybe because he was interested, or maybe because he wanted distraction.

"Pretty much." She was always happy to talk about her work. "Kind of. I started with traumatized horses before moving on to people."

"You're a horse doctor?" Dan gave a weak laugh, relaxing some more.

"That's what got me into it. Then I went for special training with a man who was one of the original practitioners of this type of therapy, and for a long time, I worked with abused children." Children who'd been victims of physical or sexual abuse who were scared to death of human touch. "I did rehabilitative work. The ability to accept physical affection is important for mental development, for healing."

"That had to be hard," Dan said. "I mean, to see kids suffer. I don't know if I could do it. I'd get angry. Might be tempted to track down the bastard..." He fell silent.

"Thinking about how the kids got hurt was difficult. But watching them recover, if I did my job right, was immensely rewarding."

And she did do her work right, because it meant way more to her than just a job.

"And now you have patients here who can't stand being touched," Dan closed his eyes. "Couple of guys don't even like if anyone's sitting next to them in the cafeteria. I'm not that bad, at least. You can help everyone?"

"For the most part, yes. PTSD is a difficult thing. Luckily, I know what I'm doing. I trained in various therapeutic methods. I can usually find something that works. And the other therapists are even better than I am." Kate finished untangling a particularly stubborn knot of muscles. "You're in good hands."

"This place is lucky to have you."

"Thanks. But it's the other way around, Dan. I'm lucky to have this place."

When she finished with the leg, she had him turn around and worked on the same muscles from the front. "What will you do when you go home from here? Any big plans?"

"College. Maybe." He kept his eyes closed. "After high school, I thought about a nursing degree but then talked myself out of it. Joined the Navy instead. It's a family thing. My daddy, my granddaddy." He opened his eyes. "Then I was lying on that deck after the accident, losing blood fast. I wasn't sure I'd live. I was sure I'd never walk again. There was a doctor at the Navy hospital, Dr. Bankole. He put me together. Right off, he told me I was going to be fine; I was too young to spend the rest of my life lazing around in a wheelchair. And then he made sure I didn't." Dan paused. "If I can, I thought I'd try premed. I always liked biology. Chemistry too. Science in general. You think I'm too old?"

Kate laughed. "I'm older than you, and if you start talking about age as an obstacle, you're going to push me right into a midlife crisis. We're young, beautiful, and we kick ass. We can do whatever we damn well want."

"Yes, ma'am."

They talked more about med school, while she mentally mapped all the trouble spots and began outlining his treatment plan.

"One of the guys said he goes to the sauna before he comes for treatment. To relax his muscles?" Dan brought up when they finished.

"You could try that if you'd like. It might help. Do you know where the saunas are?"

He shook his head.

"In the pool complex. It should be empty right now. After you get dressed, I'll walk you over and show you." She covered him with the sheet, up to his chin. "Feel free to stay for a few more minutes and relax."

At her desk, she wrote up her notes for their next session. By the time she finished, he was coming out of the treatment room with a smile.

"I'll be honest. I wasn't sure what good any of this would do. My sisters get massages. Spa days." He shrugged. "I never thought that stuff was for guys. But you made me a new man."

When he walked through her office—shamelessly showing off—his limp was barely there.

And that was why she loved her job, Kate thought as she stepped from behind her desk and clapped.

She glanced at the clock on the wall. She had fifteen minutes before her next patient. The pool complex was at the very back of the facility, but she could make it there and back.

"Let's go and see about that sauna, then."

CHAPTER FOUR

Murph

"You coming to Finnegan's tonight?" Harper stopped in front of Murph on his way to the water cooler at Hope Hill's very own gym.

Murph sat on his bench, but instead of lying back down to lift another few reps of the weights, he braced his elbows on his knees and hung his head. He was covered in sweat. He'd probably pushed himself harder than he should have. "Might as well."

He made time every day for at least a brief workout, in between handling the million management tasks that running Hope Hill required. He had shrapnel damage in his shoulder that tended to stiffen up. He needed the exercise to keep everything in good working order.

"Kate coming with you?" Harper wiped the glistening sweat off his face with the back of his hand, equipment clanging all around them.

"Probably not." Murph was at his wit's end with her. He had told her he was staying late because he had hoped she would offer to stay with him. Truth was, the grant application was nearly complete.

"Bro." Harper grinned. "Whatever you did, just apologize already. Bring her flowers. If it's beyond flowers, fancy bonbons. If it's beyond fancy bonbons, jewelry."

"Aren't you the relationship expert? Because you're, what, in your first ever serious relationship finally?"

"Hey, when I'm hanging out tonight at Finnegan's, my woman will be by my side. And then we'll go home together. And then..." He made a va-va-voom face.

Murph bit back a laugh. "Feel free to spare me the details."

Harper puffed his chest out as he sauntered away, while Murph shook his head.

He didn't know how to fix what he'd done wrong, because he didn't know what he'd done wrong. He'd proposed. Kate had run away. She'd asked for time and space, and then she bought a house and moved out of their apartment at Hope Hill.

Murph was no expert on women either, but her leaving didn't seem like a sign that she wanted to work things out with him.

He did his best not to bring up their relationship, or rather, the lack thereof, to her, because she would only remind him that they had agreed to this break. And she would say it as if it'd been as much his idea as hers.

Like hell it'd been. He'd only accepted her pronouncement because anything else—pushing, demanding answers—would have made him a jackass.

How much damn time could a woman need?

A deadline would have been nice, knowing when she'd put him out of his misery. Like, *tomorrow*. He could survive another twenty-four hours. *Maybe*.

"I'll be working a shift behind the bar," Harper said on his way back, a paper cup in his hand. His family owned Finnegan's. "Jerry's out. Emergency appendicitis surgery. Didn't tell anyone he was in pain and drove himself to the freaking hospital instead of asking for help."

"Sounds like Jerry." This was the guy whose doctor once told him he should have a suspicious mole checked out on his arm, and he went home and cut it off with his pocket knife.

Harper moved on, but called back over his shoulder, casting a meaningful glance at the weights set up for Murph. "Try not to pull anything, old man."

The words required a response, but instead of returning the smartass comment with one of his own, Murph sat there dumbstruck. Dan, the new patient, was walking across the yard with Kate, the stupid pink bag of chocolates from Sweet Beginnings swinging from *his* hand.

As they passed out of sight, Murph dropped back onto the bench, grabbed the bar, and pushed it up so violently that the weights rattled. Then he did it again, and again, and again.

By the time he was finished with his set, sitting up and breathing hard, Kate was walking back. She glanced over. Saw him through the window. Stopped.

He stared like the poor, hapless sap he was.

She'd let her hair grow, the thick locks now falling past the middle of her back. The breeze blew a few stray strands into her face. She didn't bother brushing them away.

While they'd lived in Ohio as Murphy Andrews and Katie Milano, she'd worn her hair short, colored black, but then gone back to auburn when they'd returned to Broslin, the same color she had when they'd first met.

Her sky-blue gaze held Murph's as she stood outlined against the greenery behind her. She was more beautiful in shapeless scrubs than any other woman he'd ever met in their skimpiest party gear. How often did he fantasize about peeling her out of those scrubs and the sports bra and simple cotton underwear he knew she had on underneath? Every damn night.

For a hopeful moment, he thought she might come over to talk to him, and his heart gave a big, solid bang in his chest. But instead, she pulled her cell phone from her pocket and answered a call. *Right.* She'd only stopped because her phone had been ringing in her pocket.

Murph watched as shock spread on her paling face, could read her lips as she said, *Oh my God. What?*

He grabbed his sweatshirt from the floor and was through the door and next to her just in time to hear her add, "I don't have my car. I'm stuck at work."

"Let me help." He tugged on the navy-blue sweatshirt that had the Hope Hill logo printed on the front in white. "I can give you a ride."

Her torn expression killed him. How in hell had they gotten to the point where she was hesitating to accept his help?

"Kate?" He was begging, and he didn't care.

"That was Captain Bing." Her voice rang hollow, twisting his guts. "Betty died."

He needed a second to place the name. "Your neighbor? Betty Gardner?"

Betty was a nice old woman with no family. She used to be a nurse at West Chester Hospital, then at the Broslin Free Clinic for another decade after retirement. These days, her volunteer work at church was her life. Everybody loved Betty, including Murph.

"What happened?"

"She fell and hit her head." Kate shoved her phone back into her pocket, her fingers trembling. "I have to go home," she said in rush. "I have to make sure her place is all right. I want to check that she doesn't have anything on the stove, or any windows open, or…" She huffed out a quick breath of air, paused, a lost look in her eyes. "I don't know. I just feel I should be there and do something."

"I'll drive you. Come on."

She swallowed. "Thank you." Tears sprang into her eyes. "Can you really leave right now?"

"I was taking a break from the paperwork anyway." He hurried alongside her as she took off toward her office, the gravel crunching under their shoes. "You have any appointments you need to cancel?"

"I'll cancel them while you drive. Let me grab my bag from my desk." She looked at her scrubs. "I should change too. I won't take long."

She never did. She could be ready in the morning as fast as Murph, and Murph had learned his morning routine in the US Army Reserves. She didn't wear makeup. No gel manicures, she kept her nails trim, a necessity for her job. No fancy hairdo unless she was going somewhere special. No fancy clothes either. Most of the time she either wore jeans or yoga pants with one of her soft cotton shirts that molded to her breasts, something Murph didn't need to think about just then.

He always figured her minimalism originated in the years she'd spent shuffled from one foster family to another, with nothing but a few changes of clothes stuffed in a garbage bag. He liked her as she was. Plain when it was convenient, knock-out gorgeous when she did dress up, making his heart go *bang-bang-bang*.

Although, to be fair, she could make his heart beat faster just by looking at him.

"I can't believe Betty is gone." She gripped the tan messenger bag on her lap once they were on the way. "I talked to her this morning. She was supposed to come over for tea and cookies tonight, after work."

"I didn't know you were close."

"She made it easy to be friends with her. She was always like, *How are you, honey? How was work?* Or, *I baked you some cookies.* I thought, if I had a grandmother that's what it would have been like." Kate blinked and looked out the side window. "It probably sounds stupid, but those interactions were so nice. Just…" She shook her head. "I was looking forward to running into her outside every day."

Murph understood. Kind of. Mostly, he just heard that Kate was lonely. So why wouldn't she come back to him?

He tamped down his frustration and kept that question to himself. As he passed a slow-poke farm truck, he asked her something else. "How old was Betty? Eighties?"

"Eighty-four. Healthy, other than her diabetes, and she controlled that with her meds. She had so many good years left." Kate rubbed a couple of tears away with the back of her hand. "I don't understand how she slipped. I raked the leaves from her walkway this morning. I should have told Emma to check on her."

"Sometimes, people her age fall. It's not your fault."

Kate remained silent. If her stricken expression was anything to go by, she was digging herself into guilt.

To pull her back, Murph asked, "How is Emma?"

"In between jobs. She was dating her boss in LA. Apparently, against company policy. They got caught. Guess which one of them was fired?"

"That sucks."

"It does."

Was Emma moving to Broslin? Moving in with Kate? And then what? Murph's gut tightened. Kate was just never going to come back to him?

"It's good that you two have a chance to catch up." He forced a less selfish perspective. He could be happy for Kate. He knew how much family meant to her and how hard it'd been for her to be away from them.

He wanted to say *I miss you*, the words pushing against his teeth to force a way to freedom. But he'd promised to give her time and space, so he clamped his mouth shut. The conversation he wanted to have with her could not be had right then. *Not the time.*

"How long is Emma staying?"

"Just a week."

If they hadn't run into each other at the grocery store that morning, when would Kate have told him that her sister was visiting? Never?

Kate stared straight ahead, out the window, studiously keeping her eyes away from him. "Why does the stone carving on Broslin library say Broslin Creek Library?"

"It's the original name. Mayor..." Murph clicked his tongue. "Can't remember his name. My grandfather used to talk about him... Mayor Campbell. Held office in the thirties. Biggest tightwad you'd ever seen, according to Gramps. He proposed to have the town's name changed from Broslin Creek to Broslin to save money on signage. Also, we had a couple of factories in town back then, and the creek was a travesty, the water polluted to a sludge. Apparently, Mayor Campbell didn't want to draw attention to it."

Murph tried to think what else he might remember about the guy, but couldn't come up with anything. He wanted to keep talking to distract Kate from the terrible news she'd just received, but all he could think to say was *come back, come back, come back*. The words pulsed through his heart with every beat.

"Maybe it's inevitable," she said after a stretch of silence, her tone pensive. "Rebirth requires paring back, cutting away parts that don't work."

Like hell, he thought, if she meant cutting him away.

She lifted her phone. "I'd better let people know we'll be rescheduling."

She took care of business with her usual efficiency, calling five patients by the time Murph reached her street.

The neatly lined-up sixties-style ranchers were nearly identical, differing only in the color of their front doors—red, green, or blue—and the siding—white, blue, or brown—set back about thirty feet from the sidewalk. Murph had gone to school with kids whose parents had lived in the neighborhood.

It was a nice area. Good value. He'd actually thought about buying something here once he and Kate were ready to move out of their apartment at Hope Hill.

An ambulance was pulling away from the curb in front of Betty's house, so he parked in the spot it vacated, between two police cruisers. "Is Emma home?"

Kate scanned the street. "I don't see her rental. She was going to drive to the Philly Art Museum today."

"Too bad. I would have liked to say hi to her. There's Bing." Murph nodded toward the captain out front, but Kate was no longer paying attention.

Her stricken gaze followed the ambulance, tears rolling down her face. "Do you think Betty is in there?"

Murph almost reached for her, but then caught himself and dropped his hand onto his lap. "I can catch up on paperwork tomorrow. I'm going to stay here with you. All right?"

She slipped out of the car without responding, in a haze of shock and grief.

He *hated* seeing her upset like this, especially when he couldn't do a damn thing about it.

He caught up to her and nodded at Ethan Bing by the pair of weather-beaten rocking chairs on Betty's front stoop. "Captain." Then he nodded to the policewoman who stood next to the man. "Gabi."

He got twin nods in turn.

Gabriella Maria Flores had been hired from Philly while Murph and Kate had been away, so Murph didn't know her as well as he knew the rest of the PD. From what he'd heard, she was a damn good cop, tough but fair, knew how to get the job done, a credit to the PD. The best shot on the team, according to Bing. And Bing was a fair enough guy not to say that just because she was family to him now, married to his brother, Hunter.

Kate stopped in front of the captain and visibly shored herself up, straightening, stiffening. "What happened? When did she fall? How long was she out here in the cold?" Her voice broke. "I told her a million times to keep her cell phone in her pocket."

"Let's go inside your place where you can sit down. I'll give you a full update." Bing took her elbow and walked her across the lawn.

Murph followed them over.

Gabi headed for her cruiser. "I'll start entering the report into the system."

"I wouldn't mind a few more pictures," Bing told her, waiting for Kate to find her key. "And check on Tony Mauro, would you please? He looked shook up earlier."

Kate stopped with the key in the lock, paling another shade as her gaze snapped to the house on her other side. "Betty and Mr. Mauro were close friends. I need to make sure he's okay."

"Why don't we sit down in your kitchen for a second first?" the captain suggested.

Murph caught up with them, noting every detail about Kate's new place. The freshly mulched foundation planting was neat and trimmed, the front stoop clean swept. Kate had painted the front door a cheery green and decorated it with a fall wreath of yellow leaves and orange mini pumpkins. Below that stood the house number, carefully painted in black.

She hadn't been living there long, but she'd already given the house plenty of loving attention, including an oversized welcome mat.

She made better everything she touched.

Murph caught the thought, acknowledged just how far he was gone. But, honestly, so what? He wasn't seeing her through rose-colored glasses. She *was* a nurturer, the very reason why her patients at the center thrived under her care. She was consistently one of the highest-rated therapists on the team.

"May I?" he called after them from the doorway.

"Of course." But her eyes didn't quite meet his.

Murph stepped inside. As he closed the door behind him, he tamped down his feelings—and he had plenty—about her living apart from him, about the fact that it was his first time visiting.

The interior had been completely renovated by the previous owner, no sign of old carpets or linoleum. Hardwood floors, light gray kitchen cabinets with white tile backsplash and granite countertops, appliances all next to new. There went his chance to offer to help her fix up the place.

"I'd say she fell an hour or two ago," Bing told them as he pulled out a chair for Kate.

The two of them sat at the table, while Murph stayed standing on the imaginary dividing line between the living room and the kitchen, placing himself between Kate and the front door. He acknowledged the protection reflex and didn't worry too much about it.

Kate clasped her hands together on the table in front of her. "Who found her?"

"Lilly Corrigan. Lives two streets over. She was walking her dog off leash. The dog ran between the houses and started barking. Miss Corrigan ran after him, saw Betty, couldn't make her come around, called 911."

"Did she suffer?" Kate's voice broke on the last word, and Murph had to work at staying still.

"I wouldn't think so." Bing rubbed his palm over the tired lines on his face.

He had a soft spot for Betty Gardner too. Everybody at the PD did. Betty and a few of her friends had organized the fundraising for a new police cruiser a couple of years back, when the township couldn't come up with the money in the budget.

Kate dropped her hands onto her lap. "How did it happen?"

"The best I can tell right now, she slipped, fell, and hit her head on the outside basement entry."

"Why would she go back there?"

"Taking out garbage, most likely. She was right next to the recycle bin."

Kate blinked away her tears. "I can't tell you how many times I offered to help with that."

"You and others." Bing nodded with sympathy.

They sat in silence for a moment. Then Bing asked, "Do you know who'll be making funeral arrangements for her?"

"I'd think Linda, her friend from church. They had power of attorney for each other. We were just talking about it last week. I told Betty I was going into the office supply store in West Chester to restock the cabinet at work, and she asked me if I could pick up a three-ring binder for her because she was organizing her legal papers."

"You know Linda's last name?"

"Betty said it, but… No. Sorry. It'll probably come to me later."

"No worries, I'll find her. I can call her pastor."

"He'll know. Or one of her other friends at church will." Kate wrapped her arms around her middle, her features tight. She was fighting damn hard to keep it together.

Murph fought just as hard to keep from going to her. When it became too much, he backed out and went in search of Gabi. If he were to help anybody, he needed to do more than look longingly at Kate.

A turn in the weather had put a nip in the air, the sky gray.

Other than a flock of gossipy Canada geese honking their hearts out overhead, rushing south, the street was quiet. Neighbors who were at home had probably been over already, talked to Bing, then returned to their kitchens to call everybody they knew with the news. By now, most of Broslin would have been alerted to Betty's accident—just the way small towns worked.

"Hey, Gabi." Murph found her snapping pictures between Betty's house and the neighbor's on the other side, where the garbage bins stood. "How's Hunter?"

Murph had gone to high school with him. Both of them had done tours in Afghanistan, although not anywhere near each other.

Gabi rolled her eyes. "He's refinishing the basement. Brace

yourself. We're about to have a man cave."

"Yeah? Tell him I can help, if he needs another pair of hands…"

"You can tell him at Finnegan's tonight. You going?"

"I guess."

He had no illusions that Kate would let him stay with her. And, because Emma would be there, he was mostly okay with that. Kate wouldn't be alone, at least.

"One slip and that's that." He looked around in the narrow space, pictured Betty, the fall, then dying alone. "She deserved better."

Leaves covered the ground, most of them newly fallen. From where he stood, he could see the pile Kate had started in the backyard. The brick walkway was mostly clean, passing by the outside basement entry that had a cement block frame and double metal doors.

He shook his head at the blood on the cement block. Betty's kind, smiling face floated in his mind. "A damn shame for something like this to happen." He turned to Gabi. "Mind if I go inside the house?"

She raised an eyebrow without lowering the camera, focused on what she was doing. "Miss police work?"

"Sometimes."

"Front door is unlocked. Go ahead."

Murph hurried back across the recently cut lawn to Betty's front door. He wanted a peek before the captain came back outside and told him to mind his own business.

A country-blue hooked rug protected the slate tile floor in the foyer, a small hall table to his right, with a mirror hanging above it.

Betty's house was identical to Kate's in design, but here, original finishes had been kept, from the worn brown carpet in the living room to the checkered orange linoleum in the kitchen, the fridge in avocado green. Nothing out of place. Certainly nothing that would have given Murph pause back in his Broslin PD days.

The place wasn't a crime scene, but he pulled the sleeve of his sweatshirt over his fingers as he opened the cabinet under the sink. An empty pill box sat on top of the garbage in the plastic bin, label side up. Over-the-counter sleeping pills. He didn't touch it.

He walked around until he found another garbage bin in the laundry room, this one for recyclables. He didn't touch that either, merely observed the four carefully rinsed yogurt cups that lay on the bottom, two peach flavored, two blueberry.

Murph walked out not knowing much more about Betty Gardner than when he'd walked in, but he knew this: She hadn't died taking out the garbage.

CHAPTER FIVE

Asael

Asael looked through the peephole of his room at the Mushroom Mile Motel.

Past the abandoned front parking lot, a row of houses sat quietly on the other side of the road, their inhabitants at work. Beyond those houses, nothing but unspoiled Pennsylvania countryside. Nobody in sight.

The squeaky-voiced cartoon that had been playing for hours in the next room would not quit. From chairs scraping the floor, from children shouting now and then, Asael knew exactly where each of the three kids and the two adults sat over there. He could take them out through the wall. *Five bullets*. But that wasn't why he'd come to Broslin.

And, in any case, he'd checked out already. They would no longer bother him.

He reached for the doorknob and stepped outside, right as the damn maid tootled around the corner of the building.

"Oh, hello there!" She wore a crisp yellow uniform and an entirely unwarranted, ridiculously toothy smile—the epitome of small-town cheeriness. "I'm Maisy." Her blonde ponytail swung as she stopped in front of him. "Everything all right, hon? You let me know if you need something."

He gave a curt nod. He'd asked for a room with outside entry, specifically so he wouldn't have to run into people or walk by the receptionist every time he went in and out. The damn place was crawling with nosy employees.

"Where are you from?" this one wanted to know. Then, without taking a breath, "Here for the Mushroom Festival?"

Small-town people. Everybody's damn business was their damn business. He reached back for his suitcase.

"Oh, you're leaving early."

"Got offered the guest room at a friend's place." Asael walked around her.

"Oh, okay. Maybe I'll see you at the festival!" She kept up that cheerful-to-the-point-of-grating tone that someday someone should choke out of her. Again, not Asael's job on this trip.

He drove the Altima to the parking lot of the twenty-four-hour grocery store on Route 1, switched to his other rental, an unmarked van, then drove that back to Murph Dolan's girlfriend's street.

He passed the two police cruisers in front of Betty Gardner's house, the female officer snapping photos where Betty had smacked her head against the cement block, her skull breaking with a wet crack.

She'd been kind and sweet, a small-town fool to the end, utterly unsuspecting of the man who'd knocked on her door and said he was with the county, administering a program that helped senior citizens with home upkeep. Did she have any need? Why yes, she'd offered nothing but the most grateful smile, then walked out with him and around to show him where the siding needed repair.

He'd hoped she would invite him in and show him a leaky shower or an uneven bit of floor that was a tripping hazard. He would have preferred working in private. In the end, the narrow gap between two houses hadn't been much worse. The tragic accident required only a few seconds.

Afterwards, he'd ducked into her home long enough to pull the key from the back door and drove straight to the hardware store. He'd made himself a copy, then returned the original before the body was even discovered.

Damn, he was efficient.

Katherine Concord—her friends called her Kate—bugged him. The more he watched her, the more he thought she looked familiar, reminded him of someone, a face he knew but couldn't place.

He could have let Betty live and killed Kate, but he didn't like unsolved riddles. First, he was going to figure out who Kate was, *then* he was going to kill her and her ex-cop boyfriend.

Asael wasn't in Broslin for revenge, but he *was* here. He'd been thinking about an extended vacation for years, but now that he was on one, the idleness of it left him restless. His brain preferred to be busy, laser focused on planning and execution. He missed the adrenaline wave—the rise, the crest, the afterglow.

Betty had given him a moment, the sound of her skull cracking, then the first flash of red. But Betty hadn't been enough to take off the edge for more than an hour or so. Asael craved a real hit.

As he reached the end of the street, Anthony Mauro, Kate's other neighbor, shuffled around the corner. His face was ashen, drawn with grief. He looked a decade older than that morning, the last time Asael had seen him. Yet not stricken enough to stay the hell home instead of walking the neighborhood again with his cane and that painfully slow gait, the self-appointed neighborhood watch, that one. Asael despised people who couldn't mind their own business.

The geezer had no idea how close he'd come to vacationing at the morgue right now instead of Betty.

Chances had been fifty-fifty on which neighbor Asael would eliminate. He wanted an outpost as close as possible to Kate's place. The final decision had come down to Kate's bedroom window facing Betty's house.

One of those stupid quirks of fate, Asael thought as Tony Mauro looked right at him.

"Don't be a fool, old man." *Or do.*

But Tony Mauro turned, his attention on the three kids who burst from the garage across the street with a football.

Asael moved on, right at the intersection, toward the center of town. In his khaki pants and shirt, he was invisible behind the wheel of his nondescript white van. Now that everyone ordered everything from the internet, deliverymen like him—freelancers in unmarked vehicles—were so common, nobody noticed them.

Nobody would pay attention to him at the diner either. His makeup took off twenty years, putting him at late twenties. An average guy with slightly greasy brown hair and dull brown eyes. Someone who'd just moved back to his parents' basement and made ends meet by running deliveries. Not so repulsive that they'd recall him for being the creepy dude who came in for lunch, yet not nearly attractive enough to draw the attention of the younger waitresses. There was a sweet spot he'd perfected where the eye just slid right on over him.

The cops would dick around for another hour, he figured. He had time to eat before returning to take possession of his new lodgings.

CHAPTER SIX

Kate

"Good to see you back, Scott." Kate glanced at the open file on her laptop screen as her first patient walked through the door Tuesday morning.

Scott Young. Age: 35. Former Marine. Violent physical trauma. PTSD. Second visit.

Kate forced herself to be cheerful and positive and not to think about poor Betty, not to drag like she'd spent the night without sleep, which she had. To best serve her patients, she checked her own problems at the front door. She needed to be fully available to the people she treated.

Scott nodded at her, a head taller than Kate and heavy built, with a military haircut still. He'd never cracked a smile that she'd seen. Everywhere he went on the property, he always entered tense, scoping out the room as if he was stepping into enemy territory.

"You can go in and hop on the table," she told him.

She already had her blue scrubs on, so she did a few minutes' worth of paperwork while she waited for him to call out that he was ready for her.

When her phone rang, the display showing Shannon O'Brian,

Kate picked up. She could always spare a minute for a friend. "Hi, Shannon. Everything all right?"

"The honeymoon suite is finally finished," the Broslin Bed-and-Breakfast's proprietor said. "Wendy is going to bring by a friend to take photos next week. I was hoping you could do a website update for me after that? I need to get the suite up for bookings. The contractors took forever. I lost six months' worth of income on that room. I need to catch up."

Kate ran a website for kids in foster care, so she'd learned the skills for that and helped out friends with their internet needs now and then.

She glanced at her calendar. "How about after the Mushroom Festival? My sister is here from LA, and I already spend all day at work. I want to spend some time with her, at least in the evenings."

"After the festival would be perfect. Say hi to your sister for me."

"I will." Kate made a note about the website.

Then Scott called out, "Ready!"

Kate ended the call with Shannon and went to treat her patient. She didn't light a candle. She'd learned—the hard way—that smoke and fire were triggers for him.

"Sorry about last time," he mumbled.

"We'll start slow. Any time you want to stop, Scott, you say the word, and I step back. I can even step out of the room for a few minutes if you need me to do that."

He nodded.

She smiled. "I'm going to fold the sheet back from your legs."

When he didn't protest, she gently uncovered his right leg. Scars covered him everywhere. No matter what body part she'd start with, she couldn't avoid his injuries.

Scott Young had been captured by the Taliban, tortured daily for a month, then left behind for dead when they moved camp. Kate hoped she could help him. The last time, they hadn't made it to five minutes before he bolted.

"How is your stay here so far?" She kept her tone light and professional. Patients picked up on her moods, if she was worried or uncertain.

"I like swimming and walks in the woods," he said after a couple of seconds.

Activities that he could do alone, she noted.

"I'm going to put some warm massage oil in my hands now." *No sudden movements.* She reached for the warmer next to him and lifted the bottle, poured, then spread the oil by rubbing her palms together. "I'm going to touch your right calf. I'll just lay my hand on your skin for starters. See how that feels."

His rough raised scars were uneven, as if he'd been cut by a serrated blade, the marks wide and gnarly, as if someone had rubbed irritant into his raw wounds. She couldn't even imagine. Nor would she ever ask.

She rested her hand as lightly on his skin as possible, felt his body vibrate with tension regardless. "Try to relax."

He let out a strangled laugh. But then, after a moment, he did force himself to go still. He was making an effort, giving treatment a chance. And that was all Kate asked.

"I'll start working now, okay? While I see what's going on with these muscles, can you tell me where it hurts the most?"

He laughed again—a bitter, bitter sound. "In my head."

She moved her fingers gently—no digging deep for this patient. Her primary goal was just to have him allow her to touch him. For now. Once she achieved that, they would progress from there.

As the minutes ticked by, Scott relaxed. He had to work damn hard for it. She could see him regulate his breathing.

"You're doing great."

She worked over the muscles under her hands. "I'm going to move up to your thigh. Same thing. It's not going to hurt. I promise."

God bless his immense self-control, he let her.

She worked his other leg, then covered that up too, to keep the muscles warm. "I'm going to uncover your shoulders next."

He didn't say anything, but he had his eyes closed, for the first time. They hadn't worked together long enough yet for her to learn his signs. Were closed eyes good or bad?

Definitely bad.

49

As Kate's fingertips touched his shoulder, he spun with a roar. His left hand gripped her wrist, holding her immobile, while his right hand shot for her throat and grabbed it hard.

Scott!

Her air cut off, she could only scream in her head.

She scrambled with her free hand to pry his fingers off her throat, but his muscles might as well have been made of steel. "Scott!"

He was staring at her without seeing, as he sat up and bent her back.

"Plssz," was the most Kate could manage, a wheeze, the hoarse whine of an animal in a deadly trap.

Stars sparked in her peripheral vision. Then darkness began closing in from the edges. She had seconds left before she'd pass out.

Don't panic.

Don't panic!

While they were in exile in Ohio, Murph had spent considerable time teaching her self-defense. Except, back then, not hurting her assailant hadn't been a concern. She *could* punch Scott in the throat, hard, or in other places that hurt. But she wouldn't, because he was her patient.

Against all instinct, Kate forced herself to go limp instead of fighting back.

Scott held her for another interminable moment, then his eyes cleared, and then his muscles unclenched.

She fell to the ground with a thud.

Ouch. That hurt.

As she gasped for air, she was damn glad it was over.

He was across the room, wedged into the far corner in nothing but black boxer shorts, before she could blink or catch her breath.

"Oh shit. I'm sorry." He had his hands out in front of him, palms toward her, his eyes tortured and begging. "I'm so sorry, Kate. Are you okay? I don't know why I did that."

"Are you all right?" she asked, her voice hoarse.

A strangled laugh. "Am *I* all right? Are you kidding me? Shit, Kate. I'm so sorry."

He slid down, his back against the wall, his knees pulled to the mangled skin on his chest, casting his hands away from him as if they disgusted him. His eyes that had been hard seconds before turned soft with misery, glinting with tears. "What the fuck is wrong with me?"

"Nothing we can't fix." She stood up. Smiled. *In control.* That was the vibe she wanted to project. "I'm going to go out into my office so you can get dressed. Then we talk. All right? I'm fine. Take your time."

She walked by him and turned her back on him without fear. His flashback was over, whatever images of hell it'd shown him gone. As Kate sat behind her desk and opened an incident report, her hands only shook a little.

Name of patient, name of staff, date and time, treatment involved…

Before Kate could decide exactly what to type in the *event description* field, Scott was out, wearing a US Marines logo sweatshirt and faded jeans. He stopped as far from her as the small space allowed.

"We're going to have to cancel our next appointment," she told him in the friendliest tone possible.

Wretchedness poured off him. He shoved his hands into his pockets. "I can't even tell you how sorry I am. I'll pack my stuff and leave."

"That's not how it works. You're not discharged."

"But—"

"Look at me." She waited until he finally raised his troubled gaze to hers. "I'm fine. You're fine. I'm not putting an ounce of blame on you. I'm canceling our next appointment because I want you to double up on talk therapy this week. After that, I will meet with you and Maria, and the three of us will reevaluate your treatment plan together. All right?"

His shoulders remained hunched. He looked away, then back. "Why would you do that?"

"Why did you willingly walk into enemy territory?"

He shrugged. "It was my job. What I signed up for."

"There you have it. We both know the risks of our jobs. We do them anyway, because we care."

He shook his head, and his lips *almost* curved at the very corner. "I'm batshit crazy, I fully admit it. But, and I hate to be the one to tell you this, you're not entirely sane either."

She laughed, didn't let it show that it hurt her throat. "I'll see you in a couple of days?"

"If you're sure. I swear, I won't blame you if—"

"I'm sure, Scott. It's my job. What I signed up for. Why don't you take the rest of the hour and go for a walk in the woods?"

He drew a slow breath. Nodded. "Sorry."

"Nothing to be sorry about. You take care."

After he left, Kate finished her report and sent a note over to Maria. They were going to help Scott Young and that was that. They'd fixed worse at the center. Scott's treatment might end up being a bumpy road, but it wasn't anything they couldn't handle.

As Kate typed, her gaze fell on her bruised right wrist. Bad day to be wearing a short-sleeve T-shirt under her scrubs. When she finished the report, she stepped into her bathroom to check out her neck.

The purpling skin there looked even worse, marks left in the distinct shape of fingers. She grabbed a silk scarf from the hook on the back of the door, one she'd left there after that first cold snap they'd had. Then, back in front of the mirror, she wrapped the scarf loosely around her sore neck.

There. No problem.

An overly optimistic thought proven wrong in three minutes flat when her door banged open and Murph appeared.

"What the hell happened?" He zeroed in on Kate's wrist before she could hide her hand under her desk.

"Scott Young had a brief episode."

"He said." Murph's gaze snapped to her scarf. "Show me your neck."

"It's fine."

He was the picture of simmering fury, a volcano pre-eruption, not spitting lava yet, but the earth was definitely trembling. "Kate, dammit—"

"Fine." She unraveled the silk with short, jerky movements, glaring at him all the while. "Better?"

"No, it's not better," he said between his teeth as he stepped forward, coming to a sudden halt in front of her desk. "Makes me want to punch a fucking wall."

She tilted her head. "Anger management class is at two p.m."

"Dammit, Kate—"

"You already said that."

"Why wasn't he evaluated?"

"He was. He had issues at the first session, but he wasn't violent. I'll go slower with him next time."

"No next time."

"That's a decision for me to make. He's my patient. You taught me self-defense. You have to trust me to know how to use it."

While she rewrapped her neck, he backed away a step. "Next time you treat him, I'm going to be in the room."

"We'll see."

"You'll see me because I'll be there. And I'll see you, also because I'll be there."

She fought a smile that would just have encouraged him. Instead, she let her exasperation show. "You're a stubborn ass."

"You can call me anything you want. Now or then. Because I'll be in the room."

"Fine!" God, what was wrong with her? Because while his overprotective ogre instincts annoyed her, they also turned her on. She seriously needed therapy.

Only a sick mind would remember right then how he'd once—okay, way more than once—taken her and driven her to mindless pleasure on the very desk between them.

His eyes narrowed for a second, as if he was reading her thoughts. His ridiculously wide shoulders relaxed a fraction. "And another thing—"

"There's no other thing." She shooed him toward the door. "I have work to do. Go away."

He fixed her with a hard look. "I expect an email with the date and time of your next session with Scott Young."

"Which letter in the word *go* is causing the difficulty?" she snapped, then the anger trickled away as if someone had pulled the plug on her tubful of pent-up fury. She buried her face in her hands for a second before she dropped them to look at him. "Dammit, Murph." She sounded tired. She *was* tired. "We're always fighting lately."

He just stared at her—for five solid seconds, at least. As if *she* was being unreasonable. He opened his mouth. Closed it. Held up his hand as a sign of surrender and walked away, shaking his head in that universal gesture men had when they were insinuating that a woman was too emotional to deal with.

She wanted to throw something at his back. He could be *so* freaking aggravating. "Men!"

"Can't live without us," he called back over his shoulder.

"Can't wait until you all pile onto a spaceship and go off to colonize Mars!"

His back rippled, as if he were laughing.

She waited until he was gone, then, since she had plenty of time before her next patient, she went off to the physical therapist to borrow a wrist guard. As far as her bruises went, for the rest of the day, nobody was the wiser.

She only took the wrist guard off in her car on the way home. She didn't dwell on the mild injury. She would heal. At least her car was finally back from the mechanic, radiator fixed. She disliked depending on other people for rides. She disliked depending on anyone for anything.

She stopped by the post office on her way home, and then dropped off some dry cleaning, so darkness fell by the time she reached her house.

"Hi, Mr. Mauro. How are you today?"

He was making his rounds. He liked to walk around the block several times a day. He was just this side of eighty, with a slight Italian accent—a real character, according to Betty. Betty had spent enough time sitting on his front porch, and he'd spent enough time sitting on hers, so that Kate suspected there had been a "golden years" romance going on between the two, which she thought was inspiring and sweet.

Anthony Mauro looked toward Betty's house, then sighed as if his heart was breaking.

"I know." Kate felt the same. "Can't believe she's gone."

He waved away the words with one hand while he gripped his cane with the other. "She didn't want to be cremated. You make sure you remind Linda if you see her."

"I'm sure she didn't forget, but I'll remind her."

He harrumphed. "You get to be my age and funeral homes send you a dozen flyers a day. Always trying to talk you into some newfangled bullshit. Like making diamonds out of your ashes. Or shooting your urn up into space. Like anyone would want to end up in a pawnshop or forever float in a cold and dark nothing."

Kate didn't know how to respond, so she just nodded.

"And all of it is so expensive, you'd have to win the lottery on your deathbed." He grunted with anger. "You know what the latest thing is?"

She waited for him to tell her.

"They cremate you, mix your ashes with dirt in a cardboard box, bury it, and plant a tree seedling in there. For ten thousand dollars!"

Kate made low-key outraged noises. She wasn't really in the mood for funeral talk. She smiled at Mr. Mauro, hoping this was the end of it.

It wasn't.

He frowned even deeper. Tapped his cane. Bristled. "I told Betty the other day, if I die, just bury me upside down and stick a peach pit up my ass."

CHAPTER SEVEN

Kate

"I got a job!" Emma, dancing in place by the oven with both hands covered in mitts, announced in lieu of a greeting as Kate walked into the house.

"What?" Kate was still distracted—and more than a little stunned—by Mr. Mauro's declaration outside. And now the delicious scent of dinner, something with tomatoes and oregano, distracted her even more.

Emma pulled out her earbuds and set them on the counter, but kept the victory dance going. "I was checking out the shops on Main Street today after I had lunch at the diner. I walked by the florist and saw a Help Wanted sign in the window. The lady who runs the shop, Alice, interviewed me on the spot."

Kate dropped her bag in the foyer, tired to the bone, feeling guilty that she was coming home after dark. She had promised herself she wouldn't work late while her sister was visiting. "Oh. Okay."

Hurt flashed in Emma's eyes. She stopped dancing. "I wasn't planning on living with you. I will get my own apartment."

Ah, dammit.

"Sorry." Kate hurried forward. "I'm just preoccupied. If you stay, you're definitely welcome to live here." She took her sister's mittened hands. "I just meant... Flower arranging doesn't have a lot in common with banking."

"I need a creative break. It's temporary." Emma rolled her eyes. "I'm not setting my finance degree on fire or anything."

Okay. "Okay."

"Are you sure you don't mind if I stay here for a while?"

"We're family." Kate squeezed, then let her sister go. "Of course, I'm sure. Did you tell Mom and Dad? They'll be upset that you're not going back. Mom is experiencing...um...heightened emotions these days."

"Tell me something I don't know." Emma had a giant *duh* stamp over her face. "Why do you think I needed to get out of the house and come up here for an impromptu visit?" She smiled sweetly. "A little distance will be good for them. Dad always wanted to buy into a small vineyard when he retired. But they're not going to sell the house in LA as long as I'm there."

Emma left the rest unsaid, but Kate read between the lines. Their parents had been clinging harder to Emma because they'd lost Kate, or thought they had when she had faked her death.

"Anyway." Her sister smirked. "I don't want to come between you and Murph. Like, I don't want to be in the way if he shows up for a booty call."

"No worries." Kate's entire mental library of naked Murph was under Fort Knox-level lockup. Not opening that. Not going there. "When I said we're taking a break, I meant booty calls included."

"You know he's the hottest guy in town, right?"

"Hot isn't everything." Kate stepped to the sink and washed her hands so she could set the table. "We have issues."

"Not insurmountable ones. Biggest problem is that you moved out on him. You got a new home that doesn't include him at all. How do you think that makes him feel?"

Kate turned off the tap. "Last Christmas, when we drove around to see the lights, he told me he liked this neighborhood. His best friend in elementary school used to live around here. Murph said these ranchers were a great buy. Not a ton of square footage, but you could put an addition on the back and end up with that *and* a private courtyard. He said the ceiling in the living room and kitchen could be raised to the rafters. Put in a few skylights. Lots of height and light and open space."

Emma stared at her. "Does he know you thought about him when you bought this place?" But even as the last word was out, she zeroed in on Kate's wrist. She grabbed Kate's elbow. "What the hell happened?"

"Small accident with a patient." *Might as well get it over with.* Kate pulled away and unwrapped her neck.

"Like what?" In a split second, Emma was ready to charge off to battle, eyes flashing, mittened hands on her hips. They had their disagreements, but in times of trouble, they would back each other up to the end. "An accidental hanging?"

"He's troubled."

"Did Murph knock him out?"

"That's not what we do. We help people."

"You're crazy. You know that, right?"

"That's what the patient said."

Emma pulled off her oven mitts and leaned in for a closer look. When she stepped back, concern filled her eyes. "Is there anything I can do to help?"

"Cover up my bruises with makeup tomorrow before work? I think I have an old bottle of concealer somewhere. Or I could just wear a turtleneck," Kate said on second thought.

"Oh." Emma snapped her fingers. "I forgot to tell you. While you were at work, the eighties called. They want their turtlenecks back."

"Smart-ass."

"Sisters don't let sisters walk out of the house dressed like fashion disasters."

"And that's just one of the many reasons why I love having you here."

"Once people get to know me, they often find that they can't live without me," Emma deadpanned before asking, "Any news on your neighbor?"

The second Kate thought of poor Betty, her newfound

lightness evaporated. "Funeral's on Friday."

"I'll go with you." Emma glanced out the window at Betty's house, which sat dark and silent, a cold husk with life departed. "Do you think her kids will rent out her house? We could be neighbors." Then she slapped a hand over her mouth. "Sorry, that sounded really crass. It's not how I meant it. I…"

"No kids. I think she left the house to her church. She mentioned it the other day when she was talking about her will."

"Wait. A hot priest could move in?"

"I doubt it. Also, I think her church has a pastor. Who is married."

"Oh."

So much disappointment imbued in a single word.

Then Emma flinched. "Sorry. That was also inappropriate. I didn't know her. But I know you liked her. I know none of this is funny."

Kate offered a sad smile. "Betty would have been the first to make jokes about hot priests." She moved closer to the oven and looked through the glass. "What are we having? And thank you for cooking, by the way. I feel very spoiled."

"You're welcome. Gluten-free pizza. I stopped by the Pizza Palace and bought the dough they sell. Is that okay?"

"Better than okay. I skipped lunch. My stomach is still giving me trouble."

As the oven dinged on the last word, Emma mittened up again to pull the pizza out.

Kate took care of plates and glasses, and then she put the leftovers of the giant salad they'd had the day before, in the middle of the table.

The scent of tomatoes and cheese saturated the air. Her sister was there. Her new house was becoming a home. For the first time that day, Kate relaxed.

Then Emma passed by the window with their dinner, on her way to the table, and she froze midstep, staring outside.

Kate stepped up behind her. "What is it?"

She saw nothing except darkness and that it was beginning to rain. A dozen or so drops glistened on the glass.

Emma set the pizza on the table, then went back to the window to look again. "Do you believe in ghosts? I swear I just saw Betty walk through her kitchen." She rubbed her arms. "Goose bump city."

Kate patted her sister's shoulder. "Overactive imagination. You watched *Supernatural* too much as a kid. I promise you, there are no ghosts over there."

CHAPTER EIGHT

Murph

Murph didn't enjoy making his old police captain angry, but it couldn't be helped. He stopped by the station, a square brick building that brought back a lot of memories, first thing Wednesday morning.

Bing was reading through the mail at the front desk, the rest of the main area empty.

"Where is everyone?" Murph asked as he walked in.

The captain looked up. "Leila had to take her aunt for waxing. Rest of the squad are out setting up the streets for the Mushroom Festival, dropping off cones and cordons. We're shutting off six streets this year. Vendors need room to set up their tents."

"Hard to believe it started with a single Sunday."

"Festival's growing." Bing flashed a pleased smile. "Good for local business. Restaurants are packed already. Gift shops all stocked up. No downside to adding an extra day, other than the inevitable half a dozen drunk fights around the beer tents." He set down the stack of envelopes he'd been holding.

"Wait." Murph's brain caught up with him. "Did you say Leila took her aunt for *waxing?*"

"The aunt is having some feminine surgery tomorrow, and she's…" Bing had a don't-make-me-say-it look in his eyes.

Murph didn't make him say it. "Okay!"

"Okay." There was an awkward second, then Bing rolled on. "But you didn't come in to check on Leila's aunt or the festival."

"I was wondering if you had any news on Betty Gardner."

"What kind of news?" Bing asked in a deceptively casual tone.

"She wasn't taking out the garbage when she slipped."

The captain nodded. "Gabi said the same thing. Doesn't mean much. Betty could have gone outside for any number of other things. Fill the bird feeder, check that the outside basement door was locked, fresh air."

"Nobody saw it happen?"

"Midmorning, most people are at work." The captain paused for a second before he added, "No reason to suspect foul play. Nothing's missing from her house that we can tell. All valuables are accounted for, wallet, phone, her jewelry."

"All locked up tight?"

"Kate made sure."

She would. She was good at taking care of people.

"The leaves were raked, walkway clear." Murph's instincts kept prickling every time he thought of the accident. "What made Betty slip?"

"Old age? What's this about? Anything to do with Kate?"

"How would Kate come into this?"

"If the neighborhood turned bad, you could offer to be her private security? Or talk her into moving back into your apartment? Hell, if I know, dammit." Bing pointed at Murph. "But I know a desperate man when I see one. Want to talk about it?"

Murph rolled the man's words around in his head. Was he looking for an excuse to stay near Kate? "I'd like to think I'm not that pathetic."

"Whatever this is, it'll pass."

Murph swallowed the frustration that was bubbling up in his throat. "I hope it does, before she drives me crazy."

"You want to marry her, you have to get used to the driving-crazy part. It's half the job description. The other half…" A wistful, lovesick expression came over his face. "It's worth it." He paused, as if unsure whether to say the next bit, but then he did. "Sophie and I had our ups and downs."

"Yeah. Nobody who's ever seen the two of you together will believe that."

Bing almost smiled, then that hint of amusement disappeared and he turned police-captain serious. "You focus on fixing whatever went wrong between you and Kate and leave the investigation to us."

He didn't have to show steel for Murph to know that it was there behind the still-congenial demeanor. And yet... Murph promised nothing.

While he drove from the station to work, he considered how much he really needed to be concerned about Kate's and Emma's safety. And then thinking about Kate's sister made him think of his own brother, so Murph called him.

"What's up?"

"I'm at some training the company's puttin' on. It ain't bad. Maybe I'll get a raise and buy a house down here. Wouldn't that just burn Felicia's ass?"

Felicia had divorced Doug right after Doug had been notified he'd be downsized at work at the end of the previous year. She got the house in the divorce. Then, out of the blue, Doug's company offered him a similar position at their North Carolina location, and he'd jumped on the opportunity to leave town.

"You seen her around lately?" he asked. "Lookin' good on my money, I bet."

"Really let herself go," Murph improvised. "Total hag."

Doug laughed. "You're a good brother, you know that? Listen, I can't talk right now. Call you back tonight?"

"When you have a minute. Nothing urgent here." Murph pulled into the parking lot and looked for Kate's Toyota, tensed when he didn't see it.

On his way to his office, he swung by hers. Her door stood open. And there she sat, lost in work. Just seeing her had the power of switching Murph's world from being off to being exactly right.

She'd left her scarf at home, her bruises lighter than they could have healed overnight, probably makeup. She already had her scrubs on, with a long-sleeve shirt under that to cover her wrist.

"Didn't see your car outside. Wasn't sure if you were in."

She looked up. "Parked in the back."

"Everything okay?"

"Better than."

Her smile went straight to his heart. Best damn smile in the state of Pennsylvania, perhaps the country. When she smiled, she was all soft. He liked her soft. *Soft* wasn't *mad at him*.

"Emma is staying," she said. "Alice gave her a job at the flower shop."

All hope of Kate feeling unbearably lonely and inviting him over for a nightcap flew out the window. Murph tried not to feel so damned forlorn about it.

"That's an unexpected turn," he said, then corrected. "That's good. It'll be nice for you to have family here. How are you feeling?"

"Betty's funeral's on Friday."

She was neatly redirecting him from the incident the day before.

He decided to let her. "I'll be there."

And then they had nothing else to talk about. Or rather, they had a lot to talk about, but she didn't want to talk about their relationship, and he respected her wishes. He hesitated in the doorway, hating to leave. "You need help with anything?"

The morning sun streaming through the window kissed her auburn hair with fire. He wanted to bury his face in all that hair. He wanted to see it cascading forward as she rode him and leaned forward to kiss him. Looking into her blue eyes was like looking up at the cloudless sky on a summer afternoon. He wanted to see those eyes go blind with pleasure as he moved inside her. Wanted to hear her moan as he worshipped her perfect body.

If Murph was biased, he didn't care. She was beautiful and smart, and he loved her. And she didn't want him.

Shoot me now, before I write a country song.

"Funeral is taken care of," she said, then hesitated. "Linda, Betty's friend, asked me if I could help her clean out the house. I want to get a head start on that. As soon as the will goes through probate, the church will be putting it up for sale."

"I have a pickup."

She didn't respond.

Christ. "You said we would stay friends."

"I meant it. It's just…"

"Dammit, Kate."

Tension filled the room as she pretended to look at her calendar.

He shook his head. And because he didn't want to dump his frustrations on her, he turned out of the room, but her voice stopped him before he could take a second step.

"I'm just organizing stuff for now. But a pickup and another pair of hands would be nice when I get to the stage of moving things out."

He looked back over his shoulder. "Okay."

Her gaze was nothing if not conflicted.

Conflicted was good, right? Murph reasoned as he walked away. *Conflicted* wasn't *decided.* She thought maybe they shouldn't be with each other, but she wasn't sure. He just had to find a way to change her mind, make her see how good they were together.

Aaand…there he went sounding like a freaking stalker.

If she decided to quit the relationship for good, he would have to accept the verdict. He would have to respect her choice. Otherwise, he'd be just another asshole ex-boyfriend in a world of asshole ex-boyfriends. And if he knew one thing for sure, he knew this: she deserved better.

If worse came to worst, he was going to have to find the strength to walk away from her, dammit. Even if it killed him.

* * *

Kate

Holy mocha truffles.

Kate looked after Murph, not sure if she should cry or curse, a mix of emotions pulling her down like quicksand. She wanted to move past this stage, had been trying to come out on the other side with some clarity, but clarity kept eluding her.

All right. Was she going to be a wallowing-in-stupidity person or a solutions person? She was going to be a solutions person, dammit.

She jumped up and strode down the hallway. Maybe Maria had a minute.

Her phone rang as she turned the corner. Her mother.

"It's unfortunate that men reach the age when they start snoring like banshees at the same time as their wives reach menopause," Ellie Bridges said without preamble.

"Everything okay with you and Dad?"

"It'd be fine, if I could sleep. *Murder for snoring* should be a legitimate legal defense. Like crime of passion, and not guilty by reason of insanity."

"You scare me sometimes." Kate stopped walking. "Why don't you and Dad come up for the Mushroom Festival? I miss you. Emma misses you."

"Say the daughters who abandoned me."

"We didn't abandon you. We flew the nest. You raised us to be capable, independent women."

"Mmmm."

"Your wedding anniversary is in two weeks. You could make it an anniversary trip. The bed-and-breakfast just opened a brand-new honeymoon suite. Let me reserve it for you as a gift. The house used to belong to a guy who made glass eyes for World War Two veterans. There are eyes in jars still on the shelves." Historical military curiosities were her father's weakness.

"What's in it for me?" her mother grumbled.

"Days of uninterrupted adoration from your daughters. Also, the B and B was the scene of a kidnapping this spring." Her mother was a mystery novel buff.

"Ghosts?"

"Possibly. I swear the last time I was in there, one of the glass eyes winked at me." And then Kate thought of something that would seal the deal. "Shannon, the owner, serves shoofly pie with

Sunday tea."

"Maybe we could pop up for the weekend." Then, apropos of nothing, she added, "I'm growing a mustache."

Okay? "Is that another…"

"Menopause bullshit. Yes."

There was no correct response to that.

After they hung up, Kate resumed walking while calling Shannon. "Has anyone booked the honeymoon suite for next weekend yet?"

"Can't be booked until the website is updated. Murph finally swept you off your feet?"

"It's for my parents. Can I book the room? Saturday and Sunday."

"Sure."

"Do you need my credit card information right now?" Kate had her purse at her desk, but she could turn back.

"Nonsense. Since it's not up on the website yet, I'm not making money on it anyway. How about we barter? You do that website update, and I let you have the room for the weekend?"

"Done deal."

Maria's door stood open. Kate slipped her phone into her pocket and knocked on the frame. "Do you have a minute?"

Maria shoved her designer metal-frame glasses up the graceful slope of her nose, then pushed aside the notes she was reading on her lacquered black desk. She wore a sleek black dress with a single string of pearls. She was always perfectly put together, looking more like the editor of a fashion magazine at their Paris offices than a therapist. Her office matched her, of course, and could have been on the cover of *Elle Design*. "For you? Always."

Instead of her problems, Kate started with "Why is it that you're always effortless elegance personified, a graceful swan, while I'm like a neurotic chipmunk?"

Maria laughed. "Hardly. Take a seat. Should we have the door closed?"

"This is fine." The hallway was deserted. "Thank you." Kate sat. "Okay, first, how was the date?"

Maria smiled. "Sumptuous. He's…" She shook her head. "I'm

not even going to talk about him. I'm scared I'll jinx it." She dropped her hands onto her lap. "Are you all right?"

"I might have some mild depression." *Admitting the problem is the first step.* "I just… I don't know. I feel on the edge of crying a lot of the time lately."

"It's understandable. A friend of yours just died." Maria leaned back in her saddlebag-brown leather chair. Two black frames balanced out the wall space behind her, one her diploma from Harvard, the other a picture of her immigrant parents beaming at their citizenship ceremony. "Betty Gardner, right?"

"Even before Betty died."

"Everything okay with Murph? You moved out. I didn't want to pry, but I assume that means you're taking a break. Change in a relationship is a major stressor. You and Murph have been together a long time."

"Five years." Kate sighed. "Sometimes, I get so mad at him. But then sometimes, I feel like I'm being irrational."

"Could be from a change in hormone levels—"

"I'm not pregnant." Kate cut off that whole line of thought.

"Oh, wow." Maria's eyebrows jumped. She smiled. "I think that's what they call a *vehement* denial."

"I think it's menopause. My mother is going through it. She's all wigged out. And I feel the same. My period has been irregular…"

Maria gave her a thoughtful look. "Perimenopause is not impossible. Some women start as early as their midthirties."

"That is such bullshit— Oh God." Kate pressed her fingers to her top lip. "I'll be growing a mustache?"

Maria's shoulders shook, but to her credit, she did not laugh out loud. "No mustache. I promise. It's probably not even perimenopause, but there'd be no harm in ordering up some lab work. And we could rule out pregnancy too, for sure. It's always better knowing than not knowing," the psychologist said in a mild tone, not pushing, but gently encouraging. "I'll add some thyroid labs as well. That could cause mood swings too, and it's more likely. In the meantime, how about we schedule a session for you? I know you've processed your past, but childhood trauma is a tricky issue. It can bubble right back up through time and space."

"I don't—" Kate stopped herself. *No shame in asking for help. It's the smart thing, the right thing.* Wasn't that what she always said to her patients?

"Thank you. That would be great." She needed to get her head on right. "Let's do that."

"I could stay an extra hour tonight?"

"I appreciate it. But I promised to help with packing up my neighbor's belongings. I need to start organizing things. At least make some preliminary piles."

She wasn't scared of going over there alone after dark, regardless of what Emma had thought she'd seen. Kate didn't believe in ghosts and spirits.

CHAPTER NINE

Kate

"How long do you think this is going to take?" Linda Gonzales asked from Betty's recliner Thursday morning. To spare her bad back, she was only directing the work. At ninety, the woman had earned her rest.

Kate stopped packing to stretch her own spine. "I should have started yesterday, but I ended up with a killer headache after dinner. I swear I saw stars every time I bent over."

"It's this weather front. And you can't bend over with a headache," Linda agreed. "We'll get it done. Betty kept a clean house. The place shouldn't need that much scrubbing, just packing up her belongings."

Kate taped up the box at her feet. She was working in the living room, while Emma tackled the laundry room in the back, Murph carrying the boxes to his pickup, then delivering them to wherever Linda said they should be delivered.

Mr. Mauro was walking around the kitchen island with his cane. *Dear, merciful God, please don't let him bring up funeral arrangements.*

He'd also come to help, but he couldn't bend and he couldn't reach, so mostly he just aggravated Linda. The two couldn't stand each other, possibly a residue of their rivalry for Betty's affections.

"*What* are you doing?" Linda snapped at him. "Can't you see that you're in the way?"

He rubbed his sternum with a look at her like she was a witch, and he was trying to think where he'd left his matches. "My chest's been hurting the last couple of days. I could be having a heart attack. I'm trying to walk it off."

"You should walk in the basement," Linda suggested in a sweet tone that was new to their exchanges.

He raised his bushy gray eyebrows. "How does that help?"

"Gets you used to being underground," Linda said with a straight face, then lost it and cackled.

Kate stared at them horrified, but also on the verge of bursting out laughing, which she was going to hold back if it choked her and she fell headfirst into the new box she was packing.

She cleared her throat. "Do you need me to drive you over to urgent care?"

Mr. Mauro waved off the offer. "I'm not going to die." He gestured toward Linda with his cane. "Wouldn't give her the satisfaction."

"Are you sure?"

He sighed. "Maybe I'll go home and take a nap."

Kate nodded, her worries not entirely dispelled. "I'll check in on you later."

He shuffled out of the kitchen, passing Murph in the foyer.

Kate tossed the empty tape roll onto the counter and grabbed a new one. "I think we'll get a good chunk done by the time we have to leave for work." Both she and Murph worked the afternoon shift. "We can come back tomorrow and tackle the rest. Emma won't start work at the flower shop until Monday. We should be done by then."

Murph strode into the kitchen, bringing the scent of fall air with him. Along with a boatload of fall memories, all the things the two of them usually did this time of year. He carved good pumpkin. He was a wizard with a knife. He was a wizard with peeling her out of various skimpy Halloween outfits too. She used to pick them just for him, just to see his eyes grow heavy lidded with desire.

Elvira in the corn maze…

Heat flashed across her cheeks. Kate clenched her teeth. No Elvira in the corn maze! She swallowed back a half-escaped groan. What was wrong with her?

Murph flashed her a puzzled look. "Goodwill run is signed, sealed, and delivered."

Emma came from the back with a box and handed it to him. "Towels. Gently used. Clean. For your next Goodwill trip?"

They'd had their big reunion already, when Murph had first shown up earlier. And Kate had felt like a jerk for not inviting him over sooner.

He carried the box to the foyer, put it aside, then came back to ask Linda, "What's next?"

"Church bazaar." Linda patted the pile of boxes stacked next to her, while Emma returned to the laundry room, and Kate focused on her own work.

"You can drive it straight to the back parking lot," Linda told Murph. "Louis will be waiting for you with the Tuesday Night Men's Group. I'll give him a call to let him know you're on your way. They'll carry everything down to the basement."

"Yes, ma'am."

Kate glanced over her shoulder just in time to see Murph pick up the nearest box and carry it out as if it were his first instead of his fiftieth. She missed his muscles. Missed seeing them, touching them, kissing them. Murph naked was a sight to behold.

She was a shallow, shallow woman.

"You have a good man there," Linda commented with a wistful smile. "Reminds me of my second husband."

"Not my man." The words tumbled out and made Kate halt with the tape for a second. Was she being petty? Weird? Mean? "But he is a good man."

Linda tilted her head. "I see the way he looks at you."

"We used to be…" What? A couple? Fake engaged?

"I see." A sage look came into Linda's eyes. "Well, isn't that a shame."

Unsure how to respond to that, Kate finished sealing the box in front of her. "So what's the secret to a long and happy marriage?"

Linda thought about it for a second. Hummed. Then she said, "Every time you see your husband naked, like when he's coming out of the shower or getting dressed, just look real shocked and say *How does that thing keep growing?*"

Kate had expected *Don't go to bed angry*. She choked on laughter. "Okay. I'll try to remember that." She shook her head, pushing the finished box against the wall with her foot. "What happened to the first husband?"

"Got rid of him. Always a day late and an inch short." Linda winked.

Kate might have laughed a little too hard at that. She was starting to see why Betty had been friends with Linda. Not a dull moment.

"Do you think you'll get married for the third time?" Kate asked.

Linda gestured at the door through which Tony Mauro had left. "Have you seen what's out there?"

"He's a character. I like him. He's funny."

Linda shrugged, then changed the subject. "What went wrong with you and Murph?"

That was the last thing Kate wanted to talk about. So after saying, "What didn't?" she added, "I'll do Betty's craft room next."

Except, as she stepped into the room, she stopped and just stood there. Instead of cataloging the shelves of supplies, her brain was replaying a three-month-old conversation with Murph, the one right before he'd proposed.

"I wanted you from the first time I saw you sleeping in my bed like Cinderella."

"Sleeping Beauty."

"I'll brush up on my fairy-tale princesses when we have kids."

The thought stole her breath. The image he painted…a little girl on his knee, holding up a storybook…

"I could be a terrible mother."

It was her deepest fear—that she had some defective gene, and she'd end up being the kind of parent like the monster who had given birth to her.

"You mothered your sister," Murph said. "And you did that just fine."

"That's not necessarily healthy psychologically either."

"Okay," he said. "If you don't want kids, we won't have kids."

"As easy as that?"

"You're the one making everything complicated." He didn't quite succeed at keeping the frustration from his voice. *"I fell in love with you years ago. I was clear about wanting you then, and I'm clear about wanting you now."*

"I'm not the same person I was five years ago."

"I know. I'm in love with this version too."

"A stupid woman who's scared to have kids?"

"You're far from stupid. And you're allowed to have fears."

"You don't have any fears."

"Plenty."

"Like what?"

"I'm scared to death of this conversation. That you're telling me you changed your mind about us." He stood there with his heart in his eyes. *"Look, Kate. This is it for me. I don't play games."*

Nobody could be that sure of themselves, could they?

"I'm figuring it out," Kate told the universe under her breath, then faced the shelves of yarn and fabric in front of her.

An entire see-through storage box was filled with nothing but knitting and crochet needles. She spotted *two* sewing machines. If Betty had ever gone overboard, it was in her craft room.

The towering shelves, packed with a jumble of supplies, overwhelmed Kate. She knew little about fabric arts. She was going to need help in there.

"Maybe we should save this room for tomorrow," she told Linda as she walked back out. "Let's do the kitchen next."

She marched straight to the nearest cabinet and peeked inside. "Open food boxes to the garbage, anything unopened to the Broslin Food Pantry?"

"Or to the church. We collect cans every Sunday and deliver them together the following week. We have a whole system set up for sorting, double-checking expiration dates, boxing by allergen information, and so forth. Might as well take advantage of it."

"Sounds good. I'll start with the nonperishables."

Kate set everything with old expiration dates aside on the kitchen island, then, when she was finished, she reached for the garbage can under the sink.

Since it was almost full, she decided to take it out before filling it up again. She was halfway to the front door when Murph strode in, back from his church run.

He looked at the garbage and pulled up short. "Did you eat that?"

"What?"

"Burger."

A crumpled yellow wrapper sat on top, Main Street Diner Takeout printed on it in red. "No."

"Emma?"

"Not hers either. We didn't bring any food. I figured we can just pop back home when we get hungry."

Murph looked at Linda.

"I had breakfast at home," Linda said. "Have to eat first thing so I can take my morning pills. Betty probably had the burger for her last lunch. Guess she slipped up with her diet. She told me she was cutting out fast food. She was trying to be careful with her diabetes." Linda nodded toward the three carrot muffins in a grocery-store plastic bag on the counter. "I'm even surprised she had those. She told me she started baking all sugar-free."

"I haven't eaten yet." Murph walked over to snatch the bag. "Mind if I grab these? Should be still good, right?"

Linda shrugged. "I'm sure Betty wouldn't mind."

"Thanks." Murph turned his attention to Kate and reached for the garbage can with his free hand. "Let me take that. I need to go back to my truck for a second anyway."

He was smiling at her.

Why did that make her want to cry? What was wrong with her?

Kate thrust the bin at him and turned on her heel. "I'll tackle the fridge."

She opened the refrigerator and hid behind the door. "Cheese, half-empty milk bottle, a jar of pickles with just three spears left, half a stick of butter, wilted lettuce, various condiments," she told Linda, breathing easier when she heard the front door close behind Murph. "I suppose everything will have to be thrown out from here."

The idea was enough to distract her. She *hated* wasting food. It went against her grain. Never would she ever forget the desperate hunger of her childhood years.

Aaand… She was not going to go there either. She was going to leave the past in the past.

They worked until noon, making excellent progress, then everyone went home for lunch and on to their own afternoon plans, which for Kate meant going to work.

Murph should have been there too, but his pickup wasn't in the parking lot when she pulled in.

As she removed the key from the ignition, her phone rang.

"Mom just called," Emma said. "She bought the tickets. They're definitely coming. Early. They'll be here first thing next Wednesday."

"That's great." Kate got out of the car. "I'll call Shannon at the B and B. I only reserved Saturday and Sunday."

"I can take care of it if you want me to."

"Okay." Kate had a full schedule. "Sure. But please make sure Shannon knows we're paying for the extra days."

"She sounded a little wigged out."

"Mom?"

"Yeah. She told me she just realized the reason for men living shorter isn't because they take stupid risks. It's because women go through menopause. I'm pretty sure the implication was they *take out* their husbands."

"She needs a vacation."

Emma laughed. "Seriously."

"We'll make sure they have the best minivacation ever."

Kate reached the front of the building just as they hung up.

A twenty-something man in army fatigues and a baseball hat waited at the front door, shifting from one foot to the other, drumming his fingers on his leg, his other hand gripping a metallic cell phone. Kate had him pegged as a new patient, nervous to go in, not sure what to expect. Good thing she'd arrived when she had. They could walk in together. She could chat with him a little and allay his fears.

"Hi." She climbed the front steps. "I'm Kate. I work at this earthly paradise. Are you here to check in?"

"Ian McCall." Six foot five at least, a hefty chunk of solid muscle, he stopped fidgeting only long enough to look her over. "I need to be here."

"Murph Dolan handles the intake. Let me walk you to his office."

"The woman inside said he was running late today. She said I could talk to you instead."

So, he *had* gone in already and even talked to one of the staff. He was having some first-day jitters, but he hadn't left. He was committed to treatment. *Excellent.*

Kate smiled. "I used to help Murph with evaluations. I can start the process while we wait for him to arrive. Why don't we head to my office? I don't know about you, Ian, but I could use a cup of coffee."

She walked past him, held the door open for him, noted how he kept twitching, his gaze darting around, his entire body tense. They were close enough for her to notice that his hair wasn't just messy. It was choppy—as if maybe he'd cut it himself. Possible PTSD, although that wasn't her diagnosis to make. As the head therapist, Maria would be handling that.

"Where are you from, Ian?"

"Virginia."

"Is that where you were stationed?"

He shook his head. "Fort Bragg."

"How many tours?"

"Three. Two in Iraq, one in Afghanistan. Joined at eighteen, deployed right after, back-to-back."

"Thank you for your service. We are honored to have you here."

He didn't respond, just watched her with a quiet intensity as she unlocked her office.

Three patients were gabbing at the end of the hallway, two men and a woman. The woman laughed loudly at something. One of the guys patted her on the shoulder. Ian turned his back to them and shook his head, as if the loud chatter was a swarm of flies buzzing around his ears.

"Mind if I close the door?" he asked.

"Of course not."

Kate hung up her coat and bag, then dropped her phone onto her desk. She'd set aside an hour for paperwork that morning, so she didn't have an appointment right away. She could afford to spend some time with Ian. He'd come this far; she didn't want him to change his mind and leave.

"I'm glad you're here. I think sometimes soldiers find it difficult to ask for help. You're supposed to be strong, the strongest, warriors. You're supposed to be defending others." She kept smiling. "But asking for help is not an admission of weakness. Just the opposite."

She turned to her pod coffeemaker that sat next to the printer. Sometimes she didn't have enough time to run to the cafeteria for a cup between patients, so she finally bought herself a machine. "How about coffee? I only have one kind, breakfast blend. Is that all right?"

"Yeah." He stepped over to the treatment room to peek in.

She popped in a pod, then filled the water reservoir and set one of her mugs under the spout. While she waited for it to be filled, she said, "Feel free to sit anywhere you'd like."

She had two visitor's chairs in her office, although she only ever had one patient in there at a time. She had two chairs because sometimes just offering people a choice set them at ease, made them feel as if they were in control.

"Sugar and cream? Powdered creamer, actually." She held up the box. "I've been thinking about buying one of those small dorm fridges, but I haven't had a chance yet."

"Black." He paced the small room instead of sitting.

Kate set the mug on his side of her desk, then popped in a pod for herself. "You'll like Hope Hill. We do pretty good work here. Okay, I might be biased." She gave an easy laugh as she bent down to plug in her laptop. "How much do you know about our programs?"

He clenched his jaw, unclenched it, the muscles in his cheeks tightening, then relaxing. He was watching her every move, monitoring every foot of space around them, as if expecting a surprise attack to materialize from thin air. "Saw people talking about it in an online vet group."

"Then you probably know we use nontraditional therapies in addition to traditional methods. Massage therapy, acupuncture, reflexology, ecotherapy, the works. Would you be open to something like that?"

He shrugged again. "A couple of guys online swore you helped."

"I'm glad. It's nice to know people leave here feeling healed." She smiled, but he didn't smile back.

Desperation filled his eyes, his face too tight, his muscles too tense for just a basic conversation.

Kate turned her back on the coffee, giving Ian her full attention. "All right. Let's look at your paperwork."

"I don't have any."

His fingers clenched and unclenched at his sides. He was close enough to grab her across the desk, although she didn't think he would. But maybe because of his size, she felt him looming, and she wished he would sit down and calm down instead of getting visibly worked up.

Kate calmed her own speeding heart first, seamlessly moving into yoga breaths, to change the energy in the room. *Deescalate. Make him feel safe.* "No problem. We can just talk. Like I said, Murph is the paperwork guy anyhow."

Ian's chest heaved as if he'd been running. He stared at her for an uncomfortably long moment, then went back to pacing, but kept his eyes on her. "All everybody ever cares about is the paperwork and the damn VA."

"We care about our patients. I promise you that. But here's the thing. You know how healthcare works," Kate said in the most apologetic tone possible. "It's layers of bureaucracy on top of bureaucracy. Places like this? We have to have a referral."

When he stepped toward her again, she hurried to add, "If you don't have the papers with you, I can get that done right now. Just takes a phone call." She nodded toward her phone, not quite daring to reach for it. "What do you think? Then we can move on to the important stuff."

If he let her use the phone, she could call Murph. If she

babbled on about admissions, making no sense, Murph would know something happened. He was probably in the building already. He'd be over in a minute. She could keep Ian talking until then.

Kate kept her smile going, kept her cool. "How about we get that out of the way, then sign you right up for treatment?"

"You pick up that phone, and the next thing I know, a padded van shows up." Ian's darting gaze focused, stilled. "You'll call someone to have me locked up in a looney bin."

"You can listen to every word I say."

"No phone call!" he shouted, jabbing at the air with his cell phone as if with a weapon.

Dammit, dammit, dammit.

Kate inched back, not that a few more inches would make a difference, if he became violent. She was trapped behind her desk, couldn't run.

Ian waved his hand and kept yelling. "When the government said *go*, I went. Every time. Now when I say I need help, you give me the goddamn help!"

CHAPTER TEN

Asael

"Can I interest you in a slice of fresh pecan pie?" the homey-looking waitress at the Broslin Diner asked Asael.

He sipped his decaf and shooed her away as he checked his messages, noted the code automatically forwarded from another number. The code identified one of his regular clients, an eccentric oil billionaire who used him to eliminate regulators and business rivals.

Asael called the man back, and while the call bounced from secret server to secret server, he wondered about his next project. He usually disposed of the man's overseas opponents in a straightforward manner. They didn't require much finesse. If anyone suspected foul play, it only increased the oil baron's reputation.

Western competitors needed more planning and a degree of separation. For example, if a rival executive, in the middle of negotiations, received a call that his father had died of a sudden heart attack, his mind would no longer be in the game. He'd want to close the deal and get out of there, rush home on his private jet.

"Thank you for calling me back, friend," the client on the other end said.

The overly familiar address annoyed Asael, but he never corrected the man, who got a charge out of pretending he had an assassin for a friend. Most of Asael's clients were weird in different ways. And this one paid better than any of the others.

"How can I help?"

"I wanted to talk to you about your last assignment."

Asael straightened in his booth, alert. "Any problems?"

"No, my friend. I was merely wishing I could have been there…" He trailed off suggestively.

Asael waited.

"Next time," the man said after a couple of seconds, "if there was a way for me to…"

"I'm not sure that would be safe."

"What I mean is, maybe a video could be arranged."

"And if that video proof is found in your possession?"

"Maybe not a job connected to me, then. Maybe something you do for someone else? Whatever the client pays for the hit, I'll double it for the opportunity to view live footage." The man's voice thickened as if with arousal. "I want to feel like I'm there."

Creepy fuck. Then again, the world was full of freaks. Asael sipped his decaf. The question was, did he want to keep this particular client?

He set down his cup softly, the touch of ceramic and wood not even a whisper. "I'll see what I can do, my friend."

CHAPTER ELEVEN

Murph

"Did you just dump garbage on my desk?" The captain snapped his eyebrows together.

Murph dropped into a chair and nodded at the crumpled burger wrapper in the plastic bag he'd rescued from the carrot muffins. "All I'm saying is, you didn't put this in Betty's garbage the day you were there. Gabi didn't have a burger either. I asked her. And the first time I checked that trash can, the wrapper wasn't in there."

Bing gave his long-suffering police captain sigh, kicking his feet out in front of him and leaning back in his chair. "You think you remember every piece of garbage in a nearly full can from a glance?"

"Linda Gonzales says Betty cut out fast food. She was watching her blood sugar."

"I'm watching what I eat too." Bing looked pointedly at the half-eaten grocery store coffee cake on the corner of his desk, not that far from the garbage. "We all slip up now and then." He pushed the bagged-up burger wrapper back toward Murph.

Murph left his potential evidence where it was. "What would it hurt to dust it for prints?"

"If you miss police work so much, I hear Avondale PD is hiring." But then the captain's next words were said with concern. "You had a rough deployment a few years ago. You lost friends in Afghanistan, then you came home and got caught up in Kate's mess. It's not healthy to live in a constant state of hyperawareness."

"Kate is safe. Mordocai and Asael are gone. That's all in the past."

"You had to use deadly force to save her from Mordocai."

"You say that like it's a bad thing. I'd kill the bastard again."

"I'm not implying that you didn't do the right thing, the same thing I would have done under the circumstances. I'm trying to tell you that you've been under considerable stress before you headed off for three years in witness protection with Kate, every second of which you spent looking over your shoulder. Living like that would make anyone a little paranoid. Listen, you're back in Broslin. Relax. The PD is on the job. You don't have to keep up this level of vigilance."

The man was starting to tick off Murph. "You think my brain is bored, so I'm making up shit."

"I'm saying you might be seeing things that aren't there."

He didn't want to fight with Bing, who'd always been a friend, but he couldn't let this go either. "What if Betty's fall wasn't an accident?"

"Who would push her? Why? Can't think of anyone who had problems with her. Nothing was taken from her house. What's the motive?"

"Maybe someone—" Murph began to say, but the captain's phone interrupted.

Bing glanced at the screen. "The coroner." He picked up the call and listened with an unreadable expression, before saying, "I appreciate the heads-up. Thanks."

Then he hung up and flashed an extended, assessing look at Murph. "He's sending over his report within the hour." He paused for a moment, then another, and then he finally spoke. "Betty had some subcutaneous bruising on her chest."

"Consistent with a hard shove." Murph rubbed the heel of his hand over the armrest of his chair. "I'd rather have been wrong."

Bing snapped up the plastic bag between them, then pushed a button on his desk phone. "Could you come into my office, please?"

Harper Finnegan popped in two seconds later. He had a new energy lately, an almost palpable contentment. He used to be Officer Casanova. Then he'd fallen hard for Allie Bianchi, settled down with her, and these days, he was fifty shades of happy bastard. Murph tried not to envy him too bad.

"Captain," Harper said. "Murph."

The captain handed him the bagged burger wrapper. "I need you to dust this for fingerprints. Top priority. Betty Gardner's case."

"I'll get right on it."

When Harper was gone, Murph asked, "Are you upgrading the case to suspicious death?"

Bing gave the idea consideration. "Not yet. The bruise could have any number of causes. Betty could have fallen against anything inside. A doorframe, the fridge, whatever. Maybe she was dizzy. Then she went out for some fresh air, a loop around the house. But her blood pressure dropped again, and she fell out there too, the wrong way this time, her head against concrete." Before Murph could protest, Bing added, "We have no proof that says otherwise."

"I want to help."

"I want you to stop investigating." Bing pronounced his words with a slow care that spelled a warning. "You are no longer a member of this department. If there *was* foul play involved, the perpetrator's lawyer is going to have a field day in court with your civilian interference. It's going to discredit my case."

The tension between them was new. The captain tended to be a reasonable man. The general mood at the PD was friendly camaraderie. Of course, Murph hadn't been a part of the PD for a while. They were no longer on the same team, didn't have the same goals. The captain wanted all rules and regulations obeyed, while Murph wanted to keep Kate safe, whatever that required.

He didn't want a fight, though, so he stood. "I'd better get to work."

He called Kate from his pickup to see when she might have a minute to talk. He wanted to tell her about the contusion on Betty's

chest. When he bounced to voicemail, he hung up. She was
probably with a patient.

Murph was at the center in minutes and swung by her office,
but her door was closed. He didn't knock, didn't want to interrupt
her session.

He was walking away, halfway down the hall before he heard a
man shouting in there.

He backtracked. "Kate?" He tried the door. Locked.
"Everything okay?"

"Busy, Murphy! I'll come and find you when I'm done."

Her voice was carefully calm, and yet... He knew her, her
moods and tones. She wasn't simply busy. Nor would she lock
herself into her office with a patient. "Okay. I got some paperwork,
but afterwards, maybe we could grab some coffee in the cafeteria?"

"Sure, Murphy. Looking forward to it."

Liar. He hadn't been able to grab a cup of coffee with her in
weeks. She'd gotten good at pretending that she was always busy.
She'd even brought in her own coffee machine so she could more
easily avoid him. And on top of all that, she *never* called him
Murphy. Nobody but strangers did. To all his friends, he'd always
been Murph.

He could almost taste the danger. His insides went cold, then
colder. His basic instincts pushed him to break down that door to
see what was wrong inside. His military and police training kept him
calm enough to cobble together an actual strategy instead.

"See you later," he said. Then he was hurrying down the
hallway, calling Bing.

The captain picked up with "I'm not going to involve you any
further. You're not getting updates. You're not a police officer.
You're not working this case. Dammit, Murph, do I have to—"

"Kate is in trouble. She's in her office with the door locked.
She doesn't sound right. There's someone in there with her. She had
a violent incident the day before yesterday with a patient."

"On my way." To his credit, Bing didn't waste time on a
million questions. "You find out anything else, you call me with an
update."

"I will." Murph stashed his phone, then ran out to his pickup for the Glock G19 he kept locked in the glove compartment. Weapon securely stashed in the back of his waistband, covered with his shirt, he dashed around the building, until he stood under Kate's treatment room window—a damn floor above him. He didn't even pause. He lunged for the rainspout and climbed, using the window ledges for leverage. This was where his daily visits to the gym came in handy.

When he could reach the windowsill, he grabbed on and pulled himself up until he could peer in through the glass.

Nobody in the treatment room. The door to Kate's office stood half open, angled toward Murph. He couldn't see past it, couldn't see her.

He drew a long, even breath to slow the rush of blood in his ears, and listened. He could hear a low murmur. She was talking.

Then a man responded to her, much louder than she'd been, so Murph could make out the words. "I'll calm down when you help me!"

Murph snapped into combat mode, not so much a conscious decision as training. All emotion shut off. Focus intensified. Every thought in his head locked on her. They would remain locked until she was safe.

He dropped to hanging from one hand, yanked his key ring from his pocket, and used the thinnest key to wedge under the window, wiggling it as quietly as possible, leveraging his strength. When his muscles started to burn, he switched hands.

Come on, come on, come on. The window frame quietly popped, just as the guy inside shouted at Kate about how tired he was of everyone's excuses. Murph eased the window up.

He needed about a foot of clearance. *Slow and silent. A little more.* And then he had enough space at last.

He squeezed through and didn't have to thump onto the floor. He was able to lower himself right onto the massage table—a stroke of sheer luck.

"What if I'm never going to get better?" the man was shouting.

"I can tell you for a fact that's not true, Ian. Every patient we've ever had improved during the course of their treatment."

Ian?

Two Ians resided at Hope Hill at the moment. This guy didn't sound like either one of them.

"Listen." Kate remained commendably calm. "If you want to stay here, we have rules. No shouting matches. People come here to feel safe. I'm sure you understand that."

"Fuck the rules. You give me some pills."

"I'm a massage therapist. I don't prescribe meds. Why don't we go and see Dr. Maria Gulick?"

Murph slid from the massage table to the floor without making a sound. He didn't want them to leave, not when he was finally within striking distance.

"I'm trying to help you, Ian." Kate was nothing but kindness and compassion. "Please let me. Just please give me a chance."

"You're lying like all the others." The desperation in the man's voice took on a distinctly hopeless quality.

Murph didn't like that tone. His muscles bunched, ready to propel him forward.

Then he caught Ian's reflection in the glass of Kate's massage therapy diploma that hung on the wall. Not a sharp image, just the shadowy outline of the guy, and the metallic object glinting in his hand.

CHAPTER TWELVE

Kate

"I'm going to do absolutely everything I can to get you help."
Kate held still, shoulders down. *Nonthreatening.*

She faced down the man looming tall across her desk. She'd
heard Murph walk away outside earlier. Hopefully, he'd understood
her message and had snuck back silently. She just needed to get Ian
to walk out her door.

Sweat beaded on the man's forehead and above his lips, as if
he was in pain. *That* was the reason Kate had chosen her job, to
erase pain like that.

They'd gotten off on the wrong foot. She had no file on him.
She hadn't been prepared. But she was not going to lose him. "Let's
go see Maria."

He didn't respond.

Okay. Make him relax first.

She kept her smile and her cool. "How about you sit down, we
drink our coffee, and talk?"

Her own cup had long finished brewing behind her, but she
didn't dare reach for it, not yet. She didn't move as she waited for
Ian's response.

Ian's gaze darted around the room. "You got anything stronger?"

"Sorry. No alcohol on the premises."

"Maybe it's not the place for me, then."

A joke? Good. Some humor would be a step in the right direction.

"It's not a prison. People go into town. There's a great Irish pub, Finnegan's. A beer or two is fine, as long as it doesn't interfere with your current meds. You could even go with some of the guys tonight. They're all right, you know. Even here, they've got each other's back. It's one of the many things I love about working at this place."

"Any of them as bad as I am?" Ian challenged.

"Since you haven't been evaluated yet, I can't really answer that. But we treat a wide spectrum of conditions."

"I have PTSD, don't I?"

"Is that what your doctor said?"

"He sent me for a psych eval. I don't want to be locked up in the looney bin."

"An evaluation is not the same as locking people up. It's only so we can put together a treatment plan. Nobody's locked up here. You know how we just walked in, no security at the front door? Patients can walk out any time, just like that. People stay because they want to, because we help them."

Ian considered that for a moment, but then shook his head. "I bet people like me don't ever recover. PTSD for life. I can't take this shit. I won't."

"People like you certainly do recover here, every single day. We have discharge files a mile long. And let's not get ahead of ourselves. PTSD might not be what you have. An accurate diagnosis is important, the foundation of effective treatment."

His aggression might come from TBI. Traumatic Brain Injury was often missed as an initial diagnosis and presented later as anger, anxiety, or apathy.

"What do you think I have?" he demanded.

"A rough day." No sense in overwhelming him with what was nothing more than an educated guess at this stage.

Her easy response calmed him a little. He nodded. "I can't go on like this. You people have no idea what it's like."

"I really don't. You're one-hundred-percent right about that. But you could tell me. Let's give ourselves a much-needed caffeine hit and figure out how you could be best helped."

She slowly, carefully, reached for the full mug of steaming coffee behind her and sat down with it. His was still waiting, untouched, on the edge of her desk.

"You don't have to sit down if you don't want to," she told him.

And probably because she'd put it that way, he finally dropped into the nearest chair.

"Did you bring clothes for the stay?" she asked. "Shaving kit? Stuff you'll need for a couple of weeks?"

"In the car."

"Good." He really did plan on staying, making it work, instead of just grabbing some drugs and taking off. That gave her hope.

"So, you just give massages?" he asked.

"That's what I do." *Easygoing. Relaxed.* Maybe he'd follow her example. Patients often mirrored their therapist. "Some people come here with mental issues, some with physical, some with both. We do our best to help everyone."

He rolled his neck. "I have some shrapnel damage."

"Murph Dolan, my colleague who'll be registering you, has had a piece of shrapnel in his shoulder for over five years now. His doctor said digging it out might cause more damage than leaving it in. The injury only bothers him when the weather is bad."

"Mine are all out," Ian said.

"That's good."

He nodded. *Finally*, they were in agreement about something. Now she'd just have to take it from there.

"My head hurts more than my leg. The pain is blinding sometimes. I need something for that. And this fucking anxiety. I can't sleep."

"Once we finish the coffee, we'll walk over to Maria. If you talk to her, she can probably start you on a prescription right away."

"Not right away." Resentment and impatience flashed. "I'll have to find a pharmacy first. Then they need to get VA approval."

Kate smiled. "She can get you started on her pharmaceutical samples. We have pharma reps here almost every day."

Ian swallowed a gulp of coffee, hope sparking in his bleak eyes for the first time, dots of light in a bottomless well of darkness. "She would do that?"

"For every single person who works here, Ian, our number one goal, every single day, is to help."

He put his phone on her desk so he could hold the mug with both hands. His shoulders relaxed. The tension in the room eased.

And that was when Murph burst from the treatment room, weapon in hand, a one-person commando attack.

CHAPTER THIRTEEN

Murph

"Hands in the air!" Murph threw himself on the guy, knocking him away from Kate.

Kate shouted, "Stop! Murph!"

Like hell he would.

Murph held Ian down, putting his full body weight on the man. Where the hell was Bing? They had no handcuffs at the center, an oversight Murph was going to remedy at the earliest opportunity.

"Murph!" Kate rushed around her desk, through the puddle of spilled coffee. "Ian! Are you all right? Murph won't hurt you. Just stay still."

The guy seemed to listen. He wasn't scrambling to break free. He'd given up already, the fight gone out of him. "I'm sorry." He lay there, prostrate, his gaze searching out Kate. "I shouldn't have yelled. This is not who I am. I swear."

"Are you all right?"

Was Ian all right? When the hell was she going to care about herself?

Murph gritted his teeth because blowing up would help nothing and no one, but the freaking steam building up in his head was boiling his eyeballs. At least, he *finally* heard sirens in the distance. "I'm going to turn you over. Take it easy."

He pushed up and flipped Ian to his stomach, then gathered the man's wrists behind his back. He was ready for handcuffs by the time Bing banged on the door.

As Murph reached up to unlock it with his free hand, he caught a glance of Ian's *gun* on Kate's desk. Or what he'd thought was a gun, based on its reflection in the glass earlier. Except it was a damn cell phone. He only had time to think *Shit!* before Bing burst in.

"Police! Put your hands in the air!"

Only Kate complied, more upset than when she'd been held hostage. "Don't hurt him, please. His name is Ian McCall. He needs our help."

Bing was watching Murph, "You too. Gun on the ground."

"You can't be serious."

The captain widened his stance and set his shoulders back. "Look into my eyes. Do you see comedy?"

Okay. Fine. Whatever. Kate was safe. Relief overrode all other emotion. Murph placed his gun on the floor and slid it to Bing. "If you toss me your cuffs, I can put them on him."

The captain reached down, grabbed Murph's weapon, then shoved it into his belt behind his back. "My job. Up."

"It'd be easier my way."

Bing shot Murph a look that said he was about to lose his patience. "Show me your badge."

"You know damn well I don't have a badge."

"Guess then you're not a police officer."

"When did you become such a hard-ass?" Murph snapped as he stood, bringing Ian with him. He would let the man loose with Kate in the room when hell froze over and they opened an ice-skating rink. And the devil served hot chocolate.

"I've always been a hard-ass." The captain reached for Ian's wrists. "You've just forgotten."

Murph stepped away, following orders at last, but ready to spring again. He seriously hated not being in charge when a damn stranger who'd *locked* himself in with Kate was still within three feet of her.

To Ian's credit, he didn't struggle. He was like a rapidly deflating balloon. If Bing wasn't holding him up, he might have folded to the floor, which did a lot to settle Murph's overprotective instincts. He relaxed another notch when the captain finally slapped the cuffs on the guy.

"Ian didn't mean any harm," Kate insisted. "He's just desperate for help. What's going to happen to him?" She stepped from behind her desk, stopping next to Murph. "He came here to enter treatment. He got upset when I told him he needed a referral. I don't want him arrested. Could he please have a voluntary psych eval instead?"

"He locked the door," Bing said. "I'm reading that as a hostage situation that might not have come to a good end."

"He's desperate because he's in pain," Kate told him.

While at the same time, Ian McCall protested, "I wasn't going to hurt her. I swear. I just wanted to be alone with her. People popping in and out startle me sometimes. I—"

"All right." Bing held up a hand. "We have a guy in West Chester I can call."

Murph could see the tension go out of Kate. She unclasped her hands. "Thank you. Ian needs treatment. He's not going to improve in jail. I can enter a statement on his behalf. I'll come with you."

This was how she drove him crazy, Murph thought. Then again, this was how she'd made him fall in love with her. She sincerely, passionately cared about everyone. She had a heart a freaking mile wide that could hold lost puppies and stray cats along with family and friends and strangers she'd never met, all those kids her foster website helped.

"Don't forget his phone." Kate handed it to Bing.

"Thanks." The captain drew Ian toward the door. "Let's go." He paused only to call back over his shoulder to Kate and Murph. "I'm going to need both of you down at the station at one point today to give statements."

Kate said, "Of course."

Murph stepped after the man. "My gun?"

"You'll get it back at the station. After we have a talk."

The only thing that kept Murph from responding with words

he might regret later was Kate in his peripheral vision collapsing into her chair.

He let the captain go and stepped back into her office.

"How did you get into the treatment room?" Kate asked. "Did you climb the wall?"

"Couldn't think of anything else. I was waiting in there for the right moment. I thought he had a gun. I had about three heart attacks listening to you talk him down. Good job on that, by the way." She was smart, and brave, and excellent at her job. Of course, he was in love with her. "If you ever need a side gig, you can take up hostage negotiation."

"I'll pass," she told him. "You gave *me* a heart attack, busting out like that. I thought you were in the hallway. I was trying to get him out there." She shook her head. "He didn't mean to hurt me."

"The mental state he was in, he might have done something without meaning to."

If this had happened three months ago, she would be in his arms right now, Murph thought, resenting every inch of distance between them.

They'd had a scare, but it was over, and she was safe. With all the adrenaline coursing through him still, he wanted to celebrate. In the most primal way. On her desk. Or on her massage table. It was available.

Except, he knew what she'd say if he suggested that. It started with an N, and ended with an O.

At least she was almost smiling and not sending him away. And, most importantly, she was all right. *Unhurt.* The only thing that mattered.

Because he wasn't ready to leave just yet, he said, "We've gone all year without an incident, and now two in one week. Maybe we should hire security."

"We can't put guards at the door." Not a trace of uncertainty in her voice. "This is a treatment facility. Armed men in uniforms would trigger some of the patients. I don't want Hope Hill to look like a prison camp."

They'd had this discussion before, and the last thing Murph wanted right then was to fight with her. "Okay. You're right."

But from now on, the receptionists would be veterans, carrying concealed. He was going to break that to her later. No way in hell was he going to allow her, or any of the staff or patients, to be in danger.

She was doing her yoga breathing, so he knew she was still shaken. He would have given anything if she just walked into his arms for comfort. She didn't.

"Thank you. For all of it," she said instead.

"Even if I knocked him to the ground?"

"Even so. Although, that was absolutely unnecessary."

Not when Murph had thought the guy had a weapon. He'd never been happier to be wrong in his life.

"Why did you come by?" Kate tilted her head. "Earlier, when you knocked." She was back in business mode, calm, or doing a damn good job faking it. "Did you need to talk to me about anything?"

Earlier was a lifetime ago. "Just wanted to check in."

It wasn't the right time to tell her that her neighbor might have been murdered.

CHAPTER FOURTEEN

Asael

Asael sat in the center of the middle pew at Betty Gardner's memorial service—like a spider in his web—watching the mourners and unsure why. He was not in the habit of attending the funerals of his victims. Amateurs did that. The cops were always around, hoping to nab the killer. Not a fate Asael anticipated for himself, since he was certainly not an amateur. He was a master.

Stupid cops didn't even know there'd been a murder.

Asael observed precautions anyway. He sat with friends and family instead of in the back, where he would have been a lone spectator, possibly suspicious. He was masked as an octogenarian. When people asked, he said he'd served with Betty's husband, lived in West Chester, and saw the obituary in the paper.

As the choir sang—not one good voice among the lot—he wanted to be anywhere but there. Yet he was at the funeral because, to start with, there was little else to do in the damned town other than going to their *fungus festival*. Small-town people were a waste of space, not fit to live—born in some godforsaken backwater of a place without enough brains and ambition to leave. The kind of people who'd die in the same town where they were born and go nowhere in between, doing the same damn thing every day, usually the same damn thing their parents had done before them. And they were convinced they had it best, that they had it great. All smiling and chatty and stupid and annoyingly syrupy sweet, and so damn proud of themselves.

Nauseating.

Asael couldn't walk down the street without wanting to strangle at least half a dozen of them.

Broslin was his idea of hell. The thought of a lifetime in a place like this made him want to peel off his own skin.

He couldn't imagine Mordocai enjoying this sort of environment either. He *had* to have come here for a job. And since he'd kidnapped Kate Concord, she had to have been the job. And while Mordocai had been setting up her disappearance, he'd found a gift for Asael.

What damn gift? The only thing the unsufferable town was famous for was its mushroom production. If they grew some rare poisonous mushrooms, that could have explained it, but no. Whitecap and portobello. Asael had checked.

So, what gift? And why couldn't he let all these damn questions go? Why did he care? Except that his instincts were prickling, leaving him no rest.

He watched mourners walk up to the coffin one by one. Kate and Murph were there, although not together—the bitch infuriatingly familiar, yet, for once, Asael's memory failed him.

He kept an eye on her as the infernal organ music drove him crazy. Then the choir burst into song again. He wished they'd burst into flames.

It could be arranged.

The happiest thought he'd had all day.

He sat there for another minute, then pushed to his feet and edged out of the pew. "Excuse me." He was done. He'd suffered all he could take. "Excuse me." He hadn't been to a funeral since...

It'd been a small chapel, almost like this one, on the outskirts of Los Angeles, the funeral of a woman who'd seen him taking out a mark, the only person ever to have seen him and gotten away. The only one to be able to identify him. He'd tracked her down and taken her out, had gone to her funeral to make sure she was dead. *Cathleen Bridges.* His brain readily supplied the name.

Clever little bitch, working with the FBI to fake her own funeral, as it turned out.

He'd blown her to pieces along with an FBI van, then put her behind him.

But now…

The sounds of the service faded into the background, the buzz of the funeral disappeared. Old memories sharpened.

Asael's gaze snapped to Kate Concord by the coffin.

The hair was wrong—the color, the cut, the length—and so was the style of her clothing. And yet…

As Asael watched her, he came alive, the thrill of the hunt spreading through his veins.

Well, well, well, a fellow resurrectionist.

Hello there, Miss Bridges.

CHAPTER FIFTEEN

Kate

"Coffee?" Emma asked as she and Kate walked into the house after the funeral.

"I'm trying to cut down. I've been feeling weirdly jumpy and edgy lately." Grief sat heavily on her shoulders. Betty had been gone for several days, but the service and saying goodbye at the coffin made her death more real.

Kate's phone rang. She glanced at the screen.

"Captain Bing. I was about to call you." She hung up her coat with her free hand. "I wanted to check on how Ian McCall's psych eval went yesterday."

"Our usual guy who does psych evals has retired." The captain cleared his throat. "New guy couldn't come out right away, so I had to keep Mr. McCall overnight."

Something in Bing's voice set off Kate's internal alarms. "Is he all right?"

"I put him in the conference room. He's a vet. He served his country. That means something to me."

"I know. Thank you for—"

"Should have put him in the interview room," the captain said, and as Kate wondered what the difference was, he added, "Interview room locks automatically."

Words that pretty much clued Kate in to where this conversation was going. "What happened?"

"I told the psych consult to ring me when he was done, and I'd collect McCall." A frustrated grunt popped through the line. "Idiot had a question and came over to my office. Leila was in the back, making coffee. McCall walked out."

"I should have…" Kate had no idea how to finish. She didn't know what she could have done differently under the circumstances, only that she *should* have done something more, because this outcome was unacceptable.

"Not your fault." Bing huffed. "It's mine, if it's anyone's. I have an APB on him. Everyone's out looking. I just wanted to give you a heads-up. I'm going to send Mike over to Hope Hill, in case McCall goes back there."

"I don't think he's looking to cause trouble."

"Maybe not. There's not much I can charge him with. Not sure if I want to charge him. But having that psych eval, knowing what's going on with him, would have made me feel better."

"Should I go in to work? Just in case he goes back there? I'm at home. I took the day off for the funeral."

"If he goes to Hope Hill, Mike will handle it. You might want to ask Murph to hang out at your place, just as a precaution, for a few hours. Until we locate the guy."

Kate looked at Emma, who'd already put on coffee and was paging through the stack of magazines and catalogs that had come in the mail that week. "Ian wouldn't come here. He has no idea where I live."

"Almost everyone else in town does. All he has to do is ask someone."

"Let's hope people won't give a stranger my home address."

"Most wouldn't, but it only takes one."

Maybe so, but she wasn't going to invite Murph over regardless, Kate thought as she thanked the captain for the warning, then hung up.

"Trouble?" Emma asked.

"The man I had that confrontation with at work yesterday busted out of the police station." Kate walked to the window and looked at her quiet little neighborhood. "He doesn't know where I live. We should be fine."

"You should call Murph over."

Why is that everyone's first thought?

"How about I grab my own gun and keep it within reach until Ian is located?" Not that she thought it was necessary, but maybe that would convince everyone that she could defend herself, and they would get off her back. She fixed Emma with a serious look. "But, please, don't handle it."

"What am I, twelve?" Emma rolled her eyes, poured herself a cup of coffee at last, then leaned against the counter. "Did Linda Gonzales say when she was coming over to finish cleaning out Betty's place?"

"First thing in the morning. Since I have the weekend off, I think we'll have the whole house packed."

"Is Murph coming to help again?"

Kate nodded. That was Murph. If someone he knew was moving, he offered to carry furniture. He'd mowed the lawn at Joe's house for the past month because Joe—one of Hope Hill's janitors—was allergic to grass, and Gracie, his wife, had broken her leg. Kate had seen Murph jump up and clear tables at Finnegan's before when the place had been shorthanded. Apparently, he'd bussed tables there as a teenager. He was a good guy. A great guy. His character had never been the problem.

"Let's change out of our funeral clothes, mix up some margaritas, and watch a movie." Kate headed to her bedroom. "How about *Bridget?*"

That put an instant smile on Emma's face. "I love old movies. A drink would be nice, but no food, no snacks, not so much as a single popcorn. After that church spread, I don't want to see a food item until the Fourth of July barbeque at Mom and Dad's."

"Just Mark Darcy and margaritas. And I'm going to pretend you didn't say *old movies.*"

Emma turned back from the door of the guest bedroom with a here-is-your-reality-check look. "Twenty. Years. Old."

'So mean. But guess what, baby sister? *Twilight* is thirteen. Babies who were born while you were trying to decide between Edward and Jacob are now *teenagers*." Kate smirked as she strode into her bedroom with panache.

God, she'd missed this, the teasing, the sibling one-upmanship, even the occasional fight she'd had with her sister. She was glad Emma was staying. And she was determined to enjoy every single day they were together again. She didn't think it would be permanent, just until Emma figured out what to do next.

For the rest of the afternoon and evening, Kate pretended she'd forgotten all about Ian, but she was on alert, checking her phone when Emma wasn't looking. No texts from Hope Hill about any trouble there. No calls. No updates from the captain—which meant Ian was still out there all alone, not getting help.

"What are you going to do about the Ian guy?" Emma asked as they were going to bed.

"If he reaches out? Anything I can to make sure he receives the right treatment. Right now, he's just plunging himself into more and more trouble. I wish I'd passed him my phone number before Bing carted him off yesterday. I didn't think of it at the time."

"You couldn't have predicted that he'd go on the lam."

Kate nodded and stepped into her bedroom, ready for some rest.

She slipped her gun into her nightstand drawer.

Moonlight hit her empty bed, emphasizing it as if the room was a stage set for a play called *My Lonely Life*. Since she didn't want to think about missing Murph, she turned to the window. The moon was rising, kissing Betty's roof before parting from the ridge and moving along on its celestial journey. The house that was no longer a home sat dark and silent, a sad and abandoned vibe about it already.

Kate sighed. Maybe she was just projecting.

She looked up at the sparkle of stars in the clear October sky. "I'm going to miss you, Betty."

As she settled between the sheets, she thought of the funeral service, the chapel filled to the brim. Everyone had something nice to say about Betty Gardner, about her kind heart and gentle spirit.

Kate even dreamed about her, but in the dream, Betty was her grandmother. They were having tea and cookies.

An odd sound woke her in the middle of the night, a vaguely familiar metallic snick. A few seconds passed before she could identify it: a door being unlocked.

Betty's back door, to be specific, less than a dozen feet from Kate's bedroom window.

She blinked the sleep from her eyes and glanced at her clock. *Two a.m.*

Without turning on the light, she slipped out of bed to look outside. Betty's house sat enshrouded in darkness and silence, same as when Kate had gone to bed. The neighborhood slept, all at peace.

Probably dreamt the sound.

Kate rubbed her forehead, then padded out to the kitchen for a glass of water. She was just jittery. As much as she knew Ian wouldn't come after her to hurt her, her subconscious was on alert out of habit. She'd spent too many years of her life on the run, always on her guard.

She'd barely taken the first sip when she happened to glance out the window over the sink.

"What the—" she said out loud, sputtering.

A pickup she knew all too well sat in front of her house by the curb, with Murph sleeping behind the wheel.

Dammit.

Bing must have called him too about Ian's escape.

Kate drained the glass, then set it on the counter with a hard *clink*, braced her hands on the edge of the sink, and looked at the man who was doing his best to drive her crazy on a daily basis.

The übervigilance was so completely unnecessary. Ian McCall wasn't going to come to her house in the middle of the night. He was probably back at home in Virginia by now.

Kate watched as the shadow in the truck moved, Murph shifting slightly in his sleep.

His bad shoulder is going to kill him in the morning.

Her heart twisted, because of course it did.

Her couch wasn't the best, yet it was still better than sleeping in a truck.

She *could* invite him in.

CHAPTER SIXTEEN

Murph

Murph lifted the recliner destined for the West Street Mission, doing his best not to show how much it hurt his aching back, but inside, he was swearing like a sailor who stepped on a rusty nail on deck. If he'd needed a reminder that he was no longer twenty, spending the night in his pickup had done the job.

He carried the old piece of furniture out, loaded it, then paused for a minute to roll his shoulders and stretch his muscles. Did not help. He was damn near limping on his way back inside.

Emma was still working in the back of the house. Linda wasn't coming after all. She had some emergency church meeting about an upcoming prayer retreat. But she'd written out what would go where and had given detailed instructions.

"I'll take this next." Murph grabbed the old-fashioned, solid-oak coffee table, but before he could lift it, Kate yelled at him from the kitchen.

"Stop! Wait." She wiped her hands on her jeans, pausing from finishing up the pantry. "Come over here."

He was never going to say no if she wanted to be closer to him. No-brainer. He went.

"Sit." She pulled a kitchen chair out for him. "Backwards. You can rest your arms on the back of the chair if you'd like."

He followed the order, and in a hurry. He knew that position and knew what was coming. *Thank you, God.* She was going to help him.

When she put her hands on his shoulders and dug in, he could have cried with relief.

He remembered the first time she'd done this, taken away his pain. And then afterwards… It'd been the first time he'd kissed her.

"I saw you out there last night," she said in a quietly pissed tone, clearly not strolling down memory lane. "For the hundredth time, Ian McCall is not going to come here to hurt me."

Murph didn't say anything. For one, he was afraid she'd stop massaging his stiff muscles if he started arguing. And also, Ian wasn't even the only possible source of danger he was concerned about, but he wasn't sure how much he could pass on about what Bing had told him about Betty's autopsy.

"Mmm." They could talk later.

"Why do you do this to yourself?" She dug in deeper. "I don't need a bodyguard. Please don't come here again like that. Okay?"

"Mmm."

She stopped.

His muscles protested.

"Okay," he said.

Her strong fingers moved lower on his back.

He fell into a daydream where she kept going. Where her hands then went around his waist to the front, under his shirt, up his chest. She hugged him from behind, her breasts pressed against his back.

She kissed his neck and bit his ear. And then he turned around and she straddled him and…

He groaned just as Emma sailed into the kitchen.

"Am I interrupting something?" Then, barely taking a breath in between: "Hey, did Kate tell you I saw a ghost the other day?"

Murph pulled out of his bliss long enough to respond. "I didn't realize sixties' ranchers had them. I thought you had to live in a Victorian mansion to meet things that go bump in the night. Any theatrical moaning? Chain rattling? Dire predictions?"

"Very funny. Go ahead. Laugh at me. But I saw what I saw."

He liked Emma. He didn't want to offend her. Anything was possible, right? "Whose ghost was it?"

"Betty's. I was looking out, and she passed behind her kitchen window."

"Don't bunch up your muscles like that." Kate dug her fingers in harder.

Murph barely felt it. His full focus was on Emma. He kept his tone casual as he asked, "When did you see the ghost?"

She washed her hands in the sink. "The night after she died."

"What time?"

"Sevenish?"

"How do you know it was Betty?"

"She's the only one who died over there recently?" Emma looked at Kate. "I assume."

"Probably light reflecting off the windshield of a passing car," Kate told her sister.

Who immediately responded with "Killjoy," in the same droll tone.

As much as Murph was enjoying the massage and hated the thought of Kate's fingers leaving his body, he turned around to look at her. "Is there any chance someone might have been inside Betty's house?"

Kate dropped her hands. "Linda has the backup key, and she no longer drives. If she wanted to come over, she would have called me to pick her up."

"Is there a way for someone to get in without a key?"

"No. We make sure the house is locked up tight every time we leave."

Murph held her gaze. "You didn't see anything?"

"I don't believe in ghosts."

"It could have been…"

"A leprechaun?"

Under different circumstances, her quick snark would have made him laugh. "The killer returning to the scene of the crime."

Kate stepped back and folded her arms, her blue eyes flashing.

"Betty fell. She tripped."

Murph stood up from the chair. "Or was pushed."

Her face turned ashen. "Did the coroner say she was?"

Murph said nothing.

"Murph!"

"She might have been."

"Who would do that?" Grief welled in her eyes. "Why?"

"Good question. Can you think of anyone with a reason?"

"No way."

He turned to Emma, who stood staring at them. "What time did you leave here Monday morning to go into Philly?"

"As soon as I got home from dropping Kate off at work. I put away the groceries, but that's it. I was definitely on the road by nine."

Before Betty died.

"This is crazy." Kate was shaking her head. "You can't seriously believe…"

"When I drove you home," Murph told her, "after Bing called that Betty had an accident, while the two of you were talking in here, I checked out Betty's house."

"You should stop acting like you still work for the PD."

"Bing already reminded me." He shrugged, and the movement barely even hurt. Kate had worked a miracle. "The point is, I checked the garbage containers inside, because at the time, the theory was that Betty might have been taking out the garbage when she slipped. Except the bins inside weren't empty."

Kate frowned. "You took out the garbage when we started cleaning out the place on Thursday."

Murph nodded. "And I noticed something in the kitchen garbage on Thursday that wasn't in there on Monday."

"The hamburger wrapper. That's why you asked about it."

"You sure it wasn't yours?"

Both Kate and Emma shook their heads, so he asked, "Or Linda's?"

"No. She didn't bring food."

"If someone pushed Betty, they might come back." Murph voiced his new least favorite thought.

"Why?" Emma asked.

"Some murderers return to the scene of the crime. They get off on reliving the kill."

Emma flashed him a skeptical look. "How much of a thrill can it be to push over an old woman? I doubt anyone would risk getting caught to relive that."

"There could be other reasons to return. The killer might have been trying to rob her, then got interrupted. You sure you didn't see anything that day? Any strange cars on the street?"

"I've only been here a few days," Emma told him. "All the cars are strange. It's not like I sit around memorizing what Kate's neighbors drive."

"Any car at all on the street near Betty's house that you do remember from that morning?"

She thought about it. "A black SUV. A Chevy Trailblazer, I think? Don't know. Sorry. I only remember it because it made me think how a black SUV automatically makes you look important. Like you have a bodyguard to drive it. That's what I'm getting if I ever become an influencer."

She'd clearly given a lot of thought to that particular daydream, whatever an *influencer* was. Murph would have asked, but right then, having to ask would have made him feel even older, and he was feeling plenty old already from the realization that a night spent in his pickup could do him in.

"Was the SUV parked in front of Betty's house?" he asked.

"Kind of between the next neighbor's house and hers."

Murph looked at Kate. "Anyone in the neighborhood?"

"No. Could have been the pastor's wife, Amanda. She drives a black SUV. She needs a big car because she gives people rides to church all the time, and some of them have canes and walkers. I've seen her around when she's come by to check on Betty."

A lead. Okay. Maybe Amanda had seen something. "I'll check with her."

Kate flashed him a pointed look. "Or you could leave it to Captain Bing."

He could have. If the suspicious death hadn't happened right next to Kate.

* * *
Asael

Asael stood on top of the water tower in the woods off the Northeast Extension of the PA Turnpike and brooded in the slowly falling mist.

The tower was no longer in use—abandoned.

Watered with blood.

Mordocai had died somewhere around here. A bullet from Murph Dolan had punched through his head.

Asael wrapped his cold anger around himself as he searched for the spot below where Mordocai had plummeted to an early death, but time had erased all trace of the murder.

He stood there and planned, no longer seeing the woods, but the people he'd met at Betty Gardner's funeral the day before. *Finally*, he knew why his unfailing instincts had brought him among them.

Oh, Mordocai.

For the first time in years, Asael let himself feel. He barely noticed when it began to rain, when the background noise of birds and distant traffic changed to water splashing onto leaves.

He and Mordocai had had their ups and downs. What relationship didn't? But overall, among all the others, Mordocai might have been the one.

Older, less skilled, but stubborn. That stubbornness had been at the root of most of their fights. And yet, it was the same stubbornness that had brought Mordocai to Broslin.

The gift.

Not some trivial mushroom memorabilia, after all, but a person.

Kate Bridges.

The thought filled Asael with more affection for his dead lover than he had ever felt for anyone living.

Mordocai had doggedly tracked down the bitch and found her.

Had tried to take her out, no doubt, when the local busybody cop shot him. The news hadn't used her name. *Out-of-town stranger kidnaps local resident and is killed by police in successful rescue,* the online paper Asael had read informed him.

At the time, Asael had told himself he didn't care. He had plenty of other lovers. Assassins couldn't afford to feel pain. He had chosen to be annoyed with Mordocai instead of grieving him, aggravated that Mordocai had been stupid enough to get killed.

Asael looked down.

Mordocai had drawn his last breath somewhere on the leaf-covered ground below.

Asael filled his lungs with air that smelled like rain and wet forest, and he made a decision.

He hadn't come to Broslin with the intention to avenge Mordocai. But he hadn't known then what he knew now. Mordocai had given his *life* for him.

And that changed everything.

CHAPTER SEVENTEEN

Murph

Since Murph didn't want to get on the captain's bad side, he did not stop at the church to casually interrogate Pastor Garvey's wife. But he did drive by after he'd dropped off a pickup load of Betty's furniture at the local mission that helped people who'd served their sentences restart their lives. Pastor Garvey would have approved.

The Garveys lived in a house next to the small nondenominational church with their four kids. They drove near-identical Chevy Trailblazers, Bill's white, Amanda's black. Both stood in the driveway as Murph checked out the place, noting the CONGRATULATIONS! THE WELL IS FILLED sign in front of the church next door. The giant image of a stone well was painted all the way to the top with blue, a smaller sign stuck to the brim declaring: FOUR MILLION DOLLARS RAISED!

A vague memory stirred in his brain, the proud sign reminding him of something just out of reach. He tried to figure out what all the way to the police station, but in vain.

The cleanup crew at Betty's house was done for the day, so he had time for other things. Like talking to Bing.

"Captain in?" he asked Robin at the front desk.

She looked up from her computer. "Captains don't have to work weekends."

"Since when? He used to be in here all the time."

"And now he's married with kids." Robin smiled.

"Do you think Sophie would mind if I stopped by the house?"

"Sophie knew he was captain before she married him. Anyway, she thinks he's the best thing since kiss-proof lipstick. Man can't do wrong as far as that woman's concerned. Love makes you blind. That's why I'm staying single. It's more fun to play the field."

She was sixty-five, with a sparkle in her eyes, fashionable silver bob, and artsy dream-catcher earrings. Murph had no doubt she got proposed to once a week over at the senior club.

The station had definitely softened since she'd been hired to help out Leila so they could have extended phone coverage. Back when Murph had worked at Broslin PD, when Leila had ruled the front desk uncontested, everything had been sparse and in military order. Now they had lucky bamboos all over the place, and inspirational quotes, and instead of saying *goodbye*, Robin might say *May the angels be with you* as you left, if she was distracted.

"Reading palms at the Mushroom Festival?" Murph asked. Most years she did that, volunteered as part of their fundraiser, usually next to the face-painting tent.

"Going to Lily Dale for a psychic convention. I skipped it last year and regretted it. I have a lot of friends there, and when I don't see them, I miss them. Speaking of which… How is Doug? You must miss your brother." She was the type who kept track of people's families and genuinely cared.

"Still a dumbass, but you know?" Murph drew up a shoulder, then dropped it. "He's my brother."

"And let's not forget, without him, you wouldn't have met Kate."

Murph nodded. "There's that."

"He'll be all right. He's better off without Felicia. I talked to him the last time he was up here for a visit. I think he's maturing."

One would hope.

"I'm proud of him," Murph told Robin. "He's alone for the

first time in his life, kicking ass and taking names."

They talked another ten minutes, mostly about the singing group Robin belonged to, Senior Sirens, before Murph drove over to Bing's place.

They were neighbors, technically. The back of Hope Hill's acres met Bing's backyard. Before the center had been built, Bing had owned the entire property. His elaborate log cabin stood at the top of the rise, a long line of minivans filling the driveway. As Murph pulled up to park, two ferocious Rottweilers ran to investigate him.

"Hey there, Peaches." He jumped from the pickup and petted the dogs. "What's up, Pickles?"

After they sniffed him all over and licked his hands, the three of them walked up to the house together.

Murph tapped the doorbell, had to ring twice before Bing appeared, feminine laughter and squeals following him.

"If you need help with anything, I'm available." He was jittery around the eyes, a new look for Broslin's indomitable police captain. Ethan Bing was a low-key, easygoing guy, calm under duress. Definitely had the right temperament for his job. Didn't usually appear ready to bolt for the hills.

If anyone asked Murph before this, he would have gone so far as to say that the man could not be rattled. "Everything okay in there?"

Bing stepped outside and closed the door behind him. "Sophie is throwing a baby shower for one of her friends. There are twenty women in my house. And all their kids. I thought I was prepared." He drew a ragged breath. "I was not prepared."

Murph tried not to laugh. "Hey, I've seen live combat, and I don't think I'd be prepared."

Bing nodded with gratitude at the show of support. "Listen, women are a mystery, and I usually actually appreciate that. But...they're making crafts from diapers."

"Why?" Murph stepped back on instinct, because apparently, some hidden manly-man part of him thought the insanity might be catching.

The captain followed him, putting more distance between

himself and the house, as if thinking along the same lines. "I don't know. I don't understand anything that's happened in my house in the past two hours. They just finished a baby-food-tasting contest. They wanted me to eat pureed carrot-squash medley." Bing grimaced, his eyes asking for understanding. "I'm a man."

Murph patted him on the shoulder. "I'm appalled on your behalf."

When Peaches and Pickles nosed them and jumped around at their feet to be included in the show of masculine affection, Bing frowned at the pets. "Traitor dogs. They fled as soon as the women got here." But he petted them before asking, "Anyway, what brings you by?"

Murph scratched Peaches and Pickles behind their ears. "Emma saw a ghost inside Betty's house the other night, through the window."

Bing didn't get excited about the news. He had more of a clowns-to-the-left-of-me-jokers-to-the-right expression on his face.

"Also," Murph hurried to add, "she just remembered that a black SUV was parked in front of Betty's house the day she died. Possibly Amanda Garvey's car."

"The pastor's wife? A visit wouldn't be unusual. She looks in on the older ladies and delivers casseroles if someone is sick."

"Betty wasn't sick. Have you talked to Amanda lately?"

"At the funeral yesterday. Usual funeral talk. How much everybody is going to miss Betty."

"Betty left everything she had to the church." Murph pointed out the obvious.

Bing raised an eyebrow. "You think Amanda Garvey knocked her off?"

"People kill for money." Then, on second thought, Murph added, "You know anything about that fundraiser at the church?"

"Steeple needs to be renovated. Wind damage. And they're updating the daycare center in the basement, I think. Can't remember the rest. The *Broslin Chronicle* ran an article about the project a while back."

"Something about it bugs me." Murph could almost, *almost* put his finger on it, but the vague thought wouldn't coalesce. "Didn't we have a case once that involved church fundraising?"

"Not us. Up in Lancaster. Church treasurer ran off with the funds. Almost ten million. Big church."

"Right." Memories of the case floated back. It'd been all over the local news at the time. "And not just the funds, was it? He also ran off with the preacher's wife."

"I don't see what that has to do with Amanda Garvey."

"She could have embezzled the reno money. Then she was desperate to get Betty's house sooner rather than later so she could sell it before the first bills from the contractors come in."

"Christ, Murph." Bing was professional enough not to roll his eyes, but the corners twitched. "A lot of ex-cops try their hands at writing mysteries. Maybe you should give it a go. Plotting a novel would give your imagination a healthy outlet."

"I want to talk to Amanda."

"Do we have to have another conversation about where you do and don't work?"

"I mean, if you were to go and talk to her, I would like to tag along. That's all."

"Go and talk to her based on what pretext?"

"Like I said, her car was possibly seen in front of Betty's house on the day of her death."

The sound of screaming women filtered through the front door, reaching after Bing like an invisible hand trying to pull him back in. He carried his gaze down the row of cars in his crowded driveway. "Blocked and double blocked. Can't even get my car out."

"My truck is by the curb," Murph offered helpfully as the women squealed even louder. "You could just pop back in there and tell Sophie you're stepping out for a while."

"I'll text her from the car." Bing launched himself down the steps—without as much as going back for his coat.

He glanced at Murph as they dodged their way through the jumble of minivans, the dogs on their heels. "All right. You're with me in the capacity of a temporary civilian consultant on the case, because Chase is off on a second honeymoon with Luanne as of today and Hunter took Gabi up to the Adirondacks for a weekend of snowboarding on the spur of the moment. One of Hunter's

Army buddies works at a lodge up there, gave him heads-up that they have the first good snow this season."

Hunter and Gabi had one of those relationships that was permanently stuck in the hot-and-heavy phase. They were still necking every time people turned their backs for a second. Murph envied them more than a little. "Dollars against doughnuts they won't make it out of the hot tub."

"Not betting against that," Bing said. "My point being, I'm kind of shorthanded this weekend."

"Right. I'd be happy to help."

Murph led the way to his pickup, poor Peaches and Pickles left behind where the electric fence ended their domain. They looked heartbroken, as if they just knew Murph and Bing were sneaking off for a bacon-tasting event.

"Don't go and scratch on that front door," Bing advised the dogs with loving affection. "If you go in, those women are going to try to feed you pureed green beans."

Murph shuddered as he slid into his seat. He'd never been to a baby shower in his life, and he didn't plan on changing that. In any case, he was far from becoming a father. Kate was barely talking to him.

To dispel that depressing thought, he pulled away from Bing's place and asked, "Any news on Ian McCall?"

"Not yet. I feel damn bad about losing him. The psychologist is a newbie to police work. I should have stayed with them." Bing bit off a curse. "Didn't want to make him feel like I didn't trust him to know what he was doing. Didn't want McCall to think I didn't trust the guy, because then McCall wouldn't have trusted him either. That boy's on the edge."

"What did his background check say?"

"Exemplary military service. No trouble with the law that I could find."

"Kate keeps hoping he'll come back."

"Never seen her give up on someone."

And that was Murph's number one hope, for sure.

"Anybody as bad as him at the center?" Bing asked.

"Seen worse," Murph told him, and for the rest of the drive, they discussed treatments that were offered.

Bing was the one to ring Pastor Garvey's doorbell.

The man himself answered. "Is everything all right, Captain?"

Bing had put on a smile before the door even opened, and he kept it on to indicate they weren't delivering bad news—what most people feared when they saw a law enforcement officer at the door. "Just a few questions about Betty Gardner. Sorry to disturb you at home, Bill. Would it be all right if we came in?"

"Of course." He stepped aside, fifty-something, thin in the neck, thick in the middle.

"Thank you. Is Amanda here?"

Bill ushered them in. "In the kitchen."

The house hit Murph all at once, a sensory shock. *Wow.* Tchotchke Central. Or Flea Market Chic, as Kate would call it. *He* called it claustrophobic.

Every surface was covered, more crocheted things than he would have previously thought existed in all of Broslin, if he'd ever thought to think about the town's crochet saturation. And it wasn't just crochet. All manner of crafts covered the shelves, from homemade pottery to hand-dipped candles. Overwhelmed little tables were crammed in every corner.

Bill caught him looking. "We receive a lot of gifts." He flashed an indulgent smile. "Given with love and kept in love."

He seemed to mean it.

This kind of clutter on a daily basis would have driven Murph crazy.

The pastor's wife, five or so years older than her husband, was frosting a cake on the kitchen counter.

Her smile was instant and welcoming, no worry crossing her face. "Hello, Captain. Murph, thank you for all that help with delivering furniture. Linda tells me you keep saving the day." She set the spatula down and pivoted to the counter, talking over her shoulder. "Please, take a seat. Let me put on some coffee."

"Why don't I brew the coffee?" her husband offered. "Captain Bing is here to talk to you about Betty."

"Oh?" Amanda wiped her hands on her apron and sat, genuine sadness filling her blue eyes. She tucked a few strands of blonde hair behind her ears as she blinked back tears. "Poor Betty. I still can't believe she's gone. I'll think, oh, I need to call her about something. And then I reach for the phone, and remember…"

She sniffed.

"Did you visit her on Monday?" Bing asked.

"Briefly in the morning. I was in the neighborhood and popped in to ask if she needed anything. I do my groceries on Monday on my lunch break. But she said she was set."

"Around what time did you leave her?"

"A little before eight. She was an early riser, so I knew she'd be up."

"You sure it wasn't later?" Murph pushed. Betty's time of death had been put at around nine thirty.

"Definitely not. I start Mondays with the women's prayer circle at eight thirty. By nine, I'm at the preschool. I don't get out of there until noon."

Murph wanted to push more, but Bing simply asked, "You wouldn't know if anyone from the congregation was planning on visiting her too that day?"

"We have regular volunteer visits to some of our less able seniors, but Betty was far from that. If anything, she was helping others. I'm sure if someone was out at her place the day she died, they would have mentioned it to me. You know how people are. *Oh, I just saw her that morning! She looked fine!*" Amanda pressed a hand to her chest. Tears flooded her eyes. "As if people can't die just because we've recently seen them." She sniffed. "I keep telling Bill, I was just there earlier. If only I'd stayed."

Murph watched her. Bing said she hadn't mentioned a visit at the funeral, but maybe just not to Bing. Maybe she'd been too upset to say much. She seemed pretty upset still.

Murph shifted to rise, but Bill Garvey stopped him with "Coffee is ready."

The pastor's wife swiped a quick hand under her eyes. "How about some Hungarian walnut cake? I'm trying out a new recipe from one of the ladies in the choir."

Bing looked at Murph, the words *pureed squash baby food* telegraphing from his eyes. Murph telegraphed back *you're welcome,* and settled back in his seat.

"Thank you. That would be very nice." Truth was, neither of them said no to cake if they could help it.

Bill brought over their coffee mugs, while Amanda stood and supplied them with plates and forks, then transported the cake from the counter to the table. They were a well-oiled team.

The pastor went back for napkins. "May I ask why you wanted to know if Amanda visited Betty that morning?"

The captain wrapped his hands around his mug. "I'm investigating the incident as a suspicious death. And I'm going to need you to keep that between us for now."

Bill dropped heavily into his chair and reached for his wife's hand on the table. "Do you think someone might have harmed that poor woman?"

"It's possible. I'm trying to figure it out one way or the other."

"Why on earth...?" Then a quick pause, and Bill's eyes snapped wide. "Oh. Her will has the church as her beneficiary. That's why you're here." He shook his head. "It's understandable. But we loved her. She was remarkable. The kind of woman who truly walked God's path."

Amanda wiped her eyes again. "I'm happy to provide an alibi."

She listed the names of half a dozen people who were at the church with her that morning. The captain didn't take notes. He knew all of them, Murph thought. He would remember.

"We have security cameras on the outside of the church," the pastor offered when his wife finished. "I can send you the footage. Ask someone at the office to send you the footage," he corrected. "I can work the microphone in the pulpit, but other than that, I'm not great with technology."

"No video necessary, but thank you," the captain told the man before adding in an apologetic tone, "I had to ask. I'm sure you understand."

"One hundred percent." The words were said without hesitation. The man looked right at them, his expression open. Nothing about him or his wife made Murph's instincts prickle.

"Anything else you need, anything we can do, we're always here," Amanda added. "Please, do have some cake. You haven't touched it."

So, they ate. And Murph was glad they did. Turned out he *really* liked Hungarian walnut cake. Especially with coffee.

"Have you talked to the nephew?" the pastor asked, tucking away his own slice at a good pace.

Captain Bing paused with the fork halfway to his mouth. "I thought Betty didn't have family."

"Son of a second cousin, apparently," Amanda said. "I don't think that's a nephew. Second cousin once removed? I can never remember the exact term. We were served legal papers last night. He's contesting the will."

Another person with motive.

Murph exchanged a glance with Bing as he finished his cake. "Should we stop cleaning out the house?"

Bill Garvey waved off the suggestion. "Our lawyers talked this morning. The young man agreed that the executor of the will, Linda, can go ahead. The house can be sold, but then the money is to be placed into escrow until the bank decides who is entitled to the funds."

The captain pulled his cell phone from his pocket. "I'd like to have his name and contact information, if you have it handy."

"Right here. He lives in Philadelphia." The pastor reached over to the pile of papers next to the fridge on the counter, then handed them a dozen pages of legalese.

The captain snapped a photo of the first page where the surprise heir's name and address were listed, then thanked the pastor.

Bill dropped the papers back onto the pile. "I hope to meet the young man and tell him about Betty, how great she was."

Murph didn't sense any fakeness in the Garvey's easygoing demeanor. "You don't seem upset about the possibility of losing the money."

The man smiled. "Who's to say he doesn't need it more than we do? There's Betty's will, and then there's God's will."

As Murph pulled away from the curb ten minutes later, he said, "I see what you meant. They're pretty nice."

Bing flashed a told-you-so look. "Most people would get angry if they thought you were asking them questions in relation to a murder. Especially someone in a leadership position like Bill Garvey. Men who are used to being the boss don't like being questioned, as a rule. Technically, in his congregation, the pastor is a stand-in for God. But Bill and Amanda never lord their positions over anyone. They walk the talk."

"Are you going to talk to the nephew or whatever he is?"

Bing nodded.

"Can I come with you?"

"No."

"Why did you agree to me coming along to see the pastor and his wife?"

"You know where they live. If I said no, you would have come without me."

There were probably ways to find the nephew too, Murph thought, and said nothing.

CHAPTER EIGHTEEN

Kate

Since Kate was being followed Monday morning on her way to work, she couldn't admire the profusion of colorful chrysanthemums in the front yards as usual. The yellows, whites, and maroons formed a visual delight that was the favorite part of her morning drive, but instead of reminding herself to enjoy their beauty, she glanced at her rearview mirror for the dozenth time in the past few minutes.

There. The tan Nissan two cars behind her took the right turn too.

The low sun reflected off the car's windshield, so no matter how hard Kate squinted, she couldn't make out the driver, just the general shape of a man. The gluten-free toast she'd had for breakfast suddenly felt like a hard lump in her stomach. The man's size was about right for Ian McCall.

Today was going to be a good day, she decided. Today, she was going to make progress.

"Okay, Ian. Let's talk." She stepped on the brake, let the oncoming traffic pass, then pulled into the gas station on the other side of the road, drumming her fingers on the steering wheel as she waited for Ian to make the same move.

The white pickup that had been behind her wanted the gas station too, but had to wait for another handful of cars coming from the opposite direction before making the left-hand turn, the Nissan stuck for the moment. Kate still couldn't see the driver because now the damn sign that advertised oil changes blocked him from her sight.

She reached for her phone, but then, on second thought, she dropped her hand. What would she say to Captain Bing? She didn't even know for sure that it was Ian behind the wheel.

Her nerves buzzed, but she wasn't really scared. She'd talked Ian down before. If he was upset, she could talk him down again.

Then the white pickup finally made its turn and pulled up by the nearest free pump.

The Nissan drove straight on, oncoming traffic obscuring all but a few flashes of the driver. Short hair, dark coat.

Could have been Ian.

Could be he'd followed her, wanting to talk to her, but then changed his mind. Nerves. He could be upset, distracted enough so he'd never even seen her pull into the gas station.

Kate waited five minutes on the off chance he turned around. Then she waited another five. "Come on, Ian." And she would have waited five more if that wouldn't have made her late for work.

When she walked into her office half an hour later, she was still thinking about what she could have done differently with the man. She moved on autopilot as she hung her coat and turned on her laptop, set up the coffee machine, inserting a pod of breakfast blend just as Murph popped his head in.

He checked out her bruises, which had finally faded enough so she didn't need concealer. "Everything okay this morning?"

"Good enough. And it'll be twice as good once I get my second cup of coffee. How is the grant application going?"

"Sent in."

He wore the blue shirt she'd given him last Christmas, the neon lights in the hallway backlighting him and emphasizing his shoulders. The ends of his short hair were damp from his morning shower. He smelled like the olive-oil-and-chamomile soap she'd bought for their apartment.

She missed him.

"I miss you," he said. "Am I allowed to say that?"

She stepped forward. "Don't make me out to be an ogre."

"Kate, I—"

He shifted toward her, and then he was suddenly too close. She had to raise her head to look into his eyes. But halfway there, her gaze got stuck on his lips.

God, the things those lips could do to her.

He went still.

She wasn't sure he was still breathing.

Was *she*?

She couldn't raise her gaze, because she was afraid what she'd find in his eyes, and how she would respond to it.

The masculine line of his jaw was right in front of her. If she leaned forward two inches, she could kiss it.

What a stupid thought. Of course, she wasn't going to do that.

She wasn't going to nuzzle his neck either, to breathe him in. Wasn't going to brace her hands on his hard chest. Wasn't going to lift her face just in time for him to slant his mouth over hers.

All good, but now she'd been standing way too close to Murph for way too long. And he was waiting, probably thinking this was a lead-up to something.

Mixed signals. Don't send them. It's not fair to him.

Kate shuffled back—noting, bewildered, that moving away from him made her ache. She busied herself with her coffee, hating how fast her heart was beating. "Want a cup?"

She still couldn't look at him.

She said nothing about having possibly spotted Ian. If Murph thought that she was in danger, he'd stand guard in front of her office all day.

"I'm good," he said, his voice strained.

She seriously needed to put more distance between them than her little office allowed. "I'm out of creamer. I need to run down to the cafeteria."

"All right. You have a good morning." Then he walked away.

And after a few seconds, Kate could finally breathe.

The second cup of coffee did the trick, kept her going through three massages back-to-back. She ate lunch behind her desk, the best vegetarian chili on the planet. Julia, the head cook at the center, was an artist with vegetables.

Scott Young was her first patient in the afternoon, the Marine who'd had issues the week before. According to his file, he'd had daily therapy sessions since the *incident* and showed improvement. Maria, his therapist, thought he was ready to try again.

"Sorry." He walked through the door five minutes late, rubbing his palms on the side of his pants.

Sweaty palms. Nervous. Had probably been thinking about not coming.

"Nothing to apologize for, Scott." Kate gave him an encouraging smile. "I've been looking forward to catching up with you. I hear you're making amazing progress. How do you feel? Ready?"

"I hope so. I'm really sorry about last time."

"It's a normal response to past trauma. Your brain's number one job is to prevent you from getting hurt. If you think something is a threat, you defend yourself. It's the most basic evolutionary response."

"But you're not a threat."

She kept on smiling. "No, I'm not. You think you can trust me?"

"I do. I swear."

"Well, I trust you. So in you go. Let me know when you're under the sheet."

Scott barely disappeared into the treatment room when Murph strode into her office. If he had any thoughts about her earlier strange behavior, he didn't show it. He just parked himself in the middle of the space.

Sweet chocolate chip cookies, this was so unnecessary. Also, he might be an unruffleable manly monolith, but she wasn't completely over their morning encounter yet. Kate folded her arms. "No."

"Is that Murph?" Scott called through the door. "It's okay, Kate. We've talked about it."

Murph did that standing-with-his-feet-apart thing of his, hands folded behind him, parade rest or whatever they called it, ex-cop/ex-soldier move that said a tank wouldn't be able to budge him.

"I talked to Maria earlier," he told Kate. "She said it's not a bad idea if I sit in. Scott is nervous about hurting you. If he knows he can't because I'm here to intervene, it'll allow him to relax."

Kate held her tongue. Mostly because letting loose on Murph in front of a patient would have been unprofessional, but also because he was right, dammit. If Maria had shown up and offered to stay, Kate would have thanked her and wouldn't have had a problem with the assistance.

"How about you stay out here?" she said in a low voice, fully aware that she was acting as if she and Murph were parents at odds, trying not to fight in front of the kids.

When Murph opened his mouth, she held up a hand palm out to stop him from talking. She made a series of hand gestures: pointed her finger at him, then the zipper movement over her mouth, then a slash across her neck. His nostrils flared as he struggled not to laugh. Which made her want to smile, but she did not. She meant business.

Then Scott called out, "I'm ready," saving them from further awkward moments.

Thank God. Kate walked past Murph with a this-is-not-my-happy-face glare, leaving the door open a crack. But by the time she turned to Scott, she was smiling again.

"All right. I'm going to start with your right calf like last time. I'm going to fold back the sheet." She went right ahead. "And now I'm just going to place my hand on your skin. How is it so far?"

"It's fine. Good."

She began with a soothing massage first, then dug in a little deeper, but nothing that would hurt.

"Ready for me to move to the thigh muscles?"

"Sure."

That terrible tension he'd carried in every inch of his body the last time was mostly gone. He was still tense, but less so, actively trying to relax.

"Maria, Dr. Gulick, said I could do breathing exercises while you work on me. It might help."

"Excellent idea. You absolutely can."

Scott began slow breathing, and, after a few moments, his muscles relaxed another notch.

Kate didn't hesitate when she reached for his shoulder, just warned him like before, but didn't give him any indication that she remembered his reaction from last time or that it concerned her.

After she finished with him, she covered him up. "Feel free to stay here for a few minutes to relax if you'd like."

His voice held emotion as he said, "Thank you."

"Absolutely, Scott, any time."

When she walked out into her office, closing the door behind her, she found Murph scrolling on his phone.

"Thank you," she said, because he *had* come to help.

He pushed to his feet with the controlled grace of a warrior, nodded at her without a word, and then he left. No *told you so.* No gloating that she needed him. Nothing. He just did what needed to be done. Always.

He was a man a woman could count on, no matter what, in matters small and great, which was one of the reasons she'd fallen in love with him in the first place.

Kate blew out a pent-up breath. She wasn't going to stand in the middle of her office, wishing he would come back, dammit. She was there to work.

She wrote up Scott's treatment report, pleased with his progress.

He came out, fully dressed, and stopped in front of her. "I really appreciate the help."

"It's why I'm here."

"You don't understand." He swallowed and looked at his feet. "Back at home, my wife and I have to sleep in different rooms. Before my kids give me a hug, they have to ask me if it's okay. They had to be taught not to jump on me from behind, not to shout when they play. What you're doing... What this place is doing..." He shook his head.

"You're doing so well, Scott." Kate's own throat was closing up a little. "By the time you go home, I promise, you'll be a different man."

"I just want to be myself again."

"Others have done it. I can tell you, with one-hundred-percent certainty, that it's possible."

A quiet joy filled her. This was why she got up in the morning every day. This was what made her happy. When she saw someone take that first step toward getting better, it was like fireworks going off in her heart.

While Scott shifted on his feet, looking for words, a dark blond head popped in the door, followed by the rest of a tall Irishman.

"Hey, Kate." Harper Finnegan glanced at her patient, then back at her. "Got a minute?"

Scott headed for the door, stopped on the threshold, then looked back. "Thank you again."

Once he was gone, Harper stepped inside and closed the door behind him.

Kate sat up straight. "What is it? I don't like the expression on your face. What's wrong? Is this about Ian McCall?"

"It's your neighbor, Mr. Mauro," Harper said in a tone thick with regret.

A sudden chill went through Kate. She came out of her seat. "Is he all right? Did he fall on his walk?"

"You might want to sit back down."

Bad news. In a place deep inside, she knew she did *not* want to hear what Harper was about to say. Her heart lurched into a mad rush. She gripped the edge of her desk. "What's wrong? What happened?"

"Hit-and-run. I'm not going to lie, Kate, he might not make it. He's in rough shape."

CHAPTER NINETEEN

Kate

"The captain said to come and tell you in person," Harper said. "I can drive you to the hospital, but they're not allowing any visitors at this stage. Do you want to go home?"

"Yes. I need to check on his house." Because she wasn't that great with emotions, her mind tended to turn to practicalities. Hadn't she just done this for Betty? "But I can drive myself," she added. "I'm all right."

"Is Emma home?"

"She's at work. New job. First day…"

Betty dead. Mr. Mauro possibly mortally injured. The two thoughts connected in her brain. She stared at Harper, cold dread crawling up her spine. "You think we could be in danger?"

"Both of your neighbors had serious *accidents* within a week of each other. Bing says it makes him twitchy." Harper shifted on his feet. "He's worried about you. The Ian McCall incident."

She blinked, then shook her head. "Ian wouldn't run Mr. Mauro over. It wouldn't make any sense. How would he even know where I live? And why hurt a random neighbor? This isn't Ian."

"But you don't really know him, right? Isn't he new to Hope

Hill?"

"I don't know him, but I know a hundred other guys like him. This isn't…" She couldn't finish. Tears sprang into her eyes as all the emotion hit at last, all at once. *Oh God. Mr. Mauro…*

"He hasn't tried to contact you since he ran off?"

Kate rubbed her hands over her face. "I might have spotted him this morning on the road behind me. I can't say for sure if it was Ian. And I really don't think he has murder in him."

"He's a vet. He's seen combat."

"Of course. He has. He has issues. A lot of people have issues. But vets are not ticking time bombs." She couldn't help the heat in that last sentence.

She was normally a good judge of character. She wasn't naïve, not too quick to trust. She'd come out of the foster care system, then she'd spent her early career working with abused children. She'd seen the worst humanity had to offer. Ian struck her as troubled, a man in pain, desperate, but desperate for *help*. He'd come to Hope Hill to ask for aid, not to harm anyone.

"I've neither said nor done anything to him to set him off like this. Even if I made him mad, this kind of reaction would be insanely disproportionate. Ian McCall is not killing my neighbors. Anyway, Betty died before Ian ever showed up."

"Can you think of anybody else like Ian? Other people who weren't satisfied with the help you gave them here? Somebody else you turned away?"

"We don't usually turn away people." But she thought about it for a few seconds. "There might have been one or two. I'd have to go through the records."

"You sure you don't want me to drive you home?"

Her appointment book caught her eye. "You know, I can't actually go home." No matter how much she wanted to. "I canceled a bunch of appointments when Betty died. I'm still playing catch-up. I need to stay and see patients. I can't reschedule them again."

"All right. I'm going to stick around for a while. Don't worry about Tony's house. I bet the captain already had someone out there. I'll check with him, just to make sure."

Harper stepped out, his phone already in hand, before Kate

could protest.

She called her sister. "Mr. Mauro was in a hit-and-run."

"Is he okay?"

"Harper says it's pretty bad. I'm going to drive over to the hospital after work."

"I can go with you."

"They're not allowing visitors. I'm just going to talk to his doctor."

"Okay. If you're sure." Emma paused for a couple of seconds. "Broslin is the sleepiest of all sleepy small towns in existence. Which is why you came here to hide in the first place. What is happening? Are *you* okay?"

When Kate took a while to formulate a response, Emma added, "I'm an adult. You don't have to shield me like when we were kids."

"I'm a little rattled," Kate admitted. "Harper is going to stick around here for the rest of the day. Listen, the police don't think it was an accident. They think it might have to do with Ian McCall or another dissatisfied patient. I really don't think so. But with Betty and Mr. Mauro having accidents one after the other, the police think there's a connection…"

"Oh my God. Do you think Betty's fall wasn't an accident? Like, someone killed her?"

"I really hope not. It's just the police…"

"Wild. I mean, sad," Emma rushed to add. "Seriously crazy."

"Maybe you *should* go to the hospital with me after work. I don't want you to go home and be alone in the house. I want you to be safe."

"I'll stay here and offer to help Alice clean up. I'll get brownie points. Nobody knows I'm working here. It's my first day."

All good logic, but the reassurance didn't make Kate feel any better. "Please be careful." She described Ian in detail. "Be aware of your surroundings, all right?"

"I will. You too. Call me if anything else happens."

Kate promised she would, but then she had to hang up. Her next appointment, Finn Morris, was there.

While the former sailor stripped for his massage in the

treatment room, Harper popped back in.

"Murph here?"

"No. You told him?

"Of course, I told him."

Kate bit back a groan.

Harper grinned. "Yeah, I know. Even I think he's getting a tad overprotective. Then again, I can sympathize." He shrugged as he came in all the way. "If we were talking about the love of *my* life in danger, she'd be handcuffed to me right now."

The last word was barely out when footsteps sounded outside.

Kate sighed. "Talk about the devil."

"I heard that." Murph rolled in like stormy weather, intense and promising all kinds of turbulence. He nodded toward the closed door of the treatment room. "Who's in there?"

"Finn," she said, just as Finn called, "I'm ready, Kate."

And Kate breathed a sigh of relief, because that meant she wouldn't have to deal with Murph for an hour.

As it turned out, she didn't have to deal with him after the session either. He was gone by the time she finished with the massage.

"I convinced him that I can sufficiently protect you," Harper told her, chest out, all proud of himself.

She was proud of him too. "I owe you. Big."

"Don't think I won't collect. Allie's birthday is coming up. I thought about chaps, but she already has a couple for her Calamity Jane role. Maybe spurs? But she really loves her antique Old West ones. You could do some recon and find out what she'd like. Other than me. I mean, I'm the best, but she should have other nice things."

Kate didn't hold back a heartfelt groan. "Ever get back pain from carrying around that massive ego of yours? You can come in for a chair massage if you need it." She shook her head. "And, thanks for the protection detail, but please go away. I can take care of myself."

He made puppy-dog eyes at her. "I can feel Murph's pain."

After Harper left, Kate focused on her patients for the rest of the day.

When she walked out at five, mentally exhausted, Harper was waiting for her in the lobby.

She stopped in front of him. "I thought we agreed that I could take care of myself."

"I left earlier. I swear. Murph told me to come back at five and give you an escort home."

"Sounds like Murph and I are going to have to have another talk about boundaries." She was so not looking forward to that. "All right," she said. "Thank you." No sense in giving Harper any grief. He was just trying to help. "But I want to go over to the hospital first."

"Just got off the phone with the captain, who just got off the phone with the doctor. Broken hip and concussion. Unless you're family, the doctor won't even tell you that much. Still no visitors. Might as well wait until tomorrow."

He was probably right. "Okay."

Once inside her car, Kate texted Emma to let her know she was going straight home. Then off she went.

Harper stayed behind her. When he caught her looking at him in her rearview mirror, he waved.

A police escort. Because Captain Bing didn't think Kate was safe.

Now that she wasn't working, her mind was free to run away with all kinds of dark thoughts. *Betty and Mr. Mauro.* And there was Emma… Her little sister. The most important person to her in the world. The thought of Emma in danger was unacceptable.

Kate pulled up to the curb in front of her house and made a decision.

As she got out of the car, Harper walked over, holding a hand out for her keys. "Let me walk through your house first."

Kate didn't protest. She was busy figuring out how to tell Emma what she needed to tell her. She waited in the foyer until Harper called, "All clear" from the back.

"Thanks." Kate put her bag down and hung up her coat.

Emma burst through the door. "Any news on Mr. Mauro?"

Harper responded, walking up to them. "He's resting comfortably."

"Harper Finnegan," Kate introduced him. "Harper, this is my

sister, Emma."

Emma turned to her and mouthed, *Hot.*

Kate mouthed back, *Taken.*

"Nice to meet you." Harper, none the wiser, walked up and shook Emma's hand. "You two lock up tight." He looked at Kate. "Murph says you've got a gun?"

"And I'm not afraid to use it."

"If you decide you want me to hang out with you guys, just call me, and I'll pop right over. Allie is out of town for work. They asked her back to Suntown Elementary over in Maryland to do Annie Oakley this time. I was just going to listen to a new spy thriller after work. I can do that sitting in my car in front of your house. I have nothing else planned for the rest of the day. All right?"

If she were on her own, Kate would have said no. But Emma was there. "Okay. Thank you, Harper."

"Who's Allie?" Emma watched Harper through the window as he strode back to his car, her gaze hesitating on his rangy build.

"The love of Harper's life."

"Bummer."

"Don't even think about it. She's got a fancy Old West rifle, and she's not afraid to use it."

"Why is it that all the good ones are always taken?"

"They're not all taken. Patience."

"Easy for you to say. You have Murph."

Did she? Not a topic Kate wanted to discuss right then. She wanted to talk to her sister about the decision she'd made.

She took Emma's hand and drew her into the living room, onto the couch, until they sat side by side, facing each other. "You know how much I love you. I love you more than I love anyone in the world."

"You need a kidney," Emma deadpanned.

"You know how much I love having you here."

"But you want me to move out so Murph can move in and you two can have hot countertop sex?"

That caught Kate off guard enough to make her laugh. She hated to ruin the mood. She forged ahead anyway. "No countertop sex. But would you please consider going home?"

Emma shoved to her feet and stepped back, betrayal glinting in her eyes, a hard, hard look. "No."

"I want you to be safe."

"Well, I want *you* to be safe! I'm not leaving you alone."

"I won't be alone. Bing assigned me a detail. That's why Harper is here. They'll all be keeping an eye on me."

"You don't have to protect me. Could you catch up to that now, please?" Emma's tone thickened with hurt. "I'm not a child."

"I know. But if you stay, if it is a disgruntled patient, and if he does want to hurt me by hurting people near me…"

"Why would a patient be this obsessed with you?"

"Could be transference." She'd thought about that on her way home too. "Take someone like Ian. In his mind, I might stand in as a surrogate for someone else in the past he'd gone to help for, someone who then ended up hurting him. It's extremely unlikely. But extremely unlikely things happen every day."

Kate would ask Maria what she thought the next time she saw the psychologist, but she'd spent enough time around therapists, discussing patients in staff meetings, to have picked up this and that.

"As soon as the police figure out what's going on," Kate told Emma, "you can come back."

"I just got a job."

"Alice will understand."

"I can't believe you're kicking me out."

"To keep you safe."

"Like you faked your death to keep me safe. Like you stayed away for years, letting me grieve. All to keep me safe." Emma was seething, stepping farther back, putting more distance between them.

"We've already talked about that. I explained why."

"Isn't it great for you to be deciding what's best for everyone all the time?"

"I don't want you to get hurt," Kate snapped, losing her own patience. "What's so hard to understand about that?"

"Why are you in charge of my safety?" Emma shouted.

"Because you're my little sister!" Kate shouted back, getting good and angry. "I can take care of myself better than you can. I spent three years taking self-defense classes from Murph in Ohio."

Emma rolled her eyes. "So if you won't let me stay and help because I'm younger and not a ninja, then you'll let Murph help you, right? He's older, and I bet he still has better hand-to-hand combat skills than you do, despite all your *extensive* training."

Kate gritted her teeth. She didn't want to say anything she would regret later, but dammit… "Emma, I love you. But I want you to go home to Mom and Dad until this, whatever this is, blows over."

"You're seriously uninviting me?"

"Yes. And I'm also going to uninvite Mom and Dad."

If her family was mad at her, Kate could live with that. But she didn't know what she'd do if harm came to them.

God, she *hated* to have to fight with Emma over this. "Listen. I—"

The doorbell interrupted. Maybe just as well.

Kate strode over to the window to look out. She wasn't going to open the door without checking first who was out there, not in the foreseeable future.

She swore under her breath.

"Because my day wasn't complete," she said as she stepped to the door and opened it.

"What's that?" Murph tapped his ear with a goofy grin that only made him more ridiculously handsome. "Did you say *You complete me?*"

"So not funny."

He dropped the grin. "I wanted to make sure you two were all right. I know you want distance, but how about we do the distance thing when you're safe?"

"She's protector goddess of all!" Emma shouted from the living room. "Nobody can protect her. Sorry!"

Murph raised an eyebrow.

Kate sighed. "We had a fight. I asked her to go back to LA."

"Best idea you've had lately."

"Freaking traitor!" Emma shouted.

"We love you!" Murph shouted back, then he lowered his

voice. "How do you feel about me moving in? Temporarily."

So not in the mood for this. Kate's fingers tightened on the doorknob as she struggled to keep her temper in check. "Are you trying to make me run screaming into the night?"

"Can I go with you?"

"No! Do not make light of this."

"I was going to tell you the same." Murph held her gaze. "I was supposed to go into Philly tomorrow to check out equipment for that zipline course, but I think I'm going to stick around instead."

"The accidents have nothing to do with me. I'm safe."

"Which is why you're kicking out your sister?"

"I'm not kicking her out. I'm…" Kate groaned. She hated when people turned things around on her, dammit. "Go to Philly, please. We can't stop doing our jobs. Neither of us."

"I'd feel more comfortable—"

She fixed him with a gaze so steely, they could have made medieval battle swords from it to fight dragons. "Do you ever wonder what would make me feel more comfortable?"

"I said *temporarily.*" He emphasized the word as if it were a magic spell to unlock her common sense.

She held out a hand between them, palm up. "This is a slice of *nope* bread." She whooshed her other hand over it. "Topped with some *nope* spread." She pretended to drop something on top. "And here is some *nope* bologna and *nope* cheese." She placed her other hand over all that. "And another slice of *nope* bread." She lifted her imaginary creation closer to Murph. "You know what it is? A *nope* sandwich."

He kept a straight face as he raised an eyebrow. "What? No pickles?"

Damn him for making her laugh when she meant to be good and mad at him. *Just like a man.*

CHAPTER TWENTY

Kate

"Today could be the day I finally murder someone," Kate told Maria Tuesday morning as they walked into work together.

"Want to talk about it?"

"I want to scream about it. Had a big fight with my sister this morning. She left, and I hate that her visit ended on a bad note. She decided to keep her rental and drive cross-country instead of taking a flight. Determined to have an adventure." She groaned. "Sweet cocoa bean heaven. Like right now? She has to do this now?"

"She's young. She needs fun in her life. We all do."

"But she's not picking up my calls, and that makes me worry. And my car is *coughing* again. I barely got it back from the shop." She read Maria's unspoken words on her face. "I'm *not* going to ask Murph to look at it. I have to be able to live without him, dammit."

Maria, wise woman that she was, offered nothing but supportive smiles in response to that.

"Was I unreasonable with Emma?"

"Some worry is natural. As long as it's not all the time. Have you scheduled that lab work yet?"

"Haven't had a free minute. But I'll do it. I promise."

Maria stopped in front of her office door. "Everything will feel better after your second cup of coffee."

"The truest words in the universe. Somebody should merchandise that."

"We could start a girlfriend side gig. Nothing but coffee wisdom on tea towels and pillowcases."

"Deal. All right. You have a fun day."

"You too, Kate."

Kate walked to her own door, went straight to brewing that second cup. While the black gold slowly dripped from the machine, she called the hospital.

Unfortunately, that ended her good vibes.

"We can't give out information on a patient. I'm sorry," the man on the other end said.

"I'm his neighbor. Can I at least visit him today?"

"Family only."

"Neighbors are practically family. I don't know where you live, but we're talking about Broslin here."

"Your name is not on the emergency contact list."

"But you contacted his son, right?"

"We haven't been able to reach him. Or his other emergency contact."

Mr. Mauro had only one son. Who was the other contact? *Oh God.*

"The other contact is Betty Gardner, isn't it? She died last week."

The silence on the other end confirmed Kate's suspicion.

"Look." She used her firmest tone. "Mr. Mauro's son works on oil wells in Alaska. Even when you do reach him, it'll take him days to get here. Betty is gone. That poor man needs to see a friendly face. I need to bring him some clean clothes and toiletries…"

"I'll talk to his doctor and see if we can put your name on the visitor list."

"Thank you." *Finally. Something.*

Joe Kessler, another one of Broslin PD's finest—former high school football star, still practically worshipped—stuck his head in. "Captain said I should check in on you."

Kate put down her phone. "Everything is fine here. I take it Ian hasn't been found yet?"

"Matter of time. Want me to hang around?"

"I don't think that's necessary, but thank you."

"All right. I'll be in the neighborhood. Call if you need anything."

As Joe left and Kate finished her coffee, her first patient for the day arrived. Kate had three sessions before noon. Whatever else had gone wrong that morning, all three went off without a hitch.

The first thing she did on her lunch break was to call Emma, but her sister still wasn't answering her calls. So, on her way back from the cafeteria, Kate stopped by the vending machine and grabbed some chocolate and took it back to her desk. Her stomach was improving finally, soothed by her new, restricted diet. She was back on chocolate. The smell no longer roiled her stomach. Thank God, because she didn't know how she would survive the day without it.

Maria hurried by, caught Kate with the chocolate bar halfway to her mouth, and grinned.

"I'm not using chocolate as a crutch!" Kate yelled after her. "We're in a committed relationship!"

She finished the bar, thought about going back for another one, but then talked herself out of it. Her favorite jeans were snug already. As much weight as she'd lost while she'd been figuring out her gluten intolerance issues, she'd gained the pounds back and a few extra ones lately.

When her phone rang, she grabbed it, hoping Emma was calling her back at last. Instead, a ghost rose from her past.

The name on the display made Kate's throat close. Her heart lurched into a panicked gallop. Anxiety tightened her muscles. Where was all the damn air?

"Agent Cirelli," she said as she picked up, her voice embarrassingly weak. "It's been a while."

"How are you, Kate?"

"Okay. But I have a terrible premonition that I'll be worse in a minute."

"I'm sorry."

"Just say it."

"We have reason to believe that Asael is alive."

No, no, no!

Kate squeezed her eyes shut. For a few seconds, she couldn't catch her breath. In what universe was this fair? In what universe was this even remotely possible?

"How?"

"We're looking into that. Our facial recognition software has been getting better and better, and we recently analyzed security footage at a small airstrip in Colorado during an investigation that involved a credible terror threat."

"Computers can be wrong." Denial came rushing forth. "My laptop crashes all the time. Just because some software matched Asael, it doesn't mean he's…" Kate could not bring herself to say the word *alive.*

"Partial match. We think he might have had work done."

"Like plastic surgery?" Kate gripped the phone, feeling as if a whirlpool had opened beneath her and sucked her into a bad thriller movie. The script writer of her life needed to be seriously fired. "So, he's a terrorist now?"

"We don't believe so. He just happened to come through at the same time as some men we're interested in did."

"Colorado is far from Pennsylvania." She knew it didn't mean anything, but she said the words anyway.

"Please keep an eye out. That's all I am asking," the agent told her. "Has anything unusual happened lately around where you live?"

For several seconds, Kate couldn't breathe. Blood pounded at her temples. *Betty Gardner. Tony Mauro.*

No, no, no. "A suspicious death and a hit-and-run." Her voice was high with panic. "Both were my neighbors."

"When?"

"Mr. Mauro yesterday. Betty on last Monday."

A pen scratched over paper on the other end of the line. "Could be coincidence, but I can't say it doesn't sound suspicious. I'm going to call the local police and ask some questions, to be on the safe side. Is Captain Ethan Bing still the man in charge?"

"He is."

The agent probably made a note of that too, because she paused for a second before saying, "We have no reason to believe Asael knows where you are, or even that he knows that you're alive. We have no reason to think that he's heading your way. I'm still working out of DC. If anything changes, I'll come up. I don't want you to be scared. I just want you to be alert."

"No problem there." Kate gave a weak laugh. "I'm pretty sure I'm never going to sleep again."

"Are you and Murph Dolan still together?"

Because Kate didn't want to go into all that, she simply said, "Sure."

Technically. Almost. They worked at the same place, saw each other daily.

"Good. He's a solid guy. Stick around him. I'll also ask Captain Bing to keep an eye on you."

"He keeps an eye on me already. I had a would-be patient turn violent a few days ago."

"I'm sorry to hear that. You had a difficult week."

You didn't make it any better, Kate wanted to say, but she didn't. She thanked Cirelli for the update.

She kept it together. Her old fears didn't break loose until after she'd hung up with the agent. But then old memories of her friend Marco's murder rushed her: his shocked eyes, the crimson of his blood spreading on the white carpet, the assassin's face reflected in the glass. Then when he'd tracked her down for the first time and the bullet had come within an inch of her face, how she'd swerved off the road and hit a tree head-on. How the FBI decided she should fake her death and disappear. But they hadn't fooled Asael. He'd shown up at her funeral and tried to blow her up as she sat in the FBI van. A couple of years in hiding, then Mordocai found her. Again, she escaped by a hair.

Only because of Murph.

All those years in hiding.

Then the news of Asael's death. Finally feeling safe again these past couple of years. But, of course, it was too much to hope for.

Death kept coming for her, again and again and again.

Kate stared across her office, seeing dark memories instead of her furniture and anatomy posters. A cold, bitter knowledge filled her, like poison spreading through her veins, making her limbs go numb and her stomach burn with pain.

Asael was back.

* * *

Asael

Asael followed the white Honda going west on Route 76. Traffic was light, and he liked a drive. He didn't have the radio on. He preferred silence and his own thoughts. Like what he would do with the young woman in the car in front of him, how soon, with what tools. His favorite part of the job was the planning.

Scratch that. He loved all the phases. The planning, the hit, the reminisce-and-relive phase at the end. A good job well done brought him endless joy, made life worth living.

Kate was too closely guarded. Oh well. There were many, many ways to skin a cat. If he couldn't get to Kate, he'd make Kate come to him. Traps were easy enough to set. He just needed the right bait.

When, two hours out of Broslin, Emma Bridges signaled and turned off the highway onto a quiet country road, Asael stuck behind her. And when she pulled over at a roadside farmer's market next to a seedy motel, he pulled in right next to her.

He stayed behind the wheel, pretending to scroll through messages on his phone while she went inside. Then he climbed into the back of his rented white delivery van.

He opened the sliding door on the side that faced the Honda, then crouched among a small pile of anonymous cardboard boxes of various sizes, and waited, enjoying every second of the anticipation.

If he wasn't an assassin, he could have become a serial killer. He liked what he did for a living that much. But, as things stood, as long as people were willing to pay, and pay exceedingly well for his skills, only a fool would have worked for free.

Ten minutes passed before his target returned, humming a tune under her breath. She must only have used the bathroom—not enough time to have waited in line to buy anything. *Perfect. Plan A, then.* He had a Plan B too, in case she came back with an armload of snacks.

As she walked up between his van and her car, Asael pretended to be looking for something, turning inside, kicking a cardboard box onto the ground with his heel.

"Sorry!" He grabbed for it, missed, pretended to land on his ass and laughed.

The woman laughed with him, a pretty young thing, a bonus on an otherwise already great day. "No problem. Here."

Because her hands were empty and she'd been raised to be nice, she picked up the package and handed it to him.

Except instead of the package, Asael grabbed her slim wrists, then gave her a good yank. A second later she was sprawled across his lap. Another second and the already cut-to-size duct tape he had ready was across her mouth, before she could get out a stupid *No!* or *Why?* or *Stop!*

He yanked the door shut so fast, anybody watching would have missed the whole incident if they'd blinked, but there hadn't been a soul out there. A nice piece of luck, not that he didn't have a Plan C prepared.

He rolled his full weight onto her madly struggling body to keep her down while he yanked her hands behind her back, grabbed for the waiting roll of duct tape, and wrapped a double layer around her wrists. Women always dieting, wanting to be small, was the first mistake they made. He had at least sixty or seventy pounds on her, which mattered.

She fought anyway, not one of those who froze or fainted. And he didn't mind, not at all. She got his blood moving.

"Shhhh. I've got you," he whispered into her ear.

He had to kneel on her calves to make her stop from kicking, but he managed to have her ankles bound up too, without her making too much noise. It helped that he'd padded the van with soundproofing mats. He'd picked those up at a music store at the same strip mall where he'd picked up the rental van.

"Now I want you to be quiet." He pushed off her. "I'd rather have you alive, but dead also works."

The duct tape muffled her outraged screams into pitiful whimpers.

Tamed.

They were all that at the end, one way or the other, the women *and* the men.

Or maybe not so tame, Asael thought, as she kicked the side of the van. He could have hog-tied her, he had the rope, but he wanted to get out of there.

He climbed to the driver's seat in the front, pulled his gun from the glove compartment, and showed it to her. "Do we understand each other?"

That settled her down.

"Good girl."

He backed up and pulled out, got back on the pothole-ridden country road, then on the highway, toward Broslin. He'd only left town to follow her.

"I'd decided last night that I would grab you on your way to work. But when I drove by the house this morning, I saw you swing a suitcase into the trunk. Sister trouble?"

Emma made some noises behind the tape, but he didn't think it was a response. Sounded like a curse.

"Families are a pain in the ass," he told her. An endless source of unnecessary drama, a massive drain of energy—which was why he didn't have one. But Emma Bridges's temper and troubles suited him just fine. "Grabbing you on the road worked out better, anyway. Too many damn busybodies in Broslin."

The two-hour drive before her first pit stop had gifted him with plenty of time to plan. "If I couldn't grab you at the first stop, I would have done it at the next one, or the next. I'm never in a hurry. Never desperate. I'm ready, always, to take advantage when an opportunity presents itself."

He smiled at her in the rearview mirror. "That's what a few decades' worth of experience brings to the table. It's what separates the professionals from the riffraff."

CHAPTER TWENTY-ONE

Kate

Kate wanted to talk to Murph about the possibility of Asael being alive. But not yet. She had to stop freaking out first. Murph texted that he'd be in Philly all afternoon to check out zipline equipment for the course he planned to install in the woods behind Hope Hill. His absence came in handy.

She sat behind her desk and counted to eight as she breathed in. How long was she supposed to hold that breath? Dammit, she couldn't remember. And she'd taken two different yoga breathing classes at the center—she liked to try out things before recommending them to her patients.

Forget controlled breathing. She kicked off her shoes and focused on the muscles in her neck and back. *Relax.*

She gave up after a couple of minutes and picked up her phone. Time to call Emma again to see if she'd calmed down enough to pick up.

The phone rang. But before Emma could have answered the call, footsteps sounded out in the hallway, someone running, then Joe Kessler popped in. "I think Ian McCall is in the parking lot."

The call went to voicemail. Kate clicked off without leaving yet another message. "Are you sure?"

"Fits the description. He's out of his car and pacing. Like he's trying to decide whether or not to come inside. I called it in, but I'm not going to wait for backup. I'm going to take him into custody. I want you to stay right here."

Then, before Kate could protest, Joe was gone again.

"Wait!" She scrambled up and tripped over her sneakers.

She had to plop back down and untie the laces before she could shove her feet in, then tie the laces again so she wouldn't trip and fall on her face. And then, *finally*, she was out of there, leaving her chair spinning behind her like some cartoon character. "Wait!"

By the time she rounded the corner, Joe was long through the doors on the other side of the lobby. He might not be a football player anymore, but when he ran, he ran.

"Do not hurt him!" Kate called after him, just in case he could hear.

By the time she burst outside, he was halfway through the parking lot. She stopped short because she didn't want to startle Ian, who was keeping a close eye on Joe's progress. Joe's physique was pretty intimidating, to be fair. Kate imagined having him coming at you was like watching an approaching freight train.

He slowed a dozen feet out and stopped, held up his hands, away from his weapon. "Hi, Ian. I'm Joe Kessler. Kate's friend."

He was good at this, trained for this, but Kate was still having a heart attack.

"I don't want to talk to you," Ian said, surly, backing away, completely focused on Joe, whom he saw as a source of danger. "I want to talk to Kate." He hadn't noticed her yet.

"All right. I get that. She's nice. Everyone wants to talk to her. I'm a poor substitute, but hear me out. Last time you two talked, it didn't go well."

"And I'm sorry about that!" Ian slapped his palm on the tailgate of his beaten-up black pickup.

He didn't drive a tan Nissan after all, Kate thought. She'd just been paranoid the morning before.

He said, "I feel better now. I don't want to hurt her. I don't want to hurt *anyone*. I just want to talk to someone who can give me some pills."

"Okay. You know Kate doesn't do that. Right? She told you?"

"She did."

"How about I help you get hooked up with someone who does? A psychologist. My wife goes to therapy. Makes a big difference. She had an abusive ex who left her with some issues. I can't even tell you how much she's improved over the years."

"Tried that before." Ian dropped his gaze and kicked at the dirt before looking back up at Joe and shoving his hands into his pockets. "He was an asshole."

Joe moved closer. "How about Maria, the psychologist here? She's Kate's friend. Just as nice as Kate. They do damn good work in this place."

"You gonna let me go in?"

Joe paused. "Honestly, after last time, I don't feel comfortable doing that. I'm sure you understand."

"So I'd have to go back to the station."

"I can take you. Maria might even be able to follow us right down."

I would make sure of it, Kate thought. The last time, half the problem had been waiting for the therapist to come out from West Chester. Ian had been locked in a room all that time, getting more and more worked up, more and more anxious. That certainly hadn't improved his already agitated state of mind.

He was calmer now. *Progress.* Taking a step back as he watched Joe. *Not progress.*

"I don't want handcuffs." His voice grew brittle with tension.

The negotiation was deteriorating.

Kate stepped forward from the shadows, where one of the potted evergreens by the door had mostly hidden her. "Hi, Ian!" she called from the top of the stairs as if she'd just come outside. "I'm so glad you came back."

And then she walked down the steps and toward the two men without hesitation, radiating an all-is-well vibe for all she was worth.

Joe shot her a warning look. She kept going anyway. She wasn't going to lose Ian again.

"How about if I go in the car with you? I'll call Maria on the way. And I'll stay with you at the station until she gets there."

Ian's gaze snapped from her to Joe. "Can she do that?"

"I'll have to pat you down first. Make sure you're unarmed."

Ian held his arms out to the side. "I am."

"Nothing personal." Joe stepped forward. "I have to be sure."

He was quick, but not abrupt, careful, no sudden movements. "All right," he said as he straightened. "Cuffs next."

Ian's gaze darted to Kate. He looked ready to bolt.

She stepped closer. "Are cuffs really necessary?"

"Anybody gets a ride in the back of the car gets cuffed," Joe said, keeping himself between them. "Standard procedure. It's what we do, no exceptions. Like the Army, man," he told Ian. "You get your orders, you follow your orders. My orders are, people in the back get cuffed."

"I'll be right there with you," Kate added. "Don't focus on the cuffs. By the time we're done catching up, we'll be at the station."

A moment of tension-laden silence passed. Then Ian put his wrists together behind his back. "All right."

Kate had to give it to Joe, he managed to be quick once again, without giving off any aggressive or threatening vibes. He even added, "Comfortable?"

Ian shot him a baleful glance.

Joe took the man by the elbow. "Let's go over to the cruiser. You sit in the back, Kate and I sit in the front."

Ian looked at Kate.

She nodded, and he moved forward, stopping only when Joe opened the back door for him. He slipped in without trouble. Then Joe closed the door, carefully, not slamming it.

"Thank you for being so good with him," Kate said as he opened the passenger-side door for her in the front.

"You shouldn't have come outside."

"I'm trying to help."

Joe shook his head, but if he thought she was the opposite of helpful, he didn't say it. He went and slid behind the wheel.

Kate turned around as they rolled out of the parking lot and Joe radioed the station. "How have you been doing, Ian?"

"Been better. I'm really sorry about last time. I mean that."

"I know you are. We're all right. I'm not the grudge-holding type." She dug out her phone.

Nothing from Emma. Not as much as a one-word text.

Half worried, half angry, Kate said, "Let me call Maria to make sure she can meet us as soon as possible."

She waited for her friend to pick up. "Hey. Joe and I are taking Ian McCall down to the police station. He says he'd rather talk to you than their usual guy. You think you could come down and do an evaluation?"

To her credit, Maria didn't hesitate. "I just finished a session two minutes ago. I don't have anything for the next two hours. I'm walking out right now. How is he? If he's agitated, you can put me on speaker and I'll talk to him."

Kate smiled at Ian. "He's just fine. But thanks." Then she hung up with Maria and told the men, "She's on her way. We call her Miss Lead Foot. She'll probably be there before we are."

Ian offered a weak grin. "Not if Joe pulls her over."

Even Joe laughed.

Good—everyone nice and relaxed. Kate was going to keep it that way. "What have you been up to these last couple of days?"

"Called an old Army buddy." Ian shifted into a more comfortable position. "Lives in Lancaster. Hung at his place. Played video games. He's all right, you know. Lost a leg, plays baseball anyway. He's got one of those fancy prosthetics. Like he's in some sci-fi movie."

"It's good to have friends. That makes a huge difference in recovery. One of the most important factors, in fact. I'm really glad you didn't go home. I'm glad you hung around and came back to us."

"I can't get better if I don't get help. That's what Brian said. I'm going to bite the bullet and do it."

Committed to treatment. Another harbinger of successful therapy. Ian McCall was going to do just fine. Kate would make sure of it.

"How long ago did you return to civilian life?" she asked, to keep the conversation going.

"Six months. I thought things would get better."

"They will now. Does your family know you're here?"

He shook his head. "Brother's with the Marines, deployed right now. Don't know where. Parents gone."

"Girlfriend? Wife?"

"She moved back to her parents with the kids. I didn't hurt them or anything," he was quick to add. "I should call them. I don't have a phone. I punched the screen yesterday." He looked down with a sheepish expression. "I got frustrated."

"They would probably want to know how you're doing. They'll be glad you're getting help. If you give me their contact information, I'll contact them for you, if you'd like. Explain how things stand."

Even if he and his wife had a fight, even if the wife was mad at him, he was still the father of the children. They would still be asking about him.

"Boys or girls?"

"One of each."

"How old?"

"Six and seven." He dropped his head back and stared at the roof of the car to hide the moisture that was gathering in his eyes. "I want to be back with them. I want that more than I want anything in life."

Motivated.

"You follow the treatment plan," Kate told him, "and there's a very good chance of you seeing them again. And, in the meanwhile, even the restricted facility we work with allows visitors."

His gaze snapped back to her, some of the misery slipping from his face. He was close to breathless as he asked, "For real?"

"Have I lied to you yet?"

"Wish I could just stay at Hope Hill."

"I'll set that up with the VA while you start getting better at the first facility. Then as soon as you're discharged there, you're coming to us. I'm going to make it my personal mission to make that happen. I hope to meet your daughter and your son. Why don't you tell me about them?"

"Matty is mini-me." Ian came close to smiling. "Paige is a little princess. All pink all the time. Bicycle, toy ponies, clothes…pink and sparkles. Wants to have her ears pierced." His forehead smoothed out. Memories of better times clearly made him happy.

They were at the station long before he ran out of stories.

Maria wasn't there waiting for them, but she pulled in thirty seconds later—in her silver, sporty, little BMW—like a Formula-1 driver into a pit stop. She jumped out, in silver stilettos that matched the car.

Joe raised an eyebrow at her.

She flashed an angelic smile. "Traffic was light."

Joe shook his head and led Ian toward the entrance by the elbow.

Ian looked at Kate over his shoulder, the tension back on his face, eyes and mouth tight. "You said you'd come in."

"Right behind you. Just give me a second to catch Maria up."

As the men walked through the door, Kate stayed behind with the psychiatrist. "Thanks for taking this on at short notice."

"I want to do what I can. Probably not much, right here, right now, but when we eventually get him, if we get him… Was he aggressive again today?"

"Not at all. Just unsure. He wants help, but he's scared." Kate caught Maria up on everything she knew about Ian, finishing with "I'd like it very much if he ended up with us. I think a place like Hope Hill would be beneficial to him. For some reason, he trusts me. I don't want to let him down."

"All right. Let's talk again after I check him out." Maria reached for the door and held it open.

Kate looked pointedly at her friend's shoes as she passed through. "Another hot date?"

"Third date, same guy." Maria walked in behind her, then they stopped, because Ian was still being processed at the front desk.

"It's refreshing," Maria said. "Half the time when I meet someone, as soon as they find out what I do for a living, every date turns into a free therapy session. It's all about how they got messed up when they were kids. Or they just want to talk about how certifiably crazy their exes were."

"Like the guy who wanted you to write a letter to his ex-girlfriend's employer to certify that she's a psychopath?"

"Like that and worse." Maria made an eloquent warding-off motion with her hand, as if erasing the memory. "Anyway. This guy is a psychologist like me. First date, first ground rule was that we're not going to talk shop when we're together."

"*This guy?* You're ever going to tell me his name?"

"Maybe. Someday. Still don't want to jinx it." Maria tilted her head. "Heard from Emma yet?"

Kate pulled out her phone. "No."

Zero messages. She was about to call again when Joe stepped away from the front desk and led Ian to the interview room in the back. Kate put away her phone and followed with Maria.

Once inside the small, bright room, Maria stepped forward. "Dr. Maria Gulick. Nice to meet you, Ian."

Joe Kessler pulled out a chair for her.

"I'll be staying," he said and pushed a chair in the corner for himself.

"Can Kate stay?" Ian asked.

"If she wants to."

She'd planned on calling her sister again, but Ian was looking at her so beseechingly…

"I can stay." Kate moved a chair next to Joe's before he had a chance to do it for her.

Maria pulled the smallest, thinnest, most feminine laptop possible from her bag. "All right, Ian. Why don't you start with telling me about yourself?"

He did, haltingly at first, jumping around in time, childhood in one sentence, war in the next. Then he settled into his last deployment, the attacks, the friends who were dead.

After the eval, Maria made some calls and placed Ian at the secured facility they normally worked with, in the Philly suburbs. While Kate and Maria stayed with him to wait for the pickup. They talked to Ian about what he might expect, how things worked, and then Ian wanted to know more about Hope Hill, so they told him about that.

Then Captain Bing stuck his head in the door and Joe stepped out to talk to him.

A minute later, Joe came back in. "So here's the deal," he told Ian. "As long as you promise to check in to treatment and stay there until discharged, the captain is willing to let last week's incident go."

"That's exactly what I'm gonna do, man."

The handcuffs came off. And when the treatment center's transport van arrived, Ian went peacefully with them.

Kate rode back to Hope Hill with Maria, who, considerately, drove at a speed that didn't make Kate clutch the door handle.

The second she was back behind her desk, she called her sister.

Emma still wouldn't pick up. Not on the third ring, not on the fifth, not on the tenth. Kate left another message. Then she called her mother.

"Hey, could you tell your crazy daughter to check in with your sane daughter when she stops for a driving break? She can't punish me forever."

"I'll try," Ellie Bridges said, "but she hasn't been picking up."

"You haven't talked to her yet today?"

"Not since she texted this morning to let me know you kicked her out and she was leaving."

"I did not kick her out. Okay, not like that. I asked her to leave to make sure she was safe. Same as I asked you and Dad to postpone your visit. You didn't throw a fit." Kate glanced at the time on the bottom of her laptop screen. "When was the last time you tried her?"

"Half an hour ago. Your father tried too. I know she doesn't like to pick up when she's driving, but..." Kate's mother sighed. "You know how I worry."

The rental came with Bluetooth. She doesn't have to hold the phone to talk. Kate's stomach clenched.

Emma might ignore her out of sheer stubbornness, but not their mother, and definitely not their father. She was Daddy's girl, always had been, from Little League baseball to assisting with changing the oil in the car, to choosing to study finance at college— Daddy's little shadow all the way, in a good way, a sweet way.

"Do you think she might have been in an accident?" The question came in a trembling voice from the other end of the line, but Kate could barely hear her mother over the word that roared through her mind.

Asael!

CHAPTER TWENTY-TWO

Kate

After Kate hung up with her mother—her chest tight, blood rushing in her ears—she called Murph. *Should have called the police.* Old habits were damn hard to break. She was pulling her phone away from her ear to do just that as Murph picked up.

"Kate."

His voice made her feel better, and she didn't care what that said about her, not in that moment.

"I can't reach Emma." Panic pushed the words from her in a rush. "Asael is alive."

"What?"

"Agent Cirelli called me this morning."

"And you didn't tell me?" The sound of shoes slapping on a hard floor came through the phone. He was running. His next question came on an angry snap. "Where are you?"

"In my office."

"Do you have your gun?"

"No." She never brought it in, not even after the incident with Ian. For one, they didn't allow weapons on the premises. Two, she wouldn't have risked it if they did. Locked doors could be pried open. Her patients' safety took priority.

"Is Joe there?"

"No. Ian McCall showed up and agreed to go into a restricted treatment facility. After Joe took Ian to the station and Ian went off to get better, there was no reason for Joe to come back here."

"Ian showed up." Murph's voice took on a pronounced chill. "And you didn't feel the need to tell me about that either."

"He cooperated fully. Joe and I handled him without any trouble. Maria helped."

A hard silence on the other end. "Lock your door. No more patients today. I'm going to call Bing, bring him up-to-date, and ask him to send Joe back over. He's closer. But I'll be there as soon as I can."

The line went dead.

Kate tried Emma again. "Pick up, please. I love you. You're the best sister ever."

She locked her office door while she waited for a call back that never came. The phone didn't ring.

Then she thought of Cirelli and called the agent next.

"Everything all right, Kate?"

"I haven't been able to reach my sister since this morning. What if Asael got her?"

"Emma Bridges, right? Does she still live in California? She should be fine."

"She's spent the past week with me here in Broslin. She left my house this morning to drive back to LA."

To her credit, the agent didn't waste time on telling Kate not to worry. She snapped straight to the details. "When was the last time you saw her?"

"A little after eight a.m."

"What is she driving?"

"White Honda Civic. I don't know what year or the license plate number. It's a rental. She was going to drive west on Route 76."

"I'd like to have her cell phone number."

Kate rattled it off. "You can track her location through the phone, right?"

"I'm going to do my best."

"Do you think he has her?"

"There could be a number of reasons why a person doesn't answer their phone. Maybe she put it on mute. Or she could have forgotten it at a rest stop. Or it could have been stolen."

Cirelli said all that so calmly, so reasonably, that Kate almost believed it. *Almost.* "But you'll check into the phone and the car?"

"I'll check. Are you at a safe location?"

"I'm at work. The police are on their way."

"Good. This might have nothing to do with Asael, but let's take all precautions. Let me see what I can do, and I'll get back to you as soon as I have anything. If I find any indication that this is connected to Asael, I'm going to suggest that we take you into protective custody. Are you all right with that?"

Kate couldn't think about herself, not right then. "Just find my sister, please."

After hanging up with Cirelli, she tried Emma again. Then she canceled her afternoon appointments. Then she called her mother, because she didn't know what else to do. "Any news? Did she call?"

"No. And she still won't pick up either. Hold on I'm putting you on speaker. Oh God, if she was in an accident…Do you think we should call the police?"

"I just talked to Murph. He said he'd call the local police captain as soon as we hung up."

"Good. He used to be one of them. They'll pay attention to him."

Kate didn't tell her mother about the FBI or Asael. The assassin was such a far stretch. There had to be a simpler, more likely explanation for why Emma had gone silent.

For all Kate knew, Asael was still in Colorado, the other side of the country, stalking his latest assignment. Or the whole facial recognition hit could have been just a glitch. Cirelli had said it'd been a partial match. No, a partial match didn't merit Kate giving her mother a heart attack.

She gripped her phone.

Don't think the worst.

"Maybe she lost her phone at a rest stop. Or someone could

have stolen it out of her back pocket while she was standing in line for coffee," she repeated what the agent had told her. "You know how Emma gets. Head in the clouds, lost in thought. Or lost flirting with a handsome barista."

"She's right," her father was saying in the background. "Don't worry."

Her mother drew a shuddering breath. "Of course. She'll call any minute, tell us some wild story, then we'll all laugh." But she sounded very much as if she were crying.

"Listen to Dad. Try not to worry too much, all right? And—" Kate fell silent when someone rattled the doorknob.

"It's Joe," Joe said through the door. "Just wanted to let you know I'm back."

"I have to go," Kate told her mother. "The police are here. I'll call you if I have any news. Love you, Mom. Love you, Dad!" she shouted so her father could hear.

"Oh, honey. You know how much we love you back."

As soon as Kate hung up, she opened the door, and Joe stepped inside. "Murph says I have to have eyes on you at all times until he gets here."

"Have you had a chance to have lunch? We have a cafeteria. I could walk you over."

"Grabbed pizza at the station." Joe walked into her treatment room and checked it thoroughly, as if Asael could be hiding under her massage table and she wouldn't have noticed.

"Coffee?" She needed to keep busy.

"All tanked up." He came back out. "Murph gave me a quick update as I was driving over. You think this Asael guy could have taken your sister?"

"It's a very slim possibility, but it's a possibility." Kate grabbed a clean mug and popped a pod of decaf into the machine, just for the comfort of the scent and the feel of the warmth in her hands. "Or she could have lost her phone. Or she could have been in an accident."

Maybe repeating those alternate explanations enough times would help her to believe them.

It didn't.

"Not sure about the accident," Joe said. "Caught an update from the captain on the radio just as I was coming in. State police say they had no accidents on Route 76 this morning involving a young woman."

Instant relief filled Kate. Emma wasn't hurt, in a hospital somewhere. But that small burst of relief disappeared way too fast.

Joe's news didn't rule out her worst fear.

* * *

Murph

Murph was ready to grab Kate and get on the road with her, drag her back to Ohio even to keep her safe, but she would have none of it.

"Please," she begged him. "If you care about me at all, look for Emma."

He hated seeing her scared. If she was scared, if she was in danger, then he had failed. In every way.

He squared off with her. "*You* are Asael's main target."

"Joe will protect me."

Joe Kessler was watching the hallway, while Chase Merritt monitored the lobby. Two outstanding policemen. Yet not enough for Murph.

Kate stood behind her desk, wearing the turquoise sweater Emma had knitted for her this past Christmas, with bells and ribbons, and the words Jingle Bells under them, except the "e" in bells was crooked and could be mistaken for an "a," which Murph was pretty sure had been deliberate on Emma's part.

Kate kept the sweater in her desk drawer for when she got cold. Murph thought the office was plenty warm, but she'd pulled it out and put it on regardless. Maybe just to feel her sister with her.

"I'm not leaving you." His protective instincts raged at the thought. "The whole PD is looking for her. Everyone who's not here with you, is out looking."

"I want *you* to look." She dropped her voice and held his gaze.

"If you ever loved me…"

In his imagination, he already had her over his shoulder and halfway to his truck. "I still love you."

For a moment, everything went still. Tears glistened in her eyes. She wouldn't blink, wouldn't let them fall.

"Please find Emma." Desperation thickened her voice. "Please."

He hated the living shit out of the idea of walking away from Kate. He wanted to murder the thought with his bare hands.

"Murph?"

He was flayed by the fear and worry that clouded her blue eyes. He clenched his jaw as he silently swore. "All right. But I take you home. Joe will be inside the house with you. We'll have two men outside, one watching the front of the house and one in the back. And you'll have a loaded gun in your hand at all times." He fixed her with his serious-as-the-apocalypse look. "Even when you're in the bathroom."

Some of the tension on her face eased. She nodded. But before he could relax even a shade, she came up with her next brilliant idea. "Or I could come with you to look for Emma."

"No," he said as firmly as he could without shouting. First of all, she'd be going into danger over his dead body. And also… "If Bing lets me assist, he'll be doing me a huge favor. I can't bring along another civilian."

She looked like she might cry. She didn't. Once again, she steeled herself, would not allow herself to fall apart. She gave a small nod as she accepted his logic. "Okay."

The few sentences they'd spoken to each other amounted to the longest conversation they'd had in weeks. He missed her—in his heart, in his guts, in the endless, sleepless hours of the night. Something was broken between them, and damn if Murph knew how to fix it, and that helplessness didn't sit well with him. Now more than ever. He wanted to draw her into his arms, hold her, and never let her go. But it wasn't what she wanted, so he stepped back.

"Let's go. Grab your bag."

At least she had still come to him when she needed help with something truly important to her. That was something. It spoke of trust. If they still had trust, maybe, when Emma was home safe and sound, they could rebuild from there.

"Taking Kate home," he told Joe in the hallway. "Can you follow us?"

"No problem."

The three of them walked out to the lobby together, where Murph asked Chase to join them as well.

Kate rode with Murph. He wouldn't let her out of his sight until he absolutely had to.

She said nothing on the ride, just kept checking her phone over and over. Murph called Bing to tell him what they were doing and that they needed another man.

"I'll send Hunter," Bing said without argument.

When they reached Kate's house, Murph kept her in his pickup while Joe and Chase checked out the place. Then he walked her in. Walked her to her little gun safe and checked her weapon, made sure it was loaded.

"I'm not an idiot." Her temper flared at last. A good sign. She was finding her spirit. "I remember what you taught me."

"Good. You see the bastard, you shoot. No hesitation. If he comes, he'll come for one reason only."

"I'll be fine. Hunter will be here in a few minutes. Please go and look for Emma." She put her free hand on his arm.

Need roared through Murph for more. "Kate?"

She leaned forward. And then she rested her forehead against his collarbone, as if all her energy had been sapped, as if she was exhausted beyond words.

He didn't put his arms around her, even if he wanted to, wanted so much it made his teeth ache. He let her give or take what she needed.

In the end, she only needed two seconds. Then she pulled away.

And because staring at her balefully while desperately wanting her back wasn't going to help anything, he took off without further argument. He only stopped at the door to tell Joe and Chase to guard her with their lives.

He called the captain from outside. "I'll be at the station in ten minutes."

"Everybody's out already, checking abandoned buildings. If Emma Bridges was kidnapped, if it is Asael, she could have been picked up a street or two from Kate's place. She could still be in town somewhere." Frustration sharpened Bing's tone as he added, "Damn hard to know where to start. Most of the time, a kidnapper takes his victim somewhere familiar. An abandoned house he might have played in as a kid, or a campsite in the woods he'd visited in the past."

Murph jumped into his pickup. "What would be familiar for Asael in Broslin?"

"Nothing. As far as we know, he's never been here."

"His lover had. Has anyone checked Fred Kazincky's apartment?"

"I doubt it's sitting empty. And it's in the middle of town. Hardly a hideaway."

"Asael might be trying to make a point."

"Like, he's smarter than the rest of us combined?" The captain's tone said he was warming to the idea. "All right. I'll head over."

"I'll meet you there." Murph ended the call and floored the gas.

He reached the location minutes later but got stuck behind a red light at the intersection. He could see the run-down apartment building across the road and watched as two cruisers pulled up to the front, lights flashing. Gabi and Mike ran to the door, talking on their radios. Then Bing was there, hurrying past them, going in.

No, no, no. Dammit! Not like this. Not for Asael.

Then the light was finally green, and Murph sailed through it, shot into the parking lot, and jumped from his pickup.

"Going after the captain," he told Gabi, who was securing the entrance. Mike wasn't in sight, probably securing the back.

Murph dashed up the stairs to the second floor. He'd been there before. Right after Mordocai—masquerading as Fred Kazincky—had kidnapped Kate. He'd hoped never to have the occasion to come back.

Bing was knocking on the door at the end of the hallway,

standing to the side, gun at the ready.

No response, but as Murph slowed, he could hear someone moving around in there. He pulled his own weapon.

Bing acknowledged his presence with a small nod, then knocked again.

"Who is it?" a child's voice asked, a young boy.

"Police," Bing answered. "Can I talk to your mom or your dad? Could you send them to the door, buddy?"

"My dad is at work. My mom went over to the store. I'm not supposed to open the door to anyone."

Murph tucked his gun away. So did Bing.

"Are you home alone?" the captain asked.

"I'm with my sister, but I'm in charge 'cause I'm bigger."

"How old are you?"

"Six and a half."

"All right, buddy. You did a good job here not letting any strangers in."

They backed away, then stopped at the top of the steps.

"Asael could be in there with Emma," the captain said, "holding the family hostage, but I doubt it. Kid didn't sound scared."

Murph agreed. "Would have been too easy."

"Instinct is often right. This was your first thought." Bing started down the stairs. "Worth checking out."

Murph hesitated at the top. "Not going in?"

"We will, but I'm not kicking the door down with a kid in there. We'll wait for the mother."

Definitely the right thing to do. Although, Murph was willing to kick in every door in the universe for Kate's sister.

"I talked to Betty Gardner's possible heir, by the way," Bing told him. "He was at work the morning Betty died. Has about fifty witnesses. Whether he gets the house in the lawsuit or not, he had nothing to do with Betty's death."

"Asael?"

"Don't see why. Unless it's just to rattle Kate."

"How about Tony Mauro?"

"Again, for what reason? He's awake and alert, but can't

remember being hit. Couldn't give me a description of the driver when I went in to check on him. They're keeping him for the rest of the week."

As Murph stepped outside after Bing, for a second he thought Emma was found. Gabi was holding back a frazzled young woman, Emma's age, with similar long black hair, same build. Hope about lifted Murph out of his boots for that one second before it dropped him hard.

"I have to get back to my kids," the woman who wasn't Emma insisted, gallon of milk in one hand, a jar of peanut butter in the other. Anxiety drew her every feature tight. "Did anything happen? Did something happen to my kids? Oh God." She burst out in tears without waiting for the answer.

"Kids are fine," Bing told her. "I'd like to go back up with you and check out your apartment, with your permission."

"Why?"

"We're looking for someone who knew a guy who used to live there."

"We've been living here for a year. I don't know who lived here before us."

The captain nodded. "I need to make sure my guy isn't in there, that's all. We have reason to believe he might be back in town. Want to make sure he didn't pop by for a visit. You think you can give me a minute to walk through?"

"I only ran out for milk. Just over to the gas station across the road. Five minutes."

"You're not in trouble, ma'am. I'm asking you a favor here. I'd appreciate the help."

"Okay." She drew a shuddering breath. "I can go in?"

When Bing nodded and Gabi stepped out of her way, the woman took off running.

They went after her and had her unlock the door, but they went in first.

Two small children stared at the intruders from the middle of the kitchen, eyes wide, the little boy pushing his sister behind him in a protective gesture.

"Is anyone else in here, buddy?" Bing asked in a tone as

friendly as Murph had ever heard from him. He could be a teddy bear when he wanted to be.

The boy shook his head.

"Why don't you and your sister go out into the hallway to your mom while we check?"

"It's okay, baby," came from behind them, and at the sound of their mother's voice, the kids took off running.

Bing went to the left, Gabi, who'd come up behind them, to the right, Murph forward. The apartment was clean and neat, too small to hide much. Kitchen/living room, two bedrooms, bathroom.

"Clear."

"Clear."

"Clear."

"Clear."

They filed right back out.

"Thank you for your cooperation, ma'am," the captain told the woman who was crouching, holding her kids, the gallon of milk and jar of peanut butter on the worn beige hall carpet next to them.

"Are we okay?" She held on tight. "Nobody's in there?"

"The apartment is empty. You're free to go in. Thank you again for your help, ma'am."

Gabi was heading back down the stairs already, and Murph followed, trying to figure out where they needed to check next.

"All right," the captain said once they were all outside, Mike joining them. "Back to our systematic search of the town." He pulled a printout from his back pocket and handed it to Murph. "List of abandoned buildings. Map on the back. You can have this area." He made a circle with his finger on the paper. "You can approach, but if you see anything suspicious, you call it in. You don't go into any building on your own under any circumstances. If you have a problem with that, turn around and go home now."

"No problem."

Bing shot Murph a hard look as if he thought the response was too quick to be trusted. "I know how you feel about Kate. I know Emma is like family to you. But you're here strictly on my forbearance."

"I know. Thank you, Captain."

"Don't make me regret this."

"I won't."

"We'll see." Bing looked at Gabi, then Mike. "Off we go. I expect everyone to check in from each location you inspect."

They nodded, then ran for their cruisers.

Murph slid behind the wheel of his pickup and slapped the map on the dashboard with one hand, turning the key in the ignition with the other. He waited as, ahead of him, Gabi, Mike, and the captain turned right at the intersection. He turned left. He already had his first target fixed in his mind—the ramshackle old firehouse by Broslin Creek. The new firehouse was in the middle of town, a state-of-the-art facility. The township used the old one to park the snowplows.

His phone rang in his pocket.

"Anything?" Kate asked.

"Not yet."

"You'll call me if—" Her voice broke.

"I will. I'm not going to stop looking until we have Emma back. I'm going to find her. I promise. All right?"

The sniff on the other end broke his damn heart. She never cried. She was one of the toughest people he'd ever met.

The closer Murph got to his destination, the more he convinced himself he was on the right track. Broslin hadn't seen snow since the previous winter. None of the plow operators had been called up yet. The place would be empty. *Out there, nothing too close by, isolated.* The location had been chosen over a century before, because the fire wagon tanks could be filled up from the creek.

Murph brought up the old building and its surroundings in his mind. Creek on one side, woods in the back. He was going to stay away from the long driveway. He wasn't going to play this like a cop. He was going to play it like a soldier.

Bing was a fine captain, but he'd spent his career chasing small-town criminals. Asael was ten levels above all of them, in a category of his own. The combined forces of the FBI and Interpol hadn't been able to catch the assassin yet.

Murph would. He'd promised Kate, and that was that.

He slowed as he drove by the turnoff, fumbling with his phone in case anyone was watching. But as he pretended to read a text, he stole a look down the driveway. The parking lot up front stood deserted.

He kept on driving, over the little wooden bridge that spanned the water, and took the next crossroad, a bumpy gravel path that led to a rarely used fishing spot on the other side of the creek. He and his brother, Doug, had fished there a million times when they were kids.

Murph didn't stop until he was behind tree cover, where nobody from the old firehouse could see him. The disadvantage was, he couldn't see the firehouse either. Not even when he slid out of his pickup with his gun in hand.

He maintained a firm grip on his weapon. If Asael was in the building, this was where it would end. There would be no call to the captain.

There it was. The truth. Whatever that said about Murph.

Asael had Emma. Asael was a threat to Kate. Asael needed to die.

No police custody, no hearings, no prison, no hundreds of ways to escape and come back again.

Somebody needed to take care of the Asael problem permanently. And Murph was going to be that man. If he ended up spending the rest of his life in prison for it, as long as Kate was safe, he could live with that bargain.

* * *

Asael

"Like I said, I prefer you alive, but I can work with dead," Asael told Emma Bridges, who was turning out to be a pain.

Whoever had invented the kickass-heroine genre should be shot in the head. Those books and movies gave women too many ideas these days.

"Fuck you," she spat at him.

He'd removed the duct tape because he didn't want her to

suffocate. She'd cried a little when he'd dragged her from the delivery van, down the stairs, into the basement. Her nose had gotten plugged up, her face turning blue from lack of air.

He lifted a piece of paper towel to her nose. "Blow."

She tried to bite him. Clearly, she had recovered.

"I'm going to tape your mouth shut again in a minute. If you can't breathe through your nose…" He smiled.

She got it. Blew. Then blew again.

Damned disgusting. He tossed the wadded-up paper towel aside. Then he grabbed the roll of duct tape from the floor.

"Don't!" She turned her head.

He slapped her. Just enough so she knew he meant it. He might yet have to rough her up later. He would enjoy that, but he didn't want to start too early. Didn't want to chance that he might get carried away. It'd happened in the past.

When she stilled, he taped her mouth shut again.

"No crying," he told her as he stood and walked away.

"Mfmmd."

Was she trying to swear?

He looked back at her over his shoulder. "No worries. I'll be coming back. But right now…" He smiled at her. "Time to pay a visit to your sister."

CHAPTER TWENTY-THREE

Murph

Murph jumped from rock to rock as he crossed Broslin Creek, careful not to drop his gun. The town hadn't seen any rain in the past couple of days, so the water ran low. And since the creek wasn't shaded on both sides—woods to the east, but fields to the west—enough sun reached the protruding stones so they weren't covered in moss and weren't slippery. A nice piece of luck. The last thing Murph wanted was to face-plant in the water.

He climbed up the crumbling bank on the other side, then kept in the cover of scattered bushes as he approached the building. Ed Gannon had parked the broken old plow out there. It probably didn't fit inside anymore with the big new plow and the salter.

Murph ducked as he dashed behind the salt storage shed. Adrenaline sharpened his focus and his senses. His main target, the old firehouse, stood thirty feet ahead.

He ran forward silently, in a straight line, over to the firehouse's nearest dirty window. Then he flattened himself against the wall, waiting for any sound that might indicate that he'd been spotted.

No sound came from the inside.

He inched up and looked through the glass.

No movement either. The interior appeared just as deserted as the outside, nothing but snow-management equipment.

Murph waited and watched for another minute. Then he was on the move again, carefully rounding the building.

A fine dusting of dirt covered the driveway, along with a drift of dead leaves. No tire marks. The front door was padlocked from the outside. Not a single window open anywhere. None broken either. Each time he came to another pane of glass, he looked inside, going around in a complete circle.

No sign of life. No sign of recent occupation. Nothing remotely suspicious.

He rolled his shoulders to release some of the pent-up tension in his muscles. *Dammit. It would have been too easy.*

He called the captain on his way back to the creek. "Old firehouse all clear. Doesn't look like anyone's been out here in weeks."

"Nobody's had any luck so far," the captain told him.

Murph hated the thought that Emma might not be in Broslin. Their best chance for recovery was there. Outside of Broslin…he didn't even have a guess.

When he didn't say anything, the captain added, "She might not have been taken. She could be just mad as hell, focusing on her road trip, and making a point with her silence."

"Maybe for an hour or two. But not this long. Emma wouldn't do that to Kate, and definitely not to their mother and father. She's in trouble."

"Then we're going to find her."

After they hung up, Murph made his way across the babbling water, then drove to the next possible location on his list, then the next, then the next. No sign of Asael or Emma anywhere.

Then only one address remained, an out-of-business printshop. They used to print the two local papers there, but one of the papers had folded, and the other one had gone to a bigger printer for a better price in West Chester. Murph wouldn't have been surprised if the *Broslin Chronicle* folded too and soon, or went completely online. People read the news on their phones these days.

The printshop was next to a razed strip mall right on the edge of town. Murph found a broken window and climbed in, searched every inch of the building, but found nothing.

He was walking to his truck, his mood as dark as the cracked blacktop under his feet, when he happened to glance up at the water tower across the road, and it jiggled something loose in his brain. He knew another place connected to Asael, didn't he? Connected, like the apartment, through Mordocai aka Fred Kazincky.

Years ago, when Mordocai had kidnapped Kate, Murph had caught up with them an hour north of Broslin, on the edge of another small town, in the woods. Mordocai had tied Kate out as bait, then climbed a tree to hide behind the leaves and have high-ground advantage over Murph.

It hadn't worked.

There'd been an old water tower behind the guy, which Murph had used to line up his shot.

Who the hell knew why Asael wanted Emma, what his twisted mind was thinking? Maybe the assassin meant to sacrifice her on the spot where his lover had died, to honor Mordocai's memory.

Murph slammed on the gas, flying down the road as fast in the approaching twilight as his rattling pickup could take it.

He had no doubt that Asael's end game was Kate. But killing her didn't seem to be enough for the bastard. He wanted to punish her first, for having escaped him for so long, and for being the cause of Mordocai's death.

What better place to spill Emma's blood than the very spot Mordocai's blood had been spilled? Poetic justice.

Murph picked up his phone to call the captain with his latest theory.

He hesitated.

He'd been a soldier. He'd been trained in E&E, escape and evasion. He'd been trained how to sneak through the woods unseen. He drove a beat-up pickup, not something that would be immediately suspicious if seen. But if he drove up to Asael's hiding place with the captain and a couple of police cruisers in tow...

Instead of Bing, he dialed Kate.

"Did you find her?" she asked as soon as she picked up.

"Not yet."

He could hear her gulp of disappointment before she said, "I called her again. This time, it went straight to voicemail."

"Her battery is probably dead. What's going on at your place?"

"Joe just checked all the doors and windows again. House is locked up tight. Hunter had to leave, but Mike came to spell him. He's outside, in the front. Chase is in the back. Are you still looking for Emma?"

"Going down my list of possible hiding places."

"Thank you."

"If I finish my list and don't find her… I thought I'd spend the night at your place too. I could take the living room couch."

"I already promised it to Joe."

And there Murph was, suddenly jealous of Joe, which was stupid because Joe was head over heels in love with his wife, Wendy.

"Kate…"

"Thank you for looking for Emma."

We need to talk he wanted to say. But now was not the time. It never was the time lately.

Thank God frustration didn't have calories. He would have been the Goodyear Blimp by this point.

* * *

Asael

Asael drove by Kate's house. One stupid cop up front, one inside. Pitiful.

He drove to the corner, turned right, then right again onto the street that ran parallel to Kate's. He pulled over between two houses so if the inhabitants of either one looked out, they'd assume he was visiting the neighbor. Forty yards in front of him, in line of sight with the back of her house, another cruiser sat by the curb.

Asael turned off the dome light, then slipped out of his car. He used various landscaping features as cover until he was in Betty's backyard.

He let himself in. Because his stomach growled as he walked through the dark, half-empty house, he headed straight to the kitchen. Enough moonlight filtered in to make out that the muffins he'd seen on the counter the last time were gone. He opened a cabinet. Empty. He didn't want to open the refrigerator. He could have unplugged it; that would have taken care of the fridge light, but dragging it away from the wall far enough so he could reach in there wasn't worth the bother. Kate Bridges had probably cleaned that out too, just like she'd cleaned out the cabinets.

He strode back to the laundry room and stood to the side of the window, watched as the light came on in Kate's bedroom next door.

"Optimistic," he said, "to think you're going to sleep tonight."

When she stepped into her bathroom, he scowled. The bathroom window was up high. He couldn't see in there. But he didn't have to wait long for her return.

She was back in five minutes, wearing yoga pants and a T-shirt instead of a nightgown. Maybe because she had that cop in her house. Or maybe because she expected a call at any second that her sister had been found, anticipated having to jump into her car to rush to Emma's side.

There was that optimism again. She thought she was going to get her sister back. Asael laughed under his breath.

Emma.

Had a mouth on her, that one. Pretty. Too bad it wouldn't last. He was in a mood. The town brought out the worst in him, or the best…depending how one looked at it.

He'd found the perfect lair, one nobody would suspect, and it came with a built-in torture chamber. Did he believe in fate? He believed in himself, his brain, and his skills. Although, just this once, he felt as if maybe the universe was giving him a gift.

On the other side of the gap between the houses, Kate stepped up to her window and looked out, as if looking right at him.

Asael savored the tingles that spread over his skin.

She couldn't see him. She wasn't even really looking. She stared into nothing.

She was slim, strong, with lovely breasts, he noticed as she turned. A pretty pair of sisters.

He was going to enjoy them. He could do whatever he wanted. No specific instructions from a client.

This wasn't a job.

This was a treat.

* * *

Murph

Murph drove east on the Turnpike, tearing himself apart over whether he was doing the right thing. Driving away from Kate went against all his instincts. But Emma was in mortal danger. And he couldn't ignore that either.

Took him an hour to reach the right pull-off from the highway, a strip of bare dirt curled around a stand of bushes. He could see tire tracks, fairly crisp. Could have been from earlier that day, or from a day or two ago. They didn't mean much. It was the kind of spot cops used for cover to catch speeders.

Murph jumped from his pickup and headed across the field to the stand of woods ahead, to the spot where he'd killed Mordocai and saved Kate. He swore as he went, hating to think about that day. He'd never meant to come back.

The twilight was giving way to dark. He picked up speed. He needed to be able to see.

The cursed water tower waited a few hundred feet into the woods. Higher ground. If Asael was up there, like Mordocai had been, if he had a better gun than his lover had at the time, say, a rifle with a scope, he could pick Murph off from a distance. Especially since half the leaves were off the branches.

Murph kept as many trees between himself and the tower as possible, looking for footprints on any bare spot of dirt.

He stopped behind the last line of bushes, the last line of cover. The tree Kate had been tied to stood straight ahead, twenty or so feet away. The memory made him want to shoot Mordocai all over again.

He waited and listened.

No sound. No movement.

He kept in cover and circled the tower at a distance.

Nobody up there.

By the time he approached the base, there was precious little visibility left.

Enough, however, to see the broken spiderwebs.

Somebody *had* been up there recently.

Asael.

Who else would come out to the middle of nowhere to climb a rusty tower? Murph had come for a reason. Whoever had come before him would have come for a reason as well.

To pay his respects to a fallen lover.

Murph circled the base again, this time looking down, using his phone as a flashlight. Stopped when he found a partial footprint. Not his. Deep. It had to have been left when the ground had been wet.

When had it rained last?

Saturday.

He'd helped Kate clean out Betty's house that day.

A ten-second memory snapped into sharp focus, as clearly as if he were back in Betty's kitchen. Emma's smiling face as she asked, *Did Kate tell you I saw a ghost?*

"Asael." Murph spat the name as if speaking a curse.

Asael had been in Betty's house. Within arm's reach of Kate. He could be in there right now.

Murph took off for his pickup, calling Joe as he ran.

CHAPTER TWENTY-FOUR

Murph

When Murph's phone rang with a call from Bing, he was just flying past the town-limit sign, finally back in Broslin.

"Anything?" the captain asked. "Where are you?"

"Coming back from the water tower where Mordocai died. I had a hunch."

"And?"

"A single footprint."

"More than we got."

"The print was left in mud."

"Saturday," the captain said immediately. "Okay. Say Asael was here that early... What was he doing between then and taking Emma?"

"Watching Kate. I want to get into Betty's place."

"You got a search warrant?"

"I'm telling you, something about that place bugged me when I was there to help with the cleaning."

"You try to sell that to the judge. The hamburger wrapper had no usable prints, by the way. The results just came back."

"And who would eat a hamburger with gloves on? Then there's Emma saying she saw Betty's ghost in the kitchen window the night after Betty had

179

died."

"*Broslin PD doesn't investigate ghosts.*"

"*I'm not Broslin PD.*"

"*Take that thought and meditate on it.*"

"*Emma is gone. I'm not going to let the bastard take Kate too.*"

Bing said nothing for a couple of seconds, then a couple more. The silence was followed by a sigh that indicated his strong suspicion that he expected to regret whatever he was going to say next. "*Linda Gonzales has the key. As police, I can't go in without a warrant. As someone who was there helping with packing things up, if you need to go back in for something completely unrelated to police business and Linda gave you the key...*"

"*Thank you.*"

"*Don't thank me yet. She isn't home. Her daughter collected her this afternoon to celebrate her grandson's birthday in Trenton. She won't be back until tomorrow morning.*" *Bing paused.* "*Hold on. Sophie is calling. I have to take that.*"

Murph drove straight to Kate's place. He didn't relax until he saw her through the window, crossing her kitchen.

Mike sat behind the wheel in his cruiser by the curb, wide awake, not on his phone, alert and looking around, to his credit. He rolled his window down when he saw Murph walking up. "*Nothing out of the ordinary so far.*"

"*No movement around Betty's house?*"

"*Nothing. I've been watching the place like it's the last doughnut in the break room. A dog was barking in one of the backyards a little while ago. I got out and walked around, but didn't see anyone.*" *A glint sparked in his eyes.* "*Hey, do you know why the snowman named his dog Frost?*"

"*Why?*"

"*Because it bites.*"

Murph covered his face with a hand as he shook his head. "*You should ask Harper to host an open-mic night over at Finnegan's.*"

Mike shrugged. "*He doesn't appreciate my jokes. Lost all sense of humor now that he's in loooooove.*"

"*What? He had a sense of humor before that?*"

The two of them shared a laugh before Murph said, "*Thanks for keeping watch. I'll look around too. Just in case.*"

He headed over to Betty's place, passing the OPEN HOUSE sign on the front lawn—noon to 3:00 p.m. the next day. Things were moving fast.

He checked the front door. Locked. Windows. Locked. Back door. Locked.

No scratches on the wood anywhere, no sign of any locks being jimmied, no forced entry. Every piece of glass he came across, he looked through. Enough moonlight filtered inside so that he could see shadows—furniture that hadn't been removed yet. Nothing moved. None of the shadows were man shaped.

The house felt deserted. Had Murph thought otherwise, he might have bent the law and pushed his way in there.

He walked back to his truck with a wave to Mike. Then he drove around to the next street over to talk to Chase.

* * *

Kate

Kate couldn't sleep. She stared at the ceiling and cried, then swore alternately.

Oh God, Emma. I love you. Be safe, please.

Asael coming back was her worst nightmare. That and someone she loved getting hurt. And not a damn thing she could do about it.

This was exactly what she'd been trying to avoid, why she'd spent years on the run.

She tossed and turned.

She almost, almost, called Murph. But if Asael was here and he was after people Kate cared about, then she'd do best to stay as far away from Murph as possible. She didn't want to paint a target on his back.

If anything happened to him… She couldn't bear finishing the thought.

Was she being stupid holding him off?

Maybe she was being stupid.

They needed to talk. She just needed to share her fears and doubts with him.

After Emma was found.

Kate couldn't think past that right now. Right now, finding her sister was everything. The only thing.

CHAPTER TWENTY-FIVE

Murph

Murph spent the night guarding Kate's house from the outside, circling her block over and over. When the sun came up and the new shift started to arrive to watch her, he went home to catch a couple of hours sleep, then he showered, caffeinated, and drove to Linda Gonzales's house bleary-eyed. He hoped Linda was home from her visit with her daughter early.

Nobody answered the doorbell.

While Murph waited, he called the captain. "Any news on Emma?"

"Would have called you if we had anything." Bing sounded as if Murph had woken him from a deep sleep. "We'll keep looking. Got into Betty Gardner's house?"

"Waiting for Linda to come home."

"Let me know if you find anything."

Murph promised, then ended the call because a blue minivan was rolling up the driveway.

"Oh, you don't need a key, hon," Linda told him once he presented his request. "Open house today. Realtor is probably over there already, setting up. She said she'd go early, see if she could do something to put the place in the best light. I think they usually bake cookies to make a house smell nice, don't they?"

Murph had no idea. "Things are moving fast," he commented. "That's good, I suppose. Closure."

Linda pressed her lips together. She blinked, then shook her head, struggling for words.

"You must miss her."

"We had a lot in common. I could talk about anything with Betty. She read a lot, listened to NPR, watched PBS. She used to be a teacher. She had an opinion on everything. Read romances, like I do. We used to swap books." Linda teared up.

"I don't read a lot of romance novels," Murph told her, "but if you need help with anything else, you let me know."

"You're a good man." Linda patted his arm. "Tell Kate I said hi and thank her for me for all her help. You snap that girl up and marry her."

"Working on it," Murph said, then he went on his way.

Mike sat in a cruiser outside Kate's house, with bags under his eyes, looking decidedly worse for wear.

"Not a mouse stirring last night," he said when Murph walked up to him.

Murph looked up the walkway, toward Kate's front door.

"You gonna talk to her this time? Or just shoot more pining glances?"

"Give my greetings to your amazing girlfriend."

"Not funny. It's not a sin to be single. My moment will come. It will be love at first sight. We will marry immediately and live happily ever after."

"Hey, Linda Gonzales is looking for someone to swap romance novels with." Then, since Mike started to roll up his window, Murph quickly added, "Why are you still here?"

"Harper had to wait for the liquor delivery at Finnegan's to sign for it. His parents are out of town. The truck broke down, so everyone's running late. But he just called to let me know he'll be here in ten minutes."

"Thank you for keeping an eye on Kate."

Mike nodded, somewhat mollified, before he closed the

window all the way. That he hadn't cracked a single joke spoke to how exhausted he was.

Murph walked over to Betty's house, knocked on the front door, and was let in.

The Realtor was a pretty young woman, wearing a rose-hue business suit. He didn't know her. Then again, he didn't know *everyone* in Broslin. New people moved in all the time. The town had a blue-ribbon school district, and it was an all-around great place to live.

"Mila." She offered her hand and a welcoming smile. "Come on in. Interested in the house?"

"Hi. Murph Dolan. Interested, but not in buying. I'm working with the local police on a case as a civilian consultant. Do you think I could quickly walk through the place?"

Her smile fell. She glanced past him, through the window, at Mike's police cruiser by the curb. She sighed. "This is going to be terrible for business today."

"I could call the next shift and ask them to come in an unmarked car."

Her face lit up again. "Could you, please?"

Murph pulled out his phone and texted Harper. A second later, Harper texted back. *No problem.*

"All set."

Mila stepped aside. "Look at anything you'd like. But if anyone else shows up early, please pretend you're just another prospective buyer."

"Want me to say I love it so much, I'm offering full price?" Murph joked. "Bid it up a bit?"

She laughed. "Thank you, but no. That would be cheating."

He left her at the door and walked straight through to the laundry room in the back, inspected the lock on the inside. Same as on the outside, no sign of tampering. And the key hadn't been stolen. It was hanging on a peg on the wall. Murph even tested it to make sure it was the right key.

Then he hung it back up, stood in the middle of the room, and looked around. Nothing out of place. And yet, his cop instincts kept prickling.

As he turned to leave, the window caught his eye. The orientation of the window, more specifically. He looked out. Kate's bedroom window was directly across, he realized when she appeared behind the glass, wrapped in a towel. Her curtains were open to only a small gap, no more than six inches, but it was enough. Their gazes locked.

She shook her head, her tightening eyes transmitting *What the hell, Murph?* as clearly as if she'd spoken.

He drew up his shoulders in a way he hoped conveyed *Sorry, didn't mean to be a Peeping Tom.*

She snapped the curtains closed.

Right. He had no idea what to do about her anymore. Lately, it seemed no matter what he did, he'd just screw up. Which was why he hadn't gone in to talk to her the night before.

He checked the laundry room again, without finding any sign that Asael had ever been in there, then he walked out the back to inspect the ten or so feet of grass separating Betty's house from Kate's.

No footprints that he could see. No cigarette butts or gum wrappers or any other random garbage under Kate's bedroom window, or anywhere else, no sign that anyone had been out there lately.

He walked around to Kate's front door, then knocked. They couldn't not talk forever.

She opened up, fully dressed, her cheeks tinged with red from obvious anger, her eyes narrowed to slits.

"No!" she said, but stepped back to let him in.

Hunter rose from a chair by the kitchen table, leaving his mug of coffee behind. He nodded at Murph, gauged the density of tension in the air, then strode off toward the back of the house mumbling, "Gotta use the bathroom."

Coward.

Then they were alone, the sudden storm that had risen in the foyer intensifying by the second.

Before Murph could ask what was wrong, Kate put her hands on her hips and stuck her chin out. "You are not buying that house."

What house?

"You are not moving in next door to keep an eye on me. This is not normal. This is not healthy. This is exactly why I asked for time and space."

"Kate—"

"This is not space! You can't live next door."

"Kate—"

"Dammit, Murph. This is exactly what I didn't want. Why can't you listen to me?"

And she went on. And on. The protest died on Murph's lips. He took her in, the red-hot fury, that pitch in her voice that said she was nearly in tears. She was stressed to the max, and he was part of it.

Did she really see him as a stalker? Was she this desperate to push him away? Was what he felt completely one-sided?

He wanted to be with her. But if her answer was no, which it was, loudly and emphatically... A no was a no.

Hell, if one of the staff at work came to him, told him an ex wouldn't let go, wouldn't walk away, kept stopping by almost every day to check on her... Murph would have had a talk with the guy, explained to the asshole that stalking was a crime.

And in this case...

He was the asshole of Kate's story.

Shit.

If this was how she felt, then it *was* time for him to go. And not just for her sake, but for himself too. He was tired of the two-step distance. He was tired of holding his breath, waiting for her to decide she wanted him. He was tired of walking on his knees.

He was tired period, exhausted from a long night of guard duty, short on patience due to the lack of sleep.

He held up his hands, palms out. "Okay. You know what? You're right. I haven't been giving you space. But I'm going to do that now. I'm going to give you all the space you want."

Then he turned and opened the door, looked over his shoulder and held her gaze. "This is me, walking away."

CHAPTER TWENTY-SIX

Kate

There it was. Murph mad at her. Really, truly mad.

Kate hadn't thought anything could make her feel worse, but she'd been wrong.

Her throat burned with repressed emotions as she stood in her foyer and stared at the closed front door.

God, it was a shit day. After a sleepless night, a call from Cirelli had woken her, to let Kate know that the FBI still had no idea where Asael or Emma were. Then a call from Captain Bing with an identical update.

Emma had been missing for over twenty-four hours.

Kate knew what that meant.

She'd cried in the shower. Coming out to find Murph looking through her freaking bedroom window was more than she could take. She'd lost it. And he walked away.

Murph finally did what she'd been asking of him for months. Left her alone. Gave her space.

Kate couldn't breathe.

Hunter came back from the bathroom. "Everything okay?"

"Yeah." Kate held on to her emotions with an iron grip as she turned. "I didn't get much sleep last night. I think I'll go back to bed and lie down for an hour."

She wasn't going into work. Her house was easier to secure than the rehab center. Also, ultimately, Asael wanted *her*. She had no doubt the assassin was behind Emma's disappearance. The police and FBI could have their doubts, but Kate had none at this stage.

In the end, Asael would come for her. And she didn't want to draw him someplace where others could get hurt; she didn't want him anywhere near her patients.

She avoided Hunter's eyes. "Could you please wake me up if there's any news?"

"Of course. Go get some rest."

She closed her bedroom door behind her. Then she stood there, her back pressed against the wood. She couldn't hold the tears back, or the pitiful choking noises that escaped her throat.

She hurried into her bathroom and closed that door too before she gave her emotions free rein.

She cried in big, heaving, ugly sobs.

About Emma, first of all, who was in the clutches of a killer. Her baby sister whom Kate was supposed to protect. *Oh God, Emma.*

Kate's role had always been to be the big sister who sheltered the baby from the monster who'd given them birth. She'd protected Emma in foster care too, until they'd been adopted by a good family, until they were finally safe. Taking care of Emma had kept Kate alive, gave her young life purpose. If it hadn't been for Emma, she would have run away—had thought about it a dozen times— ended up on the street. Then she would have been dead, because how long would a ten-year-old possibly make it sleeping in abandoned buildings and parks, with predators on the prowl at night?

Kate had kept Emma safe, and keeping Emma safe had saved Kate. But then Kate had let down her guard. You couldn't do that. It was *never* safe. You relaxed for a second and *that* was when the worst happened.

She couldn't trust happiness with Murph. Because what if she allowed herself to be happy with him, and then something terrible happened to him? Because that was life. Nobody was ever safe.

Something terrible could happen to Murph, like it just happened to Emma.

Murph walking away was for the best. Even if it didn't feel like that at the moment. Even if right now, Kate's heart was in a thousand shattered pieces.

She dropped onto the edge of the tub and buried her face in her hands.

She sobbed so wretchedly, sniffed so loudly, that she almost didn't hear her phone ping in her pocket.

Multimedia message from an unknown number.

The type of call she would normally ignore, but this time she clicked so fast the movement, was a blur. She held her breath. Blinked away tears so she could see.

A photo flashed onto her screen, a woman's hand bound with a plastic tie at her lower back, the skin red and raw, showing obvious signs that she'd struggled.

Kate would have recognized Emma's hands even without the turquoise turtle ring. Their fingernails were shaped the same.

Her breath whooshed out, her chest constricting. Her fingers trembled as she tried to scroll, but there was nothing more, no message, not even a single word.

She pushed to her feet and stepped toward the door on liquid knees, light-headed. She had to show the photo to Hunter, forward it to Captain Bing and Cirelli. And Murph.

Because Murph would help. No matter what. He was probably out there right now, looking for Emma. It hadn't even occurred to Kate that he would stop, regardless of the breakup. But she stopped in front of the bathroom door and didn't open it. Didn't call out to Hunter. Didn't send anyone anything. She laid her forehead against the wood instead and tried to slow the thoughts racing through her anguished mind.

Asael wanted *her*. He didn't really want Emma. He was using Emma as bait. He was using Emma to scare Kate, to make her desperate, to lure her to him.

The second photo pinging onto her phone, an eye with a fresh bruise, confirmed Kate's fears. Emma's eye, looking straight into the camera, defiant, as if saying *Don't you worry about me.*

How many more pictures did Asael mean to send?

How much more was he prepared to hurt Emma before he deemed Kate "ready" to hear him?

Kate thought about their parents, who would be arriving in less than twenty-four hours. She was supposed to pick them up at the airport, then take them to the bed-and-breakfast on Main Street.

They could get an Uber.

She hit Reply on her phone and typed with trembling fingers. *Me for her.*

Not because she thought Asael would let Emma go if Kate gave herself into his clutches. For one, Emma had probably seen his face, so she was currently in the same predicament as Kate. Asael couldn't let either of them live.

BUT… Two were better than one. And Kate had years' worth of self-defense training from Murph. She'd imagined facing Asael a million times, had mentally and physically prepared for it. Between her and Emma, they might be able to come up with a plan to escape. Kate certainly wasn't going to leave her sister alone with a killer.

She drew a slow breath to calm her racing pulse as she typed a quick follow-up message. *Let's trade.*

* * *

Asael

Asael smiled at the message popping up on his phone.

The police weren't dictating it to Kate. She was alone in the back of the house. He could see this morning's police protection in the kitchen window.

He waited a minute, just to make her sweat, then typed *If you want to see your sister alive, do exactly as I say.*

The key to a good trap was the right bait. You had the right bait, and you could catch anything.

Her response was immediate. *I will.*

Go to her room, he wrote back. *Stand in front of the window.*

190

Less than thirty seconds passed before she appeared.

Now open it and climb out, he texted. Quietly. *If I see the cop in the kitchen move, your sister is dead.*

The man in the kitchen window did not move. He kept watching the street, clueless.

When the window was all the way up, Kate Bridges sat on the sill, swung out one leg, followed by the other. Then she jumped to the ground, without hesitation. She even had the presence of mind to turn and close the window behind her.

Asael sent his next text. *Go into Tony Mauro's house from the back. The door is open. If you're seen, the game is up.*

She looked both ways before pulling into the cover of a hydrangea bush on her side. Then she darted into the cover of a large lilac bush that had lost most of its leaves already, but had enough gnarly branches to provide coverage.

He noted the slight limp. Must have landed too hard on that ankle. It didn't matter at this stage.

Asael walked through the house to the back to open the door. He stepped aside to let her in. "Hello, Kate."

For a second, they stood a foot apart, the closest he'd ever been to her. She'd evaded him for years. If he wasn't as vain as he was, he would have admired her.

She scrambled away from him, as far as she could go, until her back hit the dryer.

He hadn't realized how much it would excite him, how much the personal angle added. He found her proximity...arousing. Not in the way a man might find a woman arousing, nothing that basic. But the way the sighting of the perfect prey aroused the hunter.

"Where is Emma?" she demanded, legs slightly apart, bracing for a fight, struggling to hide how scared she was. "Is she here?"

"No."

"Why are you in this house?"

"Convenience." Asael gestured at her. "Why don't you put your phone on the washer and then pull up your shirt so I can make sure there's nothing tucked into your waistband?"

She did as he instructed. He didn't deem a pat down necessary. She wore close-fitting yoga pants.

He stepped to the window and opened it. "Go ahead. There's a van outside in the next-door neighbor's driveway. No worries, they're not home. The van's side door is open. Close the door behind you. I left a blindfold in there for you. You put that on."

She did as she was told, with grim determination. The cop who sat up front in his cruiser couldn't see her. Tony Mauro's garage hung forward, blocking his sight.

Asael went after her. He locked her into the back, then slipped behind the wheel.

As he backed out of the driveway, looking as if he'd just delivered a package, he was whistling.

When he stopped at the Stop sign on the corner, he said, "You probably think you could take that blindfold off and attack me from behind. You could. But keep in mind, if I don't take you to your sister, you'll never find her."

She stayed quiet. *Good girl.* She was one of the smart ones. She'd eluded him for years. She'd survived multiple previous assassination attempts. She understood that she was beaten. Asael appreciated that.

Ten minutes, and he was at his destination. He drove right into the building. He turned off the van and went around to open the side door. Checked the blindfold. "Give me your hand."

She didn't struggle. "Where is Emma?"

"You'll see her in a minute."

He led her to the basement door. And when they were halfway down the stairs, the door closed behind them, he said, "You can take off the blindfold."

He let her go, allowing her the use of both hands. Then he walked down the rest of the stairs after her, waited for her reaction, so eager for it that his fingertips tingled.

When she reached the bottom step and her breath caught— that quick, shocked intake of air—the way she froze on that last step, that fed him.

"Emma! Are you all right?"

He was close enough behind her to smell her fear, the sharp scent of sweat. He didn't stop her as she ran to her sister.

For a long time, almost a minute, the sisters paid attention to nothing else but their embrace. Then Kate looked around, taking in their surroundings at last before her gaze snapped to his. "What is this place?"

"A workshop. Woodwork, metalwork. All these tools…" Asael gestured dramatically because he liked drama. Life was better with flair. No need to be basic. "Enough to outfit three torture chambers, aren't they?"

Kate paled as she rose. "Please let my sister go. You have me."

Really. "Don't disappoint me now, Kate. You couldn't have thought I would go through with the trade."

She stepped in front of her sister and had her hands out to the side in a sweet if desperate gesture, like a mama bird protecting her nest. "But it's me you want."

"That's the thing about wants and needs, isn't it? No matter what you have, you always want a little more. Think you need a little more. Life is not a board game where the rules forever stay the same."

He didn't duct-tape her mouth shut. He'd even removed her sister's gag earlier. He knew how he wanted to end them. It wouldn't do if they suffocated too early.

"Over to that pipe." He pointed. "Sit down. Hands behind your back."

In a minute, he had them tied up side by side, then he walked upstairs, satisfied with himself.

He'd used Emma as bait to catch Kate. And now he would use Kate as bait to catch Murph.

He liked it when a plan came together.

CHAPTER TWENTY-SEVEN

Kate

"You're an idiot," was the first thing Emma said once Kate told her that she'd come voluntarily. "And I don't mean a village idiot. I mean on a global scale. Why? Oh my God. Are you out of your freaking mind? I'm so mad at you right now."

Asael had gone upstairs, leaving them tied to water pipes, side by side.

Kate wanted nothing more than to hug her sister again, but that would have to wait. "He's alone. We're together. We're going to escape."

"We're going to die."

"Then we die together." Kate's gaze dropped to the bruise under Emma's eye. "Are you all right?"

"Of course I'm not all right. And now you're not all right either. I don't want you to die for me! I don't want you to risk yourself, and I don't want you to risk the baby. Are you crazy? Why would you do this?"

Kate was so focused on scanning their windowless prison and staring at a workbench set up like an operating table—sharp tools laid out on the sides, a human-size empty space in the middle—that a second passed before her sister's words caught up with her. "I'm not pregnant. I told you I wasn't."

"Really? You're sticking with that?" The anger in Emma's voice mixed with disappointment. "I'm your freaking sister. Just tell me already."

"I'm not pregnant!" They didn't have time for nonsense. "How are we even arguing about this right now? Don't we have better things to do? We need to figure out how we're going to escape. Listen…" She trailed off as the look on her sister's face morphed from anger to stunned disbelief.

Then Emma shook her head and looked like she might cry. "You didn't know. Seriously? You seriously didn't know?"

"There's nothing to know." Beyond the prepped workbench under the neon lights there were others, cluttered with tools. If only Kate could get to them. She scanned the walls and ceiling. No cameras that she could see. At least that one thing was in their favor. Asael wasn't watching them.

Emma bumped Kate's shoulder with her own to force Kate to look at her. "I thought you just weren't telling me because you wanted to tell Murph first, and you and Murph are on the outs right now."

What? "We need to get out of here. I swear, I'm not pregnant. Focus! Did you see the building from the outside when he brought you in? I was in the back of a van, blindfolded. I didn't see anything. Do you know where we are?"

"Have you gotten your period?"

"I think I'm in perimenopause. I was supposed to get some blood work, but then Mr. Mauro was in that hit-and-run and all the issues with Ian McCall… I forgot."

"How many have you missed?"

"Two." Kate shrugged. "As of today, technically three." Which meant nothing. She was under a ton of stress. "I think we're in Broslin. I was only in the back of Asael's van for a few minutes."

"White van?"

Kate nodded.

"That's how he got me too," Emma told her, then gave her the whole story.

Unfortunately, that didn't mean that she was off the pregnancy topic.

"When did your stomach troubles start?" she asked.

"A couple of months ago. But it's been much better since I cut out the dairy and the gluten. I haven't had any nausea in days."

"Because you're entering the second trimester," Emma said with exaggerated patience.

"Murph wears protection. Where in Broslin do you think we are? One of the old factories that shut down?"

"Every time? Not one broke? Not ever?"

"Once."

"Let me guess. Three months ago?"

"I don't know. Maybe? About that. This is not the basement of a house. It's much bigger. What kind of business needs half a dozen workbenches? Repair shop?"

"You've been moody as fuck."

"Okay!" Kate stopped inspecting the basement and faced her sister fully. "Can we stop with that topic, please? I'm not moody!"

"So, you've been picking fights with people you love for fun?"

"I haven't been picking fights." But, honest to God, right at that moment, she could have choked someone.

"You kicked me out of your house."

"I'm sorry, all right? This was exactly what I was trying to avoid. I didn't want you to get hurt."

"You got mad at Murph because he proposed to you." Emma looked like if her hands were free she would have been tearing her hair out. "Can you say hor-mo-nal? Can you just once pretend that I'm not the baby of the family who knows nothing, and listen to me? Oh my God, I hate you so much right now."

"You can't hate me. We're sisters."

"I wish we'd been twins so I could have eaten you in the womb!"

For a long moment, they stared at each other.

Then the mood in the basement took a one-eighty in a split second, and they burst out laughing. But then Kate's emotions took another turn, and she was suddenly on the verge of crying.

"Just stop." Emma's obstinance was seriously driving her nuts.

"I can't do this right now. We have to…" She blinked away some idiot tears.

She freaking hated how emotional she'd been lately.

As that thought settled on her mind, the world spun with her. Stopped.

Hor-mo-nal.

Kate stared at her sister.

She was seeing the room and herself and Emma in it from above, an out-of-body experience. And overlaid on that image, she could see a movie montage of odd little moments from the past three months, the nausea and lack of appetite, the exhaustion and brain fog, her emotions all over the place, fighting with Murph, fighting with Emma…

The movie ended and Kate snapped back into her body, still staring at her sister, except she was finally seeing the truth in those clear brown eyes. "I—"

Kate's gaze dropped to her flat belly, feeling as if she hadn't been simply shoved onto the stained cement floor minutes before but had been dropped from a great height, from outer space. Every bone in her body, every thought in her brain, felt rattled.

A tear rolled down her face. "Oh God."

Emma misted up too. "Right?"

"Murph just broke up with me." The words tore a hole in her chest.

* * *

Murph

Murph drove back to Kate's place from the mechanic shop where Mordocai used to work. It wasn't empty or abandoned, but he couldn't think of any other place to check. Neither the owner nor the mechanics had seen any strangers lurking around. Nobody had been asking questions about Fred Kazincky.

Traffic slowed for something up ahead. For a few seconds, Murph was stuck in front of his old house. The Victorian he'd sold from witness protection, via proxy, was finally fully renovated. He noted the gingerbread trim: pink, cream, and tan. *Fancy*. Although, he liked Kate's house just as much if not more, the clean lines and the possibilities it hid.

Traffic cleared, and Murph moved on. He drove around Kate's block. He went through a mental map of Broslin in his mind, east to west, anyplace he could think of that could be a hiding place. At the same time, he scrutinized every car he saw. Nothing stuck out. No strange males around forty slowing or stopping.

When his phone rang, he grabbed for it. "Agent Cirelli."

"We found Emma's car abandoned by Route 743," the agent said. "Just outside of Hershey. She must have decided to take the scenic route. No sign of struggle. I tried to call Kate, but her phone is turned off. Everything okay?"

"We had a fight," Murph told her. "She probably turned off her phone because she doesn't want to talk to me right now."

"Local police are still watching her house?"

"Three-man team. Three-person team," he corrected. Gabi was watching the back.

"I'm assuming you're also there, fight or no fight?"

Murph cleared his throat. "Yeah." He hated to be so pitifully predictable, but there it was. "So Emma's car was just sitting by the side of the road?"

"In a parking lot. I'm looking at the spot right now. Nothing but a skeevy motel on one side and a roadside market on the other. Nobody remembers seeing her. If she parked closer to the motel, we could have caught her on the security cameras. The market doesn't have any. The guy behind the counter says she could have been there, he might not remember. It's been a busy week, people picking up their Halloween pumpkins, fall wreaths, and whatnot. He does a brisk business selling fresh cider, has signs for it all down the road. Could be what pulled Emma in."

"Could she have gone to the motel?"

"Not according to the front desk clerk. And, like I said, she's not on the security cameras."

"Do you think Asael took her?"

"I wouldn't be here if I didn't think there was at least a possibility. Asael turns up alive, then both of Kate's neighbors have accidents, then her sister disappears. All in one week." The agent paused. "But still, it could be a coincidence. Emma is a beautiful young girl, traveling alone. There are people out there who would consider her prey. Plenty of women disappear in this country each year. You know the statistics."

He did. He'd been an officer of the law for long enough to learn them.

"I'll let Kate know about the car," he said.

"I'd appreciate it. She can call me if she has any questions, but I don't have anything more right now. Okay. That's it. I want to call Captain Bing to let him know that I'll be in Broslin at one point this afternoon. I'll see you then?"

"See you then."

After Murph thanked her and they hung up, he dialed Hunter. Hunter picked up with "What's up?"

"Kate has her phone turned off."

"She's taking a nap. She didn't sleep last night. Want me to knock on her door?"

Cirelli's message wasn't time sensitive. Whether Kate found out right then or an hour from then that Emma's car was located wouldn't make a difference. And maybe, by that time, the FBI would have more information.

The last time Murph had seen her, she'd been on the edge of falling apart. She needed rest. "Let her sleep."

"You sure?"

"The FBI found Emma's car," Murph told him, then filled him in on the circumstances. "When Kate wakes up, just let her know. If she has any questions, she can call Cirelli. For now, there's nothing urgent."

* * *

Kate

"I'm pregnant," Kate said for the third time, still stunned. "I'm going to be a *mother*."

"That's nothing." Emma grinned, her eyes still misty. "I'm going to be an aunt."

"Seriously, I'm pregnant."

In hindsight… There had been other signs she'd ignored. Her breasts had been achy. They did that sometimes when she drank too much coffee, so she'd put the discomfort down to that, except, she hadn't really been drinking more coffee than usual. And she tired more easily, which she put down to depression over her troubles with Murph.

"I can't have a baby. I'm too stupid to live. I was pregnant for the past three months, and I didn't even know it." She stared, blinked, whispered, "I'm going to have a baby."

Emma's grin widened. "In about six months."

"Okay. Now we seriously need to get out of here."

"Why didn't I think of that?" Her sister rolled her eyes. "You're right. Let's go."

"God, you're snarky."

"Better than sitting here scared and crying in fear. Or worrying about *that* shit." Emma nodded toward the workbench under the neon lights that Kate had been doing her best to ignore.

"Why would he hurt us?" Kate tore her gaze away and looked at her own sneakers instead. "It's not like we have information he needs to torture out of us. Fine, we've seen his face. But to end that threat, all he needs is us dead."

"A cheerful thought. He's a *psycho*. Maybe, as a bonus, he's also a sadist?"

"It's not in his FBI profile." Kate grabbed on to that thought with all her might.

Emma didn't seem impressed or comforted. "Have the FBI caught him? No. They don't know everything about him. Anyway, that bench is not even the one I'm most worried about." She gestured with her head toward another one, in the dark shadows of the far corner, this one covered with a sheet of stainless steel.

The light above was turned off, so Kate had missed the setup until then. Five separate devices sat on the bench, some kind of electronics with wires, each about the shape and size of a brick. Her breath whooshed out of her. "Are those…"

"I think so." Emma's swallow was audible.

"For what?" Kate squinted, leaning as far forward as she was able, wanting to see better. "He's planning on blowing the building?"

"He asked me how many people I thought might attend the Mushroom Festival." Emma paled.

"Thousands." Kate felt the blood drain out of her head too.

"Thank God you canceled Mom and Dad."

"They are coming." Kate's chest was so tight, she could barely get out the words. "Because you went missing... They wanted to be here."

CHAPTER TWENTY-EIGHT

Murph

Instinct pushed Murph to *last known location*, the starting point for any missing persons investigation. He was halfway across town, heading to Hershey, where Emma's car was found, to see if he could spot something Cirelli might have missed, by the time he changed his mind. Instincts were good, and the first instinct often proved to be right, but not always. He was so sleep-deprived, his decision-making was impacted. He hadn't been thinking straight.

The drive up to Hershey would take an hour and a half, an hour of looking around and talking with Cirelli, then another hour and a half back. Which translated to *a lot* of hours away from Kate.

She was the main target. Emma had likely only been taken to torture Kate, to put her on notice. And Cirelli wasn't an idiot; she was a damn fine agent. If there was something to see in that parking lot, in or around Emma's car, she'd see it.

Murph turned around. Best to stay where he was and watch Broslin.

Kate didn't want him. He'd accepted her wishes. But that didn't mean he was going to stand by while an assassin was coming for her, while Emma was missing.

He hunted for rental cars and out-of-state license plates, faces he didn't recognize. He discounted families, pairs of girlfriends, anyone obviously too young. Asael was a master of disguise, but it'd still be difficult for a forty-something man to look like a teenage girl.

Nobody set off Murph's alarm. He gave up after an hour, figured he'd be better off circling Kate's block. If everything looked all right, maybe he could catch some shut-eye there, in his pickup. At some point, Asael would make contact. Murph wanted to be in top shape when that happened.

He was driving past Kate's house, nodding at Harper in his cruiser, when Hunter burst through the front door, talking rapidly into his phone.

His face said everything Murph most feared.

He pulled up to the curb and jumped from his truck. "What is it?" He met Hunter halfway, Harper on his heels. "What happened?"

"Can't find Kate."

Murph ran past him, heart pounding like a war drum. *How the hell?* He shouldn't have left. "Kate!"

No sign of struggle in the bedroom, window locked. He ran to the back door. Locked. He pushed through the half-closed door of the guest bedroom.

Nothing disturbed. Checked the closed window. *Unlocked.*

He backed out without touching anything and ran out of the house through the laundry room, then checked the narrow space through which Kate's home had been invaded.

Asael had come through the window, two steps to cross the hallway while Hunter had been in the kitchen, looking outside. Kate would have gone with the hitman if he threatened Emma's life. Back out the window. Then gone.

"Fuck!"

Was Hunter freaking deaf?

Except, Murph couldn't fully blame Hunter. Because where had *he* been? Driving around like an idiot.

The house on the other side of the gap stood empty. Tony Mauro was still in the hospital. Murph checked the front and back doors. Locked.

He crossed the back lawn and knocked on the sliding glass door of the back neighbor. Nobody responded. Nobody home.

The woman in the next house over waved at him through the kitchen window. She opened it with effort then stuck her head out. "Looking for the Millers?"

"Hey, Maggie. Actually, looking for Kate." He pointed at her house. "Wonder if you might have seen her out back? Or anyone else out here?"

The woman shook her head. "Is she okay? Gabi told me what happened. Did the police find her sister?"

"Not yet. Any unfamiliar cars on your street this morning?"

"No. But I was doing laundry in the basement most of the day so far. Just came up to start making lunch."

Murph thanked her, then ran up her driveway to the cruiser where Gabi sat behind the wheel.

She was jumping out of the car to meet him, rushing forward, *oh hell dammit* all over her face. "Harper just said Kate's gone."

"Have you seen anything? Have you been here the whole time?"

"Except for the five minutes I was in the bathroom. Maggie let me in, so I didn't have to go far. I can't pee in a cup." Her voice thickened with apology and self-recrimination, with a good dose of frustration.

"Not your fault. Hunter was in the house with her. I was circling the freaking block." Murph was so mad at himself, he was ready to blow, so he left Gabi and ran through the backyards again, back to his pickup.

He'd underestimated Asael. They all had. They'd thought, sure, the bastard always got his target, but his targets were unsuspecting civilians who weren't expecting him and didn't have an entire police team for protection.

If it were physically possible, Murph would have kicked his own ass. The *second* he knew Asael was in the US, he should have taken Kate and they should have disappeared again.

Hunter and Harper were still outside, up front, Hunter on his cell phone.

"Captain is checking traffic cam footage," Harper told Murph.

Yes, yes, yes.

The intersection two blocks down had a camera. If they could identify Asael's vehicle, they might be able to get a license plate reading, then put an APB out, have State Police, and everyone else, looking.

Murph jumped into his truck, yelling to Harper before he closed the door. "Tell the captain I'll be there in ten!"

* * *

Kate

"I thought I was so freaking smart." Kate teetered on the ragged edge of despair, keeping a tight rein on her emotions to prevent tumbling over. "Have you checked for cameras in here?"

Emma didn't respond.

Kate glanced at her, found her eyes closed, body slack against the wall, dozing. Probably hadn't gotten any sleep since she'd been abducted.

Kate yanked at the plastic tie that held her to the pipe behind her. It held her just as securely as it had before.

Murph would know what to do.

Murph could have taken Asael out in Mr. Mauro's laundry room. The second the hitman had been within reach.

The sad truth was, while Murph had trained Kate, she was definitely no Murph.

Had his overprotective behavior annoyed her in the past? Yes. But right then, she would have given anything to have him pop up on the staircase.

He was looking for them. When he found out where they were, he would come for them.

Murph came through. Always. That was what he did.

He'd even gone to witness protection with her.

They had made love for the first time ever that day. In his bathroom. While FBI agents were waiting in his kitchen to whisk them away.

He'd lifted her up and onto him, her back against the door. She'd reminded him of the agents.

I've been deployed for the past eight months, then titillated by you days on end, he'd said. *It'll only take two seconds.*

Words every woman wants to hear. She'd laughed.

He was inside her so deep they weren't separate entities anymore. They were welded together.

And they stayed together. Until her attachment issues and pregnancy hormones messed with her head and she pushed him away.

Once Kate got herself and her sister out of this damn basement, she and Murph were going to sit down for a long talk.

She nudged Emma. "Do you know if Asael has any cameras set up down here? I can't see any. Is he watching us?"

"What?" Emma blinked with sleep-heavy eyes.

"Never mind." Kate checked again, but didn't see anything suspicious, so she kicked off her sneakers.

"What are you doing?"

She used her toes to roll off her socks, the maneuver sending half a dozen tiny tools scattering to the cement floor.

Emma leaned toward them. "Is that my manicure set?"

"You left it on your nightstand. I didn't have time to grab anything else." Kate eyed the nail file, nail clipper, the cuticle trimmer, and another few pointy metal pieces she had no name for. "I wanted to bring my gun, but I figured he'd find that on me in a second. This was as close as I could get to having a concealed weapon on me."

She had the small items flat against the side of her feet under her socks, and the bulkier clipper under the arch of her foot. It had made her limp, but only a little.

"Wouldn't have occurred to me in a million years." Emma yawned. "What time do you think it is?"

"Noonish?" Kate's stomach was growling for her missed breakfast and lunch. She'd wasted hours not daring to reveal her little tool set, for fear that Asael would come back. But he had stayed away. Maybe he would stay away a little longer. "Listen. Do you hear any noise from upstairs?"

They both fell silent.

Nothing.

"He could have gone out to eat," Emma said.

"This could be our chance. See if you could kick some of these tools up to my hand."

Emma kicked off her shoes and socks, stretched, then swiped at the cuticle cutter with her bare toes and grabbed up the round plastic handle. Then she lay on her back and pulled her feet up and over her head, tilted to the side, and dropped the precious tool behind Kate's back.

Kate searched the ground blindly until her fingers brushed over the metal. "Got it."

"You can call me Yoga Queen."

"Thank you, Your Majesty." Kate tried to saw at the plastic tie that held her to the water pipe without stabbing herself bloody.

While she worked on that, and failed, Emma finagled over the nail clipper. "Try that."

Kate did. Dropped the clipper, picked it up, dropped it again. "The plastic is too stiff. I can't get the angle right."

She kept fiddling with it anyway, until they heard the basement door open. Of course, he would come back right at this second. Maybe he did have a freaking camera hidden somewhere.

Kate shoved the nail trimmer into the back of her waistband, then grabbed the rest of the tools her sister had deposited behind her back in the meanwhile and did the same with them. Then she just sat there with Emma and tried to look innocent. They could do nothing about their socks and footwear.

Asael appeared at the bottom of the steps, a large messenger bag slung over his shoulder. He'd definitely had work done. Cirelli had been right. His nose was narrower. His hairline straighter at his forehead. Hair plugs?

He took in their shoes and socks, then shook his head. "I don't have a foot fetish." He laughed. "I'm not going to waste time on guessing what you were hoping to accomplish here."

"Could we have some water?" Kate asked.

Emma spoke up at the same time. "I need to use the bathroom."

"Later," Asael told them. "I have a schedule I mean to keep."

He strode to the workbench in the dark corner and carefully placed his homemade devices into the messenger bag, one after the other.

Desperation choked Kate. "Are those for the festival?"

"Give the girl a cookie."

"This town has done nothing to you. The people of Broslin had nothing to do with Mordocai's death."

The muscles in Asael's face tightened at the name.

Okay, definitely don't mention it again.

"Please let my sister go," Kate begged, because the hitman might respond to that. He struck her like the type who enjoyed having power over others. "You have me to punish. You don't need her anymore."

"I'm not going to leave you with this creep," Emma spoke up. And then, as Kate stared at her, she demanded of Asael, "What the hell is the operating table for?"

Don't ask questions you don't want to know the answer to. And Kate really didn't want to know the answer. But she had to hear it anyway.

"New side business. There are people who'd like to do what I do, but don't possess the skill."

Emma stared at him. "Aspiring assassins?"

"Not many have the balls for that. More like voyeurs. Taking a life can give a person a certain rush." Asael's thin lips formed an übercreepy smirk. "Have you never thought about it?"

"Cut me loose," Kate said through gritted teeth. "I'm willing to give it a try."

"Glad to see you found your spark. It's always more entertaining when the prey fights back." His smile grew colder as he glanced toward the workbench set up with a wide selection of tools.

"You're not going to break us."

"Not down here. But be assured, by the time I'm done with you and your sister, you *will* be in pieces."

Kate held herself rigid, locking in the panic. She was not going to cry in front of him. She was not going to show fear. The bastard was not going to see her cower.

"This here…" He gestured at the setup. "Is for a more private, more protracted performance. A client who likes to watch. Believe it or not, in parts of the world, there are some sick perverts who'd pay a good amount to see just how much torture an American soldier can take."

Whatever Kate had meant to say next got stuck in her throat. Because she knew exactly what soldier Asael was referring to with that sick smirk on his repulsive face.

Oh God.

Murph.

When facing a deadly predator, play dead, had been the advice Kate had received during a family camping trip to Yellowstone National Park when she'd been in high school.

Her father had meant grizzly bears, but few predators were deadlier than the man Kate faced.

Do not challenge. Hold still. Keep your head down. No eye contact.

Couldn't do it. Kate laughed into the bastard's face instead.

"You're seriously going to call Murph here?" She sneered.

She was done with the fear, the hiding, the running. Asael had killed her best friend, Marco, then taken years from her life. Kept her away from her sister, her parents. Messed up the best relationship she'd ever had with a man. If she and Murph hadn't been forced to go into witness protection, if what was between them had been allowed to develop at a natural pace, under natural circumstances, she wouldn't be having all these doubts. Asael had poisoned everything Kate held dear.

"I thought you were smart," she taunted him. "Famous assassin. Never been caught. Always outwits everyone. But if you think you're going to take Murph Dolan down…" She shook her head and flashed a pitying look. *Come on. Get mad. Make a mistake. Step close enough so I can kick your balls behind your kidneys.* "He's *so* far out of your league."

"I'll see how tough he is when he's strapped to the table." Asael offered that sickening psycho smirk again. "You and your sister will be joining the parade. I predict you'll be an explosive success."

"Ooh." Emma took a turn, catching on. "You're so brave.

Blowing up two tied-up women and a bunch of innocent people. What a big boy you are. So tough."

That did the trick. Asael stepped back to the nearest workbench behind him and grabbed a pair of pliers, then stalked back to them, dark hate dripping from his eyes.

"Did you know that pulling out someone's teeth will not make them shut up?" he asked. "Not even if you take every last one. If you really want someone to be quiet, you have to rip out their tongue."

Kate pulled her knees up as if in a self-protective gesture, but really so the man could step even closer. She held his gaze and put every ounce of defiance into her next words. "Then fucking do it, you chickenshit!"

His smile grew sickeningly excited as he dropped to one knee next to her and grabbed her hair with his left hand, then yanked hard, tilting her head. "Open up."

She spat into his face.

He smacked her with the hand that held the plyers.

The pain was instant, excruciating, and if he shattered her cheekbone, she had no time to think about it.

The asshole was between her and her sister, severely underestimating them both.

"Now!" Emma screamed as she kicked him, tipping him forward, Kate plowing her shoulder into him with all her strength.

He smacked his head into the cement block wall behind them with a satisfying thud. Kate jammed her shoulder into his ribs. Emma kicked the gun from his waistband, then kicked it farther away. Then they used their heads, shoulders, and knees to pummel him.

If they weren't tied up, they could have beaten him senseless. But without hands, without being able to rise, they had too little leverage.

With a beastly roar, he lunged back and picked up his gun. He aimed it at Kate's head.

She didn't flinch. She wouldn't look away.

Then he pointed the gun at Emma, and that was more difficult to take.

"Go ahead, you limp-dick piece of shit," Emma taunted him, her eyes blazing with courage.

"If I didn't have a more painful plan in mind for you than just a quick bullet, you'd already be dead." He spat the words, then spat blood next.

And then, with a last vicious curse, he left them.

CHAPTER TWENTY-NINE

Kate

"He's going to blow us up at the parade." Emma pulled her knees tightly to her chest, her bravado gone.

They were both deflating and fast.

"I think so." Kate looked at her sister with one eye. The other one was rapidly swelling shut. "But first he's going to call Murph here, using us for bait."

"Murph will know it's a trap."

"He'll come anyway." Kate let fury fill her. "I'm not going to let Asael hurt my baby, or you, and I'm not going to let him hurt Murph. I'm not going to let him hurt this town either. We have to warn people."

She retrieved the pieces of the manicure set one by one. Good thing she'd been gaining the lost weight back and her pants were tight, so nothing had fallen out. Being tied to the water pipe, she could move her hand up and down, could scoot close enough so she was able to reach into the back of her waistband. "How do these plastic ties work? You thread the end through the little hole in the other end and something catches, right?"

"The plastic is serrated. I think it's the same as the green ones

Dad uses to tie out his tomatoes."

Kate went through her tool set by feel and settled on the slim metal nail file.

She tossed the file toward Emma's feet. "Hey. Yoga Queen. Do you think you could pick that up with your toes, lift your legs and bring your feet behind me, and shove the tip of the file into the plastic tie's lock mechanism?"

To give her sister a better chance at seeing where she was aiming, Kate turned to the other side, presenting her hands tied behind her back.

"I think," she said, "that the only thing keeping these ties locked is a little lip of plastic inside. It catches against the serrated side of the tie and holds. If you can slip the tip of the nail file over that lip and push it down, I could get free."

Emma pinched the nail file between her toes, then folded herself in half, lifting her feet over her head. Then promptly stabbed Kate.

"Ouch."

"Sorry. Difficult to be coordinated in this position."

"You're more coordinated than I would be. Keep trying."

Emma made another attempt. Then another and another and another, stabbing again and again and again, until Kate could feel blood running down her skin.

When she couldn't hold back a hiss at the next stab, her sister unfolded herself. She lay there on the cement floor for a few seconds, breathing hard. "I don't think this is going to work."

"It should, dammit. If you could wedge the tip of the metal right in next to the plastic tooth." Kate visualized the process. *Oh.* "Okay, hang on. I know what we're doing wrong. You need to push the file in from the bottom, not from the top."

She pulled her hands up the pipe to make room for Emma's foot under them.

Her sister folded back up and tried again. Failed. Huffed. "The angle isn't right."

No, it wasn't.

"Put the file in my hand," Kate instructed.

When she had it, she wedged the tip of the nail file into the little locking loop from the bottom, then lowered her hands until the other end of the file was resting on the cement floor. She used the floor for leverage as she yanked down her hands. And accomplished nothing.

"Let me try the clipper again." This time, she felt the plastic with her finger first, located the spot where she'd already weakened it with the cuticle cutter, and she clamped the nail clipper onto the exact same spot.

Emma sat up, craning her neck. "Is it working?"

"No. The plastic is too damn thick. I can cut into it, but I can't cut through."

"If it's damaged enough, can you just break it?"

Kate dropped the clipper and tried.

Snap.

When the tie fell away, she could have cried in relief.

She didn't waste time on rubbing her wrists or celebrating. She snapped up the file and got on her knees next to Emma to release her.

The trick was much easier to perform now that she could see what she was doing. Within thirty seconds, Emma was free.

"Shoes on." She grabbed her socks and sneakers. "We'll need to run."

"Bathroom first." Emma picked up her shoes and socks, then darted around the stairs to open a door Kate hadn't been able to see from where she'd been tied up.

"Thank God." Kate ran after her sister and took her turn.

By the time she came out, Emma was at the torture table, grabbing a large wrench. Kate grabbed a hammer.

Her first impulse was to tell her sister that *she* would protect her. But then she smiled instead. "You're so kickass."

"Thank you for noticing." Emma stole up the stairs.

Kate followed silently behind her. "In my defense, the last time we lived in the same house, you were a teenager."

She held her breath while her sister tried the door at the top.

"Locked." Emma breathed the word. "Got a credit card?"

Kate pulled the nail file from her right sock.

Emma shifted out of the way and looked up.

Kate followed her gaze to the dark lightbulb.

Neither of them dared to turn it on. If Asael was out there, he might see the light through the gap under the door, and their surprise attack would be spoiled.

Kate shoved the flat end of the nail file between the door and doorjamb, swiping down, slipping, then swiping down harder.

When the metal tongue gave, she could have kissed the damn door.

She opened it with trembling fingers, only an inch, then waited, listened. The outside was silent.

She widened the gap until she could see what was on the other side. A corrugated metal ceiling soared high above. Shelving lined the walls. Equipment Kate couldn't identify littered the cement floor—carpentry tools?

"I think we're in a warehouse." She waited and watched. Nothing moved. "I don't think he's here."

She stepped forward, gripping her hammer, into the large space, about sixty feet by a hundred. Emma came up behind her, the massive wrench in hand, at the ready. But Asael didn't pop out from behind any of the shelves stacked with old boxes that had *Nowak's Antiques* printed on them.

"I know where we are," Kate whispered. "The Broslin Industrial Park."

Then they were far enough into the warehouse so they could see the bay door to the right, the roll-up kind, the white van that had brought them there parked in front of it on the inside.

They ran to the van, Emma reaching it first. "No key."

"Come on." Kate hurried to the metal door and tried to yank it up, but it seemed to be padlocked from the outside.

"Over there." Emma took off toward the man door at the far end of the building, with the red EXIT sign above it. "Quick, before he comes back."

Let it be unlocked, let it be unlocked, let it be unlocked, Kate silently chanted as she ran.

They were just a dozen feet from the door when it swung open.

The second of surprise that crossed Asael's face didn't slow him down. He stepped inside without breaking his stride and closed the door behind him, his eyes growing cold, then colder.

Kate and Emma raised their weapons. They lunged to rush him together, screaming like a couple of banshees, but he had his gun out before they were halfway there.

And they froze, neither willing to risk that the other one might get hit.

"Drop those toys," he snapped. "I'm not going to miss. This is what I do for a living."

Emma's wrench clattered to the ground a second before Kate's hammer.

Asael reached into his back pocket and pulled out a small black container, then tossed it to Emma. "Open it."

Kate watched as the contents were revealed: a single syringe filled with a colorless liquid.

"You push half of that into your sister's arm. Now."

Emma threw it back on the ground. "Like hell I will."

"It's a sedative. Either you do it, or I'm putting a bullet in your sister's head. And then I'll put one in yours." Asael aimed his gun between Kate's eyes. "One. Two."

Emma pressed her lips together and stared him down.

Kate picked up the syringe and jammed the needle into her own arm, through her shirt. Pushed in some, pulled back a little and pushed another batch into the gap between her shirt and her arm, the liquid trickling down her skin.

Then she turned to Emma. "Give me your arm. Dead later is better than dead now."

She repeated the procedure, half the drug injected, half wasted.

Asael stepped closer and pressed the barrel of his gun against Emma's temple. "Now you two get into the van."

CHAPTER THIRTY

Murph

By midafternoon, Murph was going out of his mind with worry.

They'd gotten zip out of the traffic cameras, but he refused to give up. His instincts said Asael was keeping Kate and Emma in Broslin.

When his phone rang on the passenger seat, he snatched it up. *Bing.*

"Anything?" Murph demanded.

"Where are you?"

"About two blocks from the station. Thought the FBI might be there by now. I want to talk to Cirelli." A warm day, his window down, he could hear cheers and clapping in the distance, horns blowing. The festival had begun, with a dozen parade floats making their way down Main Street.

"Cirelli isn't here yet. But we just got a message."

"From Asael?"

"Yeah." A pause. "Okay. FBI just walked through the door. I have to go. We'll talk when you get in."

The line went dead, and Murph needed every ounce of his self-

217

control not to snap the phone in half.

What freaking message?

When he finally reached the station and parked his truck, he took off running. He burst through the door, sailed by reception with a hurried nod to Leila, past the empty desks on his left, and straight to the captain's office.

Cirelli hadn't aged a day in the past five years—same short hair, same strict suit. Murph didn't waste time on greeting the agent. He didn't apologize for interrupting either.

"What message?" He couldn't breathe until he had it. "Let me see."

The captain turned his laptop around with an ominous expression, and Murph stared at the screen. It took him a few seconds to decipher that he was squinting at an explosive device attached to a two-by-four board with duct tape. The photo was a close-up, showing little else other than plywood behind the board.

"Any text with it?"

Bing scrolled up until three characters were revealed: 1/5.

"One of five." Murph reached over and scrolled back down to the picture. "Any idea where they are? Or at least where this one is?"

"Inside some kind of a wooden structure," Cirelli pointed out the obvious. "Beyond that? No."

"It's Asael," Murph said.

The agent nodded. "Multiple crazies on this level in a town the size of Broslin, at the same time, would be highly unlikely."

Murph kept his eyes on the picture. "The wood isn't weather-beaten. Looks like something recently constructed. Do we have a list of building sites in town?"

"The two new developments," Bing said. "Then hundreds of small-time reno projects probably. I already asked the township for a list of current building permits. And then there are people who work on their houses without asking for a permit." He scratched his chin. "But why blow up something and kill a couple of innocent carpenters or a DIY enthusiast?"

"Unless Kate and Emma are in the house." Murph was ready to tear the town apart with his own hands to find them. "Who's tracing the phone that sent the image?"

"The FBI." The captain nodded toward Cirelli.

"We should have the information soon," she said. "But it's probably a burner."

"Has everyone on the team seen the photo?" Murph asked. "Someone might have a better guess than we do."

"Sent it to everyone at the PD," the captain told him. "They're all out securing the…" His right hand curled into a fist that he banged on the table. "*Parade.*"

The single word had the power to suck the air out of the room.

They stared at each other in horror.

The parade. Thousands of people.

A split second of frozen shock. Then they all launched into action.

"The device is somewhere along the parade route." Murph looked back at the picture and scrutinized every pixel. "What's new construction?"

"The spectator stand and the stage," Bing said.

Murph grabbed his phone and dialed Maria at Hope Hill. When she picked, he spoke only a single sentence. "I need everyone with explosives experience on Main Street."

Cirelli was shouting orders into her own phone. The captain was radioing the information to the rest of his team.

Murph didn't wait for them to finish. He took off running. He'd just slammed behind the wheel of his truck when his phone rang. *Unknown caller.*

"I'm having a party," a male voice said on the other end. "So far, it's just me and a couple of your friends. Why don't you join us and even out the numbers?"

Before Murph could respond, the man added, "I've got a camera on you, Dolan. I'm watching you. Now roll down your window and toss your gun and phone as far as you can. Two cars down, there's a Nissan Altima. Key in the ignition. Directions to the party on the dashboard. If you try to signal for help to anyone, in any way, I'll blow your insignificant little town off the map." He laughed. "I'm undecided on it, to be honest. Play your part and play it well, and I might just spare the town yet."

"I'm not tossing a loaded gun into the street. I'm going to take the bullets out and leave them in my truck."

"Does the good-guy stuff ever get tedious? Because the bad-guy stuff is still just as much fun after all these years. You should consider a career change."

Murph made a show of emptying the weapon and stashing the bullets in his glove compartment, sneaking out his smaller backup gun and the ankle holster at the same time. He pretended to drop a bullet. Swore so Asael could hear him, then ducked and fastened the holster under his blue jeans.

Then he opened his door and tossed his main weapon under his car.

"Phone next," the hitman ordered.

Murph ended the call, lowered the phone to his lap, snapped it out of its thick protective case, and hid it in his boot. Then he tossed the protective case under the car too. He hoped Asael wouldn't be able to tell the difference from the distance, that the man would see a flash of something small and black and the right shape, and his brain would fill in the rest.

Murph got out immediately after, to keep Asael's attention on himself.

The Altima waited for him as promised, a hand-drawn map on the dashboard. The hastily scribbled drawing showed the old industrial park as his destination. Made sense. In hindsight.

The parade floats were stored in the empty warehouses out there.

Murph hadn't thought of the place, exactly because of that. Crews were coming and going all day. But that could work for Asael too, couldn't it? If he'd found a way to blend in.

Murph had to drive around the streets that were closed for the festivities, but even with the detour, he was at the location the X on the map specified in fifteen minutes.

The building was perhaps the smallest on the sprawling lot. According to the sign on the side, it had housed an antique repair/storage shop at one point, but with its peeling paint and the weeds reaching halfway to the roof, it looked long abandoned.

The shop was surrounded by larger warehouses, the ones that

housed the floats. They must have been a bustle of activity an hour ago, but now they were deserted, the crews at the parade with their creations.

Murph pulled to a stop behind a building a hundred feet from his destination, out of sight, then he ran in a half circle in whatever cover he could find, to get himself behind the old antique repair place, marked by X on Asael's map.

At the back wall, he pulled out his phone and texted Cirelli his location, then he dropped his phone into the bushes. If Asael managed to drop a dime on him, Murph didn't want the bastard to know that reinforcements were on their way.

I'm coming, Kate.

Murph climbed up the cement block wall, just enough mortar missing from between the old blocks for a fingertip or toehold here and there.

He was on the corrugated metal roof in under two minutes, thanking the wind that made enough noise to cover him as he bent down over the edge to the aluminum vent. His pocket knife came in handy to unscrew three corners of the vent cover.

He worked slowly, stopping frequently, trying to coincide with the wind brushing the branches of a couple of dogwoods against the siding below him. Once three screws were removed, he rotated the vent cover on the fourth, and just like that, it was out of his way, yet secured, not falling off, not making a sound. Since the bug screen—to keep out creepy crawlers—was glued to the back of the vent cover, that too went with it.

If the attic fan box were the standard twelve-inch residential size, he would have been shit out of luck. The industrial building, however, had an industrial-size fan, twenty-four by twenty-four inches. Not a particularly spacious fit, but not an unsurmountable challenge for Murph.

Since the hot days of summer were long gone, the fan wasn't on—another piece of good luck. Murph unfastened it, then pushed in one side, enough so he could grab the plastic-coated wire, and then, using that, he quietly lowered the fan against the wall on the inside.

The roof's edge pressed against his groin as he slipped a little lower. He ignored the discomfort. His focus was on finding Emma and Kate.

He stuck his head in the hole.

A man wearing blue overalls stood inside the front door, gun in hand.

Asael.

Murph's fingers itched to put a bullet through the guy's head then and there. There were at least two problems with that, however.

One: His backup weapon was a Glock G19, a nice compact 9mm with excellent accuracy up to fifty yards or so. Unfortunately, Asael stood at close to three times that distance, across the warehouse.

Two: Murph didn't know where Kate and Emma were. He couldn't kill Asael until he got the location out of the bastard.

The building was one open space, except for a small area portioned off with a Sheetrock wall in the back. Could be storage, could be stairs leading to a lower level. Maybe Emma and Kate were down there, maybe they weren't. Taking Asael would have to wait until Murph had eyes on the women.

He twisted so his shoulders would fit through the opening, shoved, then pulled, working himself through silently, until he was lying facedown on the main support beam.

Shelves lined the walls, filled with boxes, most of which were taped shut. The few that were open held myriad spare parts, work overalls, and cans of varnish. Nothing that screamed *possible weapon.*

Murph measured up the nearest shelf to see if he could lower himself onto it, but it wasn't tall enough. None of them were. He'd have to jump, and he'd make too much noise, possibly knock the whole shelf over. Asael might open fire. Then Murph would have to shoot back. And he might accidentally kill the bastard too soon.

Below, the hitman stepped up to the door, looked out, then moved back inside again.

Murph shoved his gun into the back of his waistband, then crawled toward his target. The spur-of-the-moment plan was to get right above Asael, drop down on him, take his weapon, then do what it took to make him give up the women's location. Murph was prepared to get as creative as he had to be, had no qualms whatsoever.

When he switched to a cross beam and finally reached the right spot with Asael directly below him, Murph lowered himself until he hung from the beam by his arms. This was as far as he could go with stealth. Up to this point, his success had depended on silence. From here on, it would depend on speed and skill.

He let go, dropping, but Asael stepped toward the door again at the same time. Instead of landing on top of him, Murph landed right behind him. Instead of Asael breaking Murph's fall, nothing took the shock of hitting the cement floor from thirty feet up.

Murph ended up on one foot and one knee, pain shooting through him. Then Asael's gun was at his forehead.

Murph's weapon—he *had* managed to pull it—was pointed at Asael's groin—as high as he had time to raise it. "Standoff."

"A standoff would indicate equal sides," Asael said in a droll tone. "I have bargaining chips. You don't."

"Then let's bargain." Murph overcame the pain enough to stand and straighten, keeping his weapon pointed at Asael. The only reason his ankles weren't broken was because he'd put on his old Army boots that morning. He gave thanks to whoever designed them to handle shock. "I want Emma and Kate."

"You toss your weapon, come downstairs with me, and I promise I'll let you see them."

"Are they in the basement?" Say *yes*, and it's game over.

"No. You can't just shoot me and free them. They're nowhere around here."

"Where are they?"

"You go downstairs with me, and I'll tell you. Then we negotiate."

Play for time.

Murph had sent Cirelli the address ten minutes ago. FBI agents would be on their way by now.

"All right." Murph had plenty of hand-to-hand combat training. Even without the gun, he'd be hardly defenseless.

He tossed his weapon as far as he could so Asael couldn't just pick it up. The Glock landed halfway across the warehouse.

Asael pointed toward the door in the back. "After you."

Murph strode ahead, then down the stairs. No Kate. No Emma. Asael hadn't lied about that. Nothing down there but workbenches. And the one set up under the light in the middle made the short hairs stand up at the back of Murph's neck.

"I have a client who is willing to pay generously for a live performance," Asael said behind him.

Play for time.

"Like what?" Murph walked farther in.

The hitman stopped to his left, leaving plenty of room between them, so Murph couldn't grab his gun. He was a murderous bastard, but he wasn't an idiot. "Let's call it an endurance test."

He pulled what Murph recognized as a detonation device—with a dramatic red button in the middle—from his pocket. He put it away and pulled out his phone next, scrolled, then turned it toward Murph.

The image on the screen showed Kate, tied up and staring into the camera with wide-eyed terror, crammed into a narrow wooden space, surrounded by two-by-fours and plywood.

Ice spread through Murph, a deadly calm. Because hot fury wouldn't be useful to Kate. "I'm going to kill you."

"I don't think you will."

"Where is Emma?"

"They're together. I wouldn't separate sisters."

That setup…the two-by-fours, the plywood… "They're in a parade float." *Shit.* "The captain got your picture. He figured it out." Murph bluffed. "Broslin PD are already there. And so is the FBI. They got in earlier today."

"There are two dozen floats. I have five devices, hidden where they can't be seen without the whole structure being taken apart. Same with your girlfriend and her sister. Those floats were put together in the warehouse next door. I had access to them for half an hour when there was a small fire." Asael's smile was calm and confident. "How long before your friends start taking apart the floats and come across the float with Kate and Emma inside? An hour is my guess. You spent fifteen minutes driving here, then fifteen crawling in through the back."

"What do you want?"

"You lie on that table and let me entertain my client. I will not push the red button for as long as you last. Hang in there for more than half an hour, and Broslin PD or the FBI will probably find the women. Grit your teeth and show me how tough you are. Buy their lives with your blood. That's the deal."

Murph had been a small-town cop and soldier with the Army Reserves. He was a simple guy at heart. Protect the weak. Eliminate the bad guys. He didn't think in elaborate evil plans. He sure as hell hadn't seen this coming.

The problem with fucking evil geniuses was that they were geniuses.

Bottom line: He would die to save Kate and Emma. That wasn't even a question.

He walked to the workbench. *The FBI is on their way.* He lay down and put his feet and hands through the prepared restraints. The cold neon light above blinded him. He had to squint.

Asael came over and tightened the straps.

"Think of it as a chance to test yourself," he said as he set up his phone to livestream, then shoved it into his chest pocket, the camera on top free and unobstructed. "Are you as tough as you think you are? In the next half an hour, you will have your answer."

And then he put away his gun and picked up a box cutter.

CHAPTER THIRTY-ONE

Kate

"No, no, no, no, no!" Kate's protest came out as "Nnnnnnnn" because her mouth was taped shut.

She lay wedged tightly between sheets of plywood, in a dark space, paralyzed from the drug Asael had made her inject into her arm. It hadn't been a sedative as he said. It was a paralytic.

Normally, she didn't mind dark, tight places. When she was young, she used to hide from the monster's beatings in the gap behind the washer. But this current hole reminded her a coffin. And if that wasn't enough, Emma suddenly kicked her on the head.

"Mmmmmmmmmmm," came from that direction.

Oh good. Maybe Emma's shot was wearing off. It'd be nice if at least one of them had working muscles.

Then Kate felt a tingling in her limbs, and her control returned too, little by little. Of course, she still couldn't crank her neck back far enough to check on her sister, and even if she could, there was precious little light to see by. Only a thin sliver filtered through a crack over her knee, just enough to make out the phobic dimensions of the space, and the red light blinking on a familiar black device at her feet.

Their deadly prison was moving. And outside, people cheered. After Asael had put them in the back of his van, once they lay in there unable to move or speak, he'd driven them over to the warehouse next door and stuffed them into the internal scaffolding of a parade float.

Death was his verdict, he'd said. But death was too fast. *This,* the anticipation—lying paralyzed for hours while Kate waited to be blown to pieces, knowing her sister was going to be blown up with her, along with friends who were there for the parade, knowing Murph was on the torture table in the basement—was the true punishment.

Kate didn't have enough space to pull back either her hands or her feet to bang on the wood, to make a sound loud enough to be heard over the roar of the souped-up engine of the truck that pulled the float, over the cacophony of the parade. So she banged her head on the wood under her. The volume was pitiful and not worth the pain.

Emma kept squirming, then there was a ripping kind of sound, then Emma said, "Brush the side of your cheek against your shoulder like you're trying to wipe it until you curl up the edge of the tape."

"Mmmmmm."

Minutes passed before Kate succeeded, then more time before she rolled the tape off enough to speak. "Are you all right?"

Instead of responding, Emma shouted, "Help!"

Kate joined her sister. "Help!"

Nobody responded. Nobody heard them over the marching band that burst into music nearby.

Emma kept wiggling and kicked Kate in the head again. "Sorry."

"I'm going to turn over. Let me see if I can untie your feet with my teeth." They had to shout now, just to hear each other.

"Okay."

Kate banged the crap out of her shoulders doing that, but then she was in position and tore at what felt like plastic clothesline. "I'm going to lose some teeth."

"Keep going," Emma said. "Murph will love you even

toothless."

Kate didn't pause to comment on that. She didn't know how much time they had left. The damn device didn't have those convenient little countdown numbers like in the movies.

By sheer dumb luck, she yanked the right spot, and the rope gave. Then she pulled back so Emma could shuck off the restraints.

"Kick up," she told her sister. "As hard as you can."

Emma did.

Crack.

"Again."

Emma didn't have to be told twice.

And then something popped, and the top busted. More dark space opened up above them, with a few more slivers of light. Kate pushed with her tied feet and hands. Until she was able to sit up at last, just as the float stopped moving and a loud murmur went through the crowd outside.

Emma was tearing at the rope around her wrists with her teeth, but paused long enough to ask, "What is it?"

"I don't know." Kate attacked her own restraints.

Emma finished first, then helped.

They were at the core of the float, inside the platform, a forest of two-by-fours and plywood around them, forming chimneys above. That seemed like the easiest way out.

"Up. Move." Kate nudged Emma toward one rabbit hole while she wedged herself into another.

It was a tight fit, but Kate wiggled up until she saw something above that was thin enough to let light through. Hope hammered at her heart. *Papier mâché.*

She braced her feet, then burst through headfirst and found herself in another enclosed structure for a second, this one yellow and sparkly. Then that fell away in sections, and she was out in the open. People were clapping.

She'd come through a giant daffodil—probably the Longwood Gardens float—and sat there for a second in the middle of the yellow petals like a demented ninja fairy while people cheered, thinking her part of the spectacle.

Then Emma broke through in a tulip next to her, and people

cheered louder.

Kate gulped the fresh air, leaning closer to Emma so she could shout into her sister's ear. "Find the police! Tell them about the devices. Then find Mom and Dad and make sure they're safe."

She was already sliding to the ground when Emma called after her. "Where are you going?"

"Back to the warehouse to warn Murph."

Kate dove into the confused crowd and yelled, "Bomb! Run!"

A panicked wave of people carried her forward, everybody shouting. A sign of the times that nobody for a second thought it was a prank. Which, actually, was damn lucky.

Kate separated from the mob at the first alley, darted through, then ran like the crow flies, through front lawns and back gardens. If she were at the Olympics, they would have given her a gold medal in hurdle jumping.

She didn't stop until she was at the industrial park, dozens of hangars and warehouses occupying several acres.

She ran around, desperate.

Then she caught sight of an old sign on the side of a building in the distance to the left, a logo with a colonial-style sideboard and faded letters above it. Nowak's Antiques.

Heart banging, lungs fighting for air, she took off toward that.

* * *

Murph

"I wouldn't mind a coffee break." Murph stretched the restraint that held his right hand to the table. The progress was maddeningly slow, one millimeter at a time, but it was progress. Asael only half paid him attention. He was discussing with his client what they should do to their torture victim next.

He'd started by cutting off Murph's clothes and made such a theatrical performance out of it, it took at least three or four minutes. Fine with Murph. But then the rest was rougher. Asael had tried every tool he had on Murph's skin for sharpness, slashing at least two dozen cuts of various depths. And that still wasn't anything serious, just a test before they got going.

The distant client had an obsession with pliers. So far, Murph was missing a thumbnail and one of his bottom teeth. Both had been extracted with excruciating slowness, as if Asael couldn't bear rushing the performance. Both had been saved in a jar so they could be mailed to the client later as keepsakes.

Murph focused on his breathing to block the pain. His body was brimming with adrenaline, so that helped. He turned his head sideways and spat blood on the floor. He was lying flat on his back and didn't want to choke.

The client made up his mind. "Cut off his balls."

Asael looked at Murph.

Murph said, "Let's not be rash."

Where the hell is the FBI?

Probably at the parade, and Murph couldn't blame Cirelli. The lives of thousands of people were at stake. All hands were needed there. He hoped they'd found Emma and Kate.

Asael picked through his instruments of torture and lifted a carving knife with a smile. "How is this?"

"Better find something bigger." Murph slurred a little because his mouth was swollen. "Match the size of the tool to the size of the job."

"I didn't think this would be so entertaining." Asael sounded genuinely pleased. "I might do it again. Of course, I might not find another one like you."

The hitman had started out with sneering arrogance and cold-blooded assholery, but the more Murph endured, the more the guy had warmed to him.

The most surreal part was how much he seemed like just a regular guy, going about an average job. The way the FBI had talked about him, Murph had expected more of a TV villain, a flamboyant psychopath.

If they'd run into each other at the Broslin Diner, Murph wouldn't have looked at the guy twice. Maybe that was how it worked. Why he'd never been caught.

Asael picked up an antique screwdriver and held out the

wooden handle toward Murph. "Want something for biting down?"

"Your carotid artery."

Asael laughed. He set the tool down. "I guess then just relax. I don't know if that makes it hurt less or not, but that's what the doctors always say."

Every muscle in Murph's body clenched tight, then tighter yet when Kate stole soundlessly down the stairs, stopping a dozen feet behind the unsuspecting hitman. She had Murph's backup weapon in her hand.

Oh hell, love. You shouldn't be here.

Murph hadn't broken down through the whole torture, but he almost did at the sight of her. And not just because her right eye was purple and nearly swollen shut. Although, somebody was going to die for that.

Don't hesitate.

Like I showed you. Feet apart. Both hands on the weapon. There you go, honey. Aim for center mass. Don't give the fucker time to turn around.

That was the key. Except, civilians always hesitated. Killing another human being went against instinct. Most decent people needed a few seconds to override their lifelong beliefs.

Kate was the most decent, kindest person Murph had ever met.

Shoot. He silently begged her. *Don't think. Drop the bastard dead.*

He held his breath.

Shoot!

He flexed his arm, almost out of the damn restraint. He needed another minute, time he wasn't going to get.

Asael picked up the carving knife again. Then he paused.

Run!

Kate pulled the trigger.

Perfect hit. The bullet went in through Asael's back and tore a chunk out of his chest in the front. The hitman's eyes snapped wide with surprise, then he staggered forward and fell on Murph, nearly stabbing him in the liver.

"Left pants pocket!" Murph shouted.

Kate lunged forward, pinned the guy in place with her body weight, and got the detonation device. Then she let Asael fall, trembling and panting, looking as if she was on the verge of a panic attack.

"There's a toggle on the side." She looked at Murph, eyes impossibly wide, voice shaking. "In the Off position. I don't think it was armed." She showed it to him before gingerly setting it down on the workbench above his head.

"Breathe. It's over. You did it." He yanked his hand free at last. "Hell of a shot."

She put the safety back on the gun, laid that next to the detonator, then attacked Murph's other restraints. "You're okay."

"Then why are you crying? Do I look that bad?"

"No," she lied through her teeth as she freed him.

He sat up, and the cuts on his chest pulled, but he ignored the pain. He couldn't take his eyes off Kate. *Safe*. She was safe. Asael was dead.

"Did he hurt you?" He swung his legs over the side of the table and slid off, went to his knees next to Asael and grabbed the phone from the man's shirt pocket.

He looked into the camera.

"Show's over, Fucker. Now I'll be coming for *your* balls next." Then he turned the phone off. He had no time to waste on the bastard. "Where's Emma?" he asked as he stood. "Is she all right?"

"She's fine. I'm fine." Kate's voice cracked. She hugged him carefully. Held him with heartbreaking tenderness. "I was so scared I wouldn't reach you in time."

"I swear my heart stopped when you popped up behind him." Murph luxuriated in the sheer relief of having her safe. "Let's not do this again."

"Deal." Kate pulled away, and Murph glanced down at the gaping hole in Asael's chest, at his blank, frozen face. The bastard had gotten off too easy. "He died so damn fast, it's almost anticlimactic."

"And that's a bad thing?"

"I'd be lying if I said I didn't hope for some last-minute hand-to-hand combat between the two of us."

She flashed him an incredulous look. "You got Mordocai. I got Asael. That's how partnerships work. We share."

Partnership. Murph liked the sound of that. "Screw him." He picked up his gun. "Let's go."

Her gaze slid to his chest. She flinched. "I think I should call an ambulance for you."

"I'm not going to the hospital over a broken fingernail." He swallowed the blood running down his throat.

"Ripped out fingernail. Among other injuries." She scooped his clothes up from the floor, started to hand them over, but then noticed the shape they were in and dropped them again. "Now what?"

He pulled her back, careful not to get blood on her, although, she didn't seem to care. God, he'd missed this—the smell of her, the feel of her, her pliant softness. "I'm naked and I have a beautiful woman in my arms. Sounds like the beginning of something great."

He kissed her cheek and wiped off the small smudge of blood his lips left behind. He'd forgotten about his tooth there for a second. Dammit, he wanted to kiss her. Badly. So much that it hurt to have to hold back. "Sorry."

Before she could respond, an explosion shook the ground, startling them apart.

"The bombs were on a timer." He swore. "The detonator was for show. Let's go."

She grabbed his arm. "Naked?"

"There are work overalls upstairs."

She pressed her lips together, as if marshaling her arguments, but in the end, she nodded. "You clean up in the bathroom under the stairs, and I'll find you something to wear."

She took off, and he headed to the bathroom. When he caught sight of himself in the chipped mirror over the sink, he did a doubletake. He looked like an extra from a B-rated horror flick. Blood covered his chin. His chest too, from all those cuts. He looked like someone had tried to skin him.

Okay. So kissing Kate would definitely have to wait.

He washed off and used an ancient roll of paper towels on the sink to dab himself dry. Some of the cuts still oozed, but nothing was gushing.

By the time he left the small bathroom, Kate was there with a pair of worn blue overalls and a first aid kit. "Found it on the wall by the front door, next to the fire extinguisher."

She handed him the clothes first. "Relatively clean. I shook out the dust, but you're going to have to bathe in disinfectant at the earliest opportunity. Hope you know when you got your last tetanus shot."

Murph kicked off his boots—which Asael had left on—then stepped into the much-needed covering and pulled it up. He slipped Asael's phone into his pocket. "That's going straight to the FBI."

"You think they can track down the guy on the other end of the call?" Kate held out the first aid kit.

Murph waved it away, yanked up the front zipper of his overalls, then put his boots back on. "I trust Cirelli to give it a hell of a good try."

Then he headed back to the table, stepped over Asael, accidentally kicking him in the head, and grabbed the bloody jar. He picked out his tooth, put it over the hole in his mouth, and bit down to force the root back into place.

Hurt like a sonofabitch, but it seemed to stop the bleeding.

Kate rushed to him. "What are you doing?"

When Murph turned, he accidentally kicked Asael in the head again. Accidentally even harder. "If you get a tooth knocked out, sometimes it can be saved if you put it back." He went for the stairs. "You have a car up front?"

"I ran."

"All the way?" He was never going to be able to thank her enough. She'd come back for him. God, he loved her. And the second they had a minute alone together... "I have an Altima stashed around the corner. I'll take you home where you'll be safe, then I'll head over to see what I can do to help at the parade."

"I'm not the kind of woman who stays home safe while others are being hurt." She kept up with him. "Especially when my sister and parents could be in danger. I'll drive. And you're not getting out of the car."

He smiled at her as they stepped outside. Then snapped his mouth closed. His teeth were probably bloody. "I'm not the kind of guy who doesn't get out of the car."

"I know." She smiled back at him. "It's one of the things I love about you."

That last thing she said made a lot of Murph's pain go away. "We're going to talk about this at the earliest opportunity. Right now, I have to grab my phone." He hurried around the building.

The second he had the phone in hand, he called Cirelli. "I'm all right. I'm with Kate," he said as he headed back to her. "Asael is dead."

"Where the hell are you?" Cirelli demanded. "I sent agents to the location you texted."

"They didn't come."

A pause while Cirelli talked to someone on the other end. "There are two Nowak's Antiques. Their old place and their new place. I'm sorry, Murph. How dead is Asael?"

"Bullet through the heart. Would be hard to be deader. I gotta go." Murph hung up and ran toward the car with Kate next to him.

"You're bleeding through your overalls." She grabbed his wrist. "Give me the phone. I'm calling 9-1-1."

He glanced at the dark stain spreading on his chest. "It's barely anything. I'm sure the ambulances are busy." Then they were at the car, the key still in the ignition, thank God. He stopped with his hand on the roof. "Tell me you know I love you and it has nothing to do with forced proximity or any other bullshit, and I promise to heal instantly."

"What if I just activated your protective instincts, which, let's face it, are pretty overdeveloped from having been a police officer and a soldier?" She pushed him out of the way to get to the driver's-side door. "I'm driving."

He went around to the passenger side. "First of all, I'm hurt that my protective instincts are the only overdeveloped thing I have that you noticed." He got in. "Second of all, I've protected plenty of people when I worked in the PD, and plenty of people when I was in the Reserves. A lot of them were women. I never felt about any of them like I feel about you. So, please, give me some credit here that I know my own mind."

"Okay." She turned the key in the ignition.

He stared at her. "Okay? Just like that? After putting me

through hell for the past three months?"

She swung the car around. "I could have lost you for real. Permanently. I don't want to live without you. Even if I could, I don't want to." She handed him the first aid kit from her lap. "Please bandage yourself up. I can't think when you're bleeding."

"We're starting over." He laid down the law as he rifled through the contents. "Once a month, we're going to have a fight. We're not breaking up again because you get worried that we never argue. We'll have a spirited disagreement about something. And then we'll have makeup sex."

God, he couldn't wait to get his hands on her.

"We're in the middle of an emergency." She reproached him, but didn't sound terribly offended. "Don't look at me like that."

CHAPTER THIRTY-TWO

Kate

"Are you sure you're all right?" Kate glanced at Murph as she drove.

She'd gotten to him in time. Murph was alive, and Asael was dead. Little else mattered.

"Good as new." He finished bandaging the thumb with the missing nail. He'd already slapped Band-Aids on all the cuts on his chest. "What I want to know is, how did Asael get you? How the hell did he get past Hunter?"

She winced. "He didn't. I did."

And then she explained to Murph how all that happened.

He grew quieter and quieter, a tornado brewing on the passenger seat.

She told him about the part when Asael had forced her to inject herself and Emma. "Some kind of paralytic, but I'm not sure what."

"What the hell?" His voice was low, tight, dark. "What the…" He shook his head as if he didn't trust himself with more. "Kate…"

"I know! Okay? What other choice did I have? He was pointing a gun."

"You shouldn't have been there in the first place. What were you thinking? Why would you risk yourself like that?"

"I had to try to save Emma. Like you had to come to save me. Like I had to come back to save you."

He looked away from her, out the windshield, as if he didn't trust himself to look at her. She had a feeling this wasn't the last fight they were going to have about the subject.

Then, thank God, they were as close to Main Street as Kate could get. Temporary reprieve.

She parked, and they both shot out of the car, hurrying through the barricades while throngs of people were coming from the opposite direction, looking rattled, everybody talking. Nobody seemed alarmed by the dark blood splotches on Murph's chest. Then again, on the blue of the overalls, they could easily be mistaken for oil stains. But Kate knew the truth, and every time she looked at him, she could have shot Asael all over again.

Maybe one day she'd feel guilty over taking a life, but that day was in the far distant future. She was pretty sure she'd be dead herself before that happened.

They had to pause in crossing a side street to let a fire truck pass.

Murph took her hand. "I love you."

Her heart turned over in her chest. Emotions rushed her. A tear rolled down her cheek.

"I'm pregnant." *Aw, dammit.* She should have told him sooner. She should have started with that.

One second of stunned staring, then a smile that made her heart melt, then a drill sergeant look came over Murph's face, and he turned her right around. "I'm taking you to the hospital."

"You're crying."

"Men cry now. It's the twenty-first century." Exasperation thickened his voice. "Dammit, Kate. You were drugged. You've been through trauma. You're pregnant…"

"I keep forgetting." But he was right. Arguing with him would have been stupid, and she wasn't stupid. "I'll go to the bed-and-breakfast. Emma was supposed to find Mom and Dad. They're probably there. Be careful," she added, then stepped into his arms and kissed his jaw, on the side that wasn't hurt. "The baby and I need you back in one piece, so don't take any chances."

His arms tightened around her, his gaze searching her face. "Okay. Let's summarize. We're okay. We're having a baby. And you love me. Just to make sure I didn't misunderstand anything."

"Yes."

"Thank fuck. I want to kiss you more than I want my next breath, but my mouth tastes like blood, so… Rain check?"

"Rain check."

She watched as he ran off toward danger. Then she ran in the opposite direction, toward the bed-and-breakfast.

At least two dozen people crowded the lawn, the front door wide open. Shannon O'Brian was directing everyone, her gray bun wagging in the air as her head moved back and forth. "Minor injuries inside! We have first aid kits. Serious injuries stay out here. Ambulances are on their way."

The carpet that used to be in her foyer covered the grass to the left of the front door, several people sitting or lying on it, one woman holding her arm, another tilting her face so someone could press a wad of gauze to a deep gash on the woman's face.

When the Good Samaritan stepped aside, Kate spotted Emma behind her and hurried over, grabbed Emma's arm.

"Are you all right?" She scanned her sister for injuries, found none, and breathed a little easier, threw her arms around Emma for a moment. Then she had to let go, because Emma was pressing a tea towel to a man's bleeding temple.

"Thank God, you're here," she said. "I wasn't near the explosion. I was halfway down the street by then. How is Murph?"

"I got to him in time. He's right back in the thick of it. Asael is dead. Where are Mom and Dad?"

"Helping inside. Worried sick about you. Go talk to them."

So Kate went.

And there they were, in the living room, in the middle of the bustling mess. Everybody she loved accounted for. Tears sprung to her eyes all over again.

"Mom! Dad!"

"Oh my God, honey. Your eye! You and Emma both." Ellie

Bridges shook her head and looked near weeping. "Are you all right? Murph?"

"Injured but alive. He's off to save the world, because, you know, he's Murph."

Tears did roll then, from all parties involved. A hoarse "Sweetheart" from her father. A round of tight, tight hugs, but no more. The need around them was too great.

"Here." Kate's mother handed her a roll of bandages and pointed at Linda Gonzales, who was sitting on a chair and holding her wrist. "Can you help that woman?"

"Linda!" Kate rushed over. "What happened?"

"The explosion knocked me down." Her hair stuck out all over the place. "I used my hand to brace myself."

"Do you think it's broken?"

Linda rolled her wrist. "I don't think so. Have you seen Tony? Do you know if he came to the parade?"

"Mr. Mauro? Definitely not. Still at the hospital. How about I stabilize your injury, then you'll have the EMTs take a look when they get here?"

"Sounds like a plan. I'm really glad you're here."

Kate began rolling on the bandage, firmly enough to hold any pulled ligaments, but not so tight that it would restrict circulation. She tucked the end of the bandage in, then patted Linda's shoulder. "All set."

"Thank you. I'll go outside and wait for that ambulance."

Kate was going to walk her out, but a little boy with a badly scraped knee took the chair, confidently announcing, "I'm next."

Kate's father came by and handed her and the boy bottles of water from a plastic bucket, kissed her on the temple. "I don't know what I would have done if anything happened to either of my girls."

Kate gave him a quick hug. "I love you, Dad."

Then she knelt in front of the boy. "Are you okay? I'm Kate. What's your name? How old are you?"

"Zak. I am seven." He eyed the peroxide warily. "I was running, and I fell. I can't find my mom."

"I'm sure she'll be here by the time I fix you up and find you a snack in the kitchen. You know Broslin—somebody probably already saw you here and called her."

The boy nodded with a serious expression. "Like how Mrs. Moses told her that she saw me skipping school?"

"Exactly like that." Kate caught him glancing at a jar of glass eyes on the windowsill. "Have you ever been in here before?"

He shook his head.

"How cool are those eyes?" she asked as she cleaned the dirt from his wound.

He winced, but then he said, "Creepy cool. You think I could touch one?"

"I bet Mrs. O'Brian wouldn't mind. I'll ask her for you when we finish here."

Kate found some antibiotic cream in an open first aid kit on the floor a few steps away and dabbed that on, Zak taking it like a soldier. Then she hunted down an oversized Band-Aid and covered the still-seeping wound.

"Zachary!" A disheveled woman who had the boy's blue eyes just about flew through the room to reach them.

"Mom!"

She hugged him fiercely first before examining every inch of him, then turning to Kate. "Is he okay?"

"Just the abrasion on his knee. I gave him first aid. He's as tough as a Navy SEAL."

Zak grinned at her, but the grin disappeared as his mother tried to pick him up. "Mom! You're embarrassing me."

"Sorry, baby."

"I'm not a baby!" He flushed. "Kate just said I'm as tough as a SEAL."

He looked to Kate for help.

She winked at him. "Actually," she told the mother, "I promised him a treat. If that's okay."

The mother nodded, tears in her eyes. And as Kate led Zak off toward the kitchen, the woman collapsed onto the chair her son had just vacated.

Kate liberated a cookie from the counter just as Shannon ran in. "We need more bottled water."

"I hope this is okay," Kate said, caught, literally, with her hand in the cookie jar.

"Of course. Hi, Zak. Take two."

"Thank you, Mrs. O'Brian."

"Also," Kate said, this seeming as good a time to push their luck as any, "I told him you might let him touch one of the glass eyes? He was very brave when I was picking dirt out of his wound."

Mrs. O'Brian was stuffing water bottles into the deep pockets of her knitted cardigan. "You can take one, if you want."

"For real?" Zak pumped the air, like he'd just found Willy Wonka's golden ticket. "Thank you, Mrs. O'Brian!"

Shannon had time for one last smile before she rushed on her way.

Zak eyed the mason jar with a dozen or so eyes on the shelf next to the pantry door.

Kate lifted it off for him. "Pick one."

"I want blue."

"Go for it."

He did, admired it for several seconds, then stashed it into his pocket before skipping out, perfectly contented.

Kate figured he wasn't going to show it to his mother until they were at home, in case Mom was of the opinion that they needed to give it back. But the second he reached the still-sniffing woman, he showed off his treasure.

"Look into my eye!"

The poor mother shrieked and almost tipped her chair over.

"Mrs. O'Brian gave it to me." Zak's grin kept growing until the smile took over his entire being.

A variety of responses flitted across the woman's face. She settled on "How wonderful."

Then she thanked Kate. And on their way out, she thanked Mrs. O'Brian, while Zak turned to wave.

"You've always been wonderful with children," Kate's mother commented from behind her.

"It's a good thing."

"Thinking about going back to pediatric treatment?"

Sounded like Emma hadn't told her the news yet. She'd probably thought Kate should be the one.

Kate turned and held her mother's gaze. She drew a deep breath and smiled. "Maybe someday. But not for a while. First, I'm going to be providing child care at home."

Her mother stared at her in confusion for a second, but only for a second. Then she screamed. Which gave the already shaken people in the B and B a heart attack, every head snapping to them and her father rushing over.

Then her mother shouted, "I'm going to be a grandmother!"

And that roused a round of clapping and cheers, while Kate's father collapsed into the chair Zak's mom had left available next to them.

"I'm going to be a grandfather?"

Kate kissed his clean-shaven cheek. "Yes, Dad."

The mood around them changed. People congratulated her. Her news managed to dispel the darkness and fear from the room.

"And how are things with Murph?" Kate's mother asked over her shoulder as she began cleaning up another patient.

"We're fine." Kate picked up a pile of soiled bandages and other discarded medical supplies. "I might have been a tad overemotional."

"You can be as emotional as you need to be. You're going through massive hormonal changes Murph doesn't have to deal with." Then her mother looked behind Kate, and her eyes snapped wide, worry washing over her face. "Oh my God. Is that blood on your overalls?"

Murph stepped up next to Kate and took her hand. "Brief encounter with a homicidal maniac." He smiled, and it was even brighter than when Zak had received the glass eye. "Hi, Ellie. Did Kate tell you I'm going to be a dad?"

CHAPTER THIRTY-THREE

Murph

Much, much later, when the last of the injured had either gone home or were taken to West Chester in an ambulance, Murph scanned the living and dining rooms of the bed-and-breakfast that looked like it had seen war, the furniture all over the place, empty bandage boxes littering the floor, along with empty water bottles.

"You all right?" Shannon came from the kitchen. "What a day. Let's not do this again anytime soon. Or ever." She leaned against the broom she carried. "Kate just ran up to take a shower. Room 202. The people who had it checked out and went home. I suppose that's understandable." She sighed. "What's the final tally?"

"About a hundred people injured. Nobody dead. There were multiple devices, but only one blew, the float that Kate and Emma had escaped. It helped that they yelled 'bomb' as they ran. People got out of there."

The rest of the devices had been found and disarmed in time, thanks to SEAL demo expert Dan Washington from Hope Hill. The mayor had better give the man a medal. In fact, Murph was going to make sure that happened.

"Nobody dead." Shannon repeated the words, as if she needed to hear them again. "Nobody dead."

Murph had been holding on to that thought for the past few hours since he'd last checked on Kate. Along with the thought that he was going to be a father.

"Let me help," he offered.

Shannon shook her head. "You see to Kate. I'm going to take my time down here. I need it to calm down. But you can help me with the furniture in the morning. You should stay."

"Yes, ma'am."

Shannon smiled. Clearly, he'd given her the right answer.

Murph ran upstairs and knocked on the door of room 202. "It's Murph."

The door opened. "I was just calling around trying to find

you."

"My phone battery went dead." He stepped inside, closed the door behind him, and pulled Kate into his arms. "I love you. I can't tell you how nice it is to be able to say that and not have you argue. I'm going to be saying it a lot."

"I'm going to be saying it a lot back."

He held her and held her. She was the perfect fit for him, the perfect partner, the perfect woman.

When he could finally let go, he still didn't let go all the way. He kept her hands. "Tell me again that you're pregnant."

"I'm pregnant."

"And you're feeling all right?"

"I'm feeling all right."

"Are you sure I don't need to take you to the hospital?"

"I'm not worried about me," she told him. "I'm worried about you."

He shook his head. "I walked some people over to Dr. Cameron's office. He took a look at me. Stitched me up. Drugged me up. I'm good to go. I'll call my dentist tomorrow." He smiled at her. "Right now, I feel no pain."

"One of the EMTs checked me out," she told him in return. "He said I looked all right. And I just called my ob-gyn. She asked a bunch of questions. She also doesn't think that the baby is in imminent danger at this stage, but she wants to see me first thing tomorrow morning."

"I'm taking you. I mean, can I take you?"

"Yes, please."

"You weren't sure if you wanted children. Are you okay with this? I thought you'd be more freaked out."

"The day's freak-out load is already pretty high. Maybe I just don't have room for more today. It could still hit me. But I don't think it will."

She laid her palm over her still-flat belly. "I'm happy about the baby. I figured it out in the basement of the repair shop. Actually, Emma figured it out for me." She smiled. "I wasn't about to give up before that, but once I knew in my heart that this baby was real…" She shook her head. "I can't explain it. The connection was instant.

Limitless love and fierce protectiveness. A switch flipped. This baby is mine, and I'm going to protect my child, always."

"You did. You escaped. You're the bravest woman I've ever known."

He brushed a kiss over her lips. He'd had a brief meeting with a large bottle of mouthwash at the doctor's office, so he figured it was all right. "I guess we won't know for a while if we're having a boy or a girl."

"We might find out tomorrow." She brushed a kiss back. "The doctor mentioned an ultrasound."

They grinned at each other like two lovesick fools.

Then her gaze dropped to the blood stain on his chest. "Now, honestly. How do you feel?"

"Like I'm the luckiest son of a bitch in the country."

* * *

Kate

"I'd like to name her Ellie after my mother," Kate said, pulling Murph farther into the room.

"I'm going to buy him one of those baby Jeeps." Murph indicated the size with his hands.

Did they even have toy cars that big?

"That's your first thought?" She laughed. "Boys and their toys."

"Not my first thought. My first thought, now and always, is that I want you."

The way his voice deepened and his gaze heated sent a delicious shiver down her spine. "I want you too. And I will have you, when you recover." Soon please. She was desperate to have her hands on his body. "You're in no shape right now," she said, more to herself than to him, to bolster her self-restraint. "You've been hurt."

"I'm fine."

"You're not fine. I—" She broke off when he took her hand

and put it on the undeniable proof of just how fine he was. "We shouldn't," she finished weakly.

He raised an eyebrow. "Are you trying to tell me what I can and cannot do with my own body?"

A desperate laugh bubbled up her throat.

"But only if you're sure you're okay," he told her. "You've been kidnapped. You're pregnant."

"At least I'm clean. I just took a shower."

"I cleaned up at the doctor's office, but I have to keep my stitches dry for a couple of days."

"I could always give you a sponge bath." Which might have sounded helpful and selfless, but really she just wanted to see him naked again.

"Definitely, yes. Later." He maneuvered her to the nearest flat surface, the wall behind her. "I'm going to undress you now."

"Then I'm going to undress you. I've never peeled you out of workman overalls before. It's sexy. Like plumber porn."

He narrowed his eyes at her. "What do you know about plumber porn?"

"Nothing?"

A sound of warning rumbled up his chest as he put his hands on her hips to hold her in place.

She squealed under his dark gaze, then confessed. "Allie's bachelorette party had a plumber stripper. He came to the door and pretended it was a repair call, then ripped his overalls off and—"

"I'm going to have to have a talk with Harper," Murph said with mock outrage.

"Later." Kate began divesting him of the overalls. Stopped. "Oh God."

She'd seen his cuts on the torture table, but not fully. His blood had covered them. Now they were out in the open. "How many stitches did you get?"

"What stitches?"

"You should lie down."

"Maybe for round two. Seriously, I'm fully anesthetized. I feel no pain. And I mean to do things before that changes." His intent gaze promised a wealth of pleasure.

"Why are you orange?"

"I've been swabbed with iodine."

"I feel like I'm about to make love to Garfield, the cat."

"Now that hurts my feelings." But he was struggling with a grin as his seeking fingers caressed her skin.

She didn't know what to say. Then, as he stood before her, naked, magnificent even in his battered and orange state, Kate remembered Linda's marital advice, and she made her eyes go wide with wonder. "How is that thing getting bigger every time I see it?"

Murph burst out in a shocked laugh. "Marry me."

She didn't have to think about it. "Yes."

God, the immolating look he gave her. The heat of it seared through her. And the endless love in it made her heart melt. Then she was naked too, and they were touching just about everywhere.

He only let her go to check her over. He was careful with her, tender, scrutinizing every inch of skin, swearing at every bruise, every scratch.

"I want to make love to you. But if you think we should wait—"

"Don't wait." She was weak, that was what she was. She wanted him with a desperate need. She couldn't even pretend to play hard to get.

"Are you sure?" he asked.

"Do you want me to beg?"

"After what you've put me through these past months? Definitely."

"Please." There. Apparently, she was also shameless.

He hooked her right knee over his hip and unerringly positioned himself at her opening, his boiling gaze holding hers. "I've missed you." He pushed inside, a tight inch, and her breath caught. They hadn't been together like this in three months. Her body needed to adjust to him being back.

He gave her time. Held.

Until she grew impatient at last. "Murph!"

That evil gleam was back. "I'm not going any farther until you say you're sorry for torturing me, and you promise not to torture me again. Promise that you're not going to change your mind before the wedding."

"Are you seriously blackmailing me while you're *inside* me?"

He didn't say anything. He held.

Fine. Time to find her backbone. They would just have to see who could hold out longer. She drew her hands from his neck and braced them on the wainscotting, a move that gave her more leverage and put enough distance between them so he could have a better view of her breasts.

His nostrils flared. "You don't fight fair."

He withdrew his hand from under her thigh and braced them on either side of her head.

Since she lost some of her support, she had to hold his waist tighter with her legs, but he would not let her pull him in. He stood his ground, even when her traitorous body squirmed for more of him.

His biceps bulged in her peripheral vision. His wide chest blocked the sight of the rest of the world. She didn't miss anyone or anything in it.

His head was tilted slightly down to hers, tendons protruding in his neck from the effort to hold the line.

"You're going to bust your stitches."

"I don't care." He was a hulking beast, piercing her with his hungry gaze, ready to devour her.

She wanted to be devoured, dammit!

Trouble was, she had no room to maneuver. She considered shoving off the wall and pushing herself onto him. She wanted, desperately, for him to fill her. But if she jumped on him and slid down on his…

What if she broke *it*?

For some reason, in the moment, she found the thought hysterical, and a peal of laughter escaped her.

His eyes narrowed dangerously. "You find this funny?"

She found none of it funny. With him pressed a single maddening inch inside her, she found everything *urgent*. She shook her head, pressing her lips together. "My emotions are all over the place. Do you think I'm hormonal?"

His eyes narrowed further. "Is this a trap? I don't think that's a word a man should ever say to a woman."

"Did they teach you that in some police self-defense class?" How were they still conversing? She was about to lose her damn mind, if he didn't fill her the next second.

"They should have. It's a shame how many things men are forced to find out about women the hard way."

A perfect pun floated somewhere in her brain about something else hard, but her brain was shutting down rapidly.

He bent his head closer.

Oh, a kiss. Yes, please.

Instead, he dipped lower, and sucked her nipple into his mouth. Her extremely *sensitive* nipple. Because, had she not mentioned, her nipples had been growing more and more sensitive lately—thank you, pregnancy.

He not only sucked the throbbing, aching peak of flesh, he sucked it in hard. And then he bit it.

Pleasure rushed through her, a blinding heat. When he sucked again, at a more leisurely pace this time, she nearly came.

She waved an imaginary white flag. "I promise I'm not going to change my mind about the wedding."

He was inside her before the last word left her lips. All the way. *Sweet truffle paradise.* Had he grown? She wasn't even joking.

Her body stretched to welcome him back. "I missed you. Does that sound stupid? We saw each other every day."

"Not like this," he said as he made love to her with a thoroughness that deserved a commemorative plaque, or a newspaper mention at the least.

When he dedicated his mind to something, he got the job done. That was Murph.

Her back bowed, her body drowning in pleasure. As she held on to his shoulders, she could barely gasp out the words, "Not like this."

Her body flew. Her mind cleared of all thought. For endless moments, she floated in bliss.

Then thoughts returned, one by one, awareness, little by little.

They'd met under unusual circumstances. They'd spent years in forced proximity. Shared danger had brought them together.

All true.

But as they walked to the bed—she refused to let him carry her—she acknowledged a greater truth yet. She sincerely and completely loved Murph Dolan. And she believed that he loved her. And suddenly it seemed incredibly stupid to have worried so much about how they'd gotten there.

She turned to him on the bed to tell him that.

He was watching her with some serious heat in his eyes.

"Now what?" she asked.

"I've been promised a sponge bath."

EPILOGUE

Kate

"You should have one of those fancy bridal umbrellas," Murph whispered after he kissed Kate in front of Pastor Garvey and all the dearly beloved who had gathered for their big day. "In case there's an unfortunate accident with the love doves."

"I haven't even worried about that until now," Kate whispered back. "Thanks."

Yet despite the fact that she'd been a ball of nerves all day, she did have a smile on her face as they turned around to the cheers of their family and friends.

Then the doves were released, a flutter of white wings that filled the sky. They circled above for a moment, the sunshine filtering through their feathers like some special effect in a movie or angels gathering to bless the ceremony. Until the birds took off for home, a local farm, as they were trained to do—a gift from Annie Murray, Hope Hill's ecotherapist who ran a growing animal sanctuary on the side.

Since nearly everyone in Broslin wanted to attend the fastest-arranged wedding in history, they held the event outside Broslin Chapel, aided by an unseasonably warm November day and outdoor heaters. The only person invited who hadn't come was Agent Cirelli—up to her eyebrows in work. The FBI had finally cracked Asael's phone and had his client list. Cirelli had sent her best wishes with a generous gift.

"I love you, Mrs. Dolan," Murph whispered into Kate's ear as they walked to the receiving line that had formed.

Every eye was on them. Except Kennan Finnegan's. Harper's brother, a US Marine in full dress uniform, only had eyes for the maid of honor. For once, Emma noticed the interest and seemed to return it.

That kept Kate smiling.

"My cheeks are going to hurt by morning," she told Murph under her breath.

Heat flared in his eyes.

She choked on shocked laughter. "Oh my God, you're such a pervert."

"I really think the word is *hopeful*," he responded with exaggerated innocence.

"We're practically in church. I'm wearing white!"

He wiggled an eyebrow. "But what are you wearing underneath?"

She couldn't respond because there were hands to shake and hugs and congratulations to accept. All she managed to do was whisper, "I'm going to get you back later."

Murph pressed a hand to his heart as he gazed at her. "I feel so married right now."

And that, of course, set her off laughing again, her nerves settling a little.

Her parents came first, and the hugs lasted forever.

Then Doug, Murph's brother, who also had his eye on Emma, though Kate doubted he was going to have any luck there.

Then Linda Gonzales and Tony Mauro stepped up. Together. As in *together*. A bewildering development.

Mr. Mauro was fully recovered, telling everyone who listened that Captain Bing had caught the idiot driver of the hit-and-run that morning. That crime, at least, couldn't be laid at Asael's feet.

Ashley Price and Jack Sullivan wished Kate and Murph happiness next.

"Thank you for your very generous gift, again," Kate told Ashley, who was becoming a known name on the global art stage. She and Jack had delivered one of her paintings the night before because it was too large to drag it to the reception.

The painting showed Kate's house, Murph and Kate walking through the front door together, holding hands. A single, breathtaking rose bloomed in her front yard in the painting's foreground. The title of the piece was a quote from Anaïs Nin. *"And the day came when the risk to remain tight in a bud was more painful than the risk it took to blossom."*

The art could probably pay for the baby's college education someday, but Kate would never ever sell it.

"Honestly, it's too much," she told Ashley. "But I love it, and I'm not going to give it back. You'd have to kill me first."

Ashley smiled, holding her own baby, while Jack herded their three older children. "It's yours. It's you. It was inspired by you. I could never sell it to someone."

They hugged again, then Allie Bianchi was next.

"Where is Harper?" Kate asked.

"I don't know. I don't care." Allie huffed. "You know what he told me while you were exchanging wows? At our wedding, he wants me to wear chaps."

"To be fair, your ass looks great in chaps." Kate grinned.

Allie rolled her eyes. "That's what he said."

Then Captain Bing came with Sophie. Since Murph's parents were gone, he'd stood in for father of the groom, although he wasn't that much older than Murph. It was the sentiment that counted.

Then Chase and Luanne and the kids. And the girls, in middle school, immediately announced that they loved Kate's dress and wanted to get married as soon as possible. Chase's hair was turning gray as he stood there.

Then Hunter and Gabi.

"Sorry," Gabi said as she hugged Kate. "Just got the call that there are four siblings at CPS in West Chester that need a family by tonight. We accepted them, so we want to drive over right now. I don't want them to be sitting there and wondering what will happen to them."

Kate hugged Gabi that much harder. "You're welcome to bring them to the reception."

"Thank you. But I think they need to settle in, just get to know us first, until they feel comfortable."

She was right, of course. Kate could still remember the despair and fear, the sheer overwhelmingness of each transfer. "When they're ready, we'd love to have you over for dinner. I could talk to them about my time in the system."

"I would love that. Thank you. I was actually going to ask."

Then Joe Kessler came to congratulate, with his wife, Wendy, and their kids. And it was a good thing Murph had been looking at

Kate all day like she was Venus reborn, because one could develop a serious inferiority complex when standing next to a professional model.

"You look ravishing," Wendy said, as if she could read Kate's thought.

"Thank you for doing my makeup."

Then Maria moved up the line. With her date. Who could have been…double-take…Jason Momoa's twin.

"He's a psychologist?" Kate asked her friend under her breath, and must have sounded stunned, because Maria laughed.

"Were you expecting an academic with wire-rim glasses?"

Kate had no idea what she'd expected. She just tried hard not to stare.

She was hugged and kissed a hundred times more as the line progressed. Then another hundred.

She was surrounded by friends. These were her people. This was her town. *Roots*. She had something in Broslin that she'd never had any place else.

For once, life was ridiculously, unexpectedly perfect. Even at work.

People credited the vets at Hope Hill with saving the town at the Mushroom Festival. Donations were pouring in. Hope Hill was going to get its zip-line course and so much more. Maybe even their first expansion, a whole new wing.

Too good to be true. Too good to last. Definitely don't deserve this. That exhausting voice that haunted survivors of childhood trauma had been whispering all day. But as Kate received warm hug after warm hug, she finally told the damn voice to stuff it.

Emma stopped by. "I love seeing you this happy."

"Thank you, sis. Hey, has anyone introduced you to Harper's brother yet? His name is Kennan."

Time passed in a blur. Kate only snapped out of the rose-colored fantasy at the reception when the bride and groom's first dance was announced and Murph led her out onto the dance floor in the middle.

"Why did I agree to this?" She panicked. "I can't do this."

Murph remained his own unflappable self. "You can."

"Oh God," she said as she looked over his shoulder. "Only like a hundred people are recording us on their cell phones."

Her muscles locked up. She wasn't like Allie, who could go on stage in front of an audience and reenact Calamity Jane for two hours. Kate wasn't a performer.

"Relax," Murph whispered into her ear. "Dance like nobody's watching."

"I can't."

He pulled her closer. Flush against him. Ran a hand down her back. Way down. And said in a rumbly voice, "Think of something else."

Oh. Well. She could pretty much guess what *he* was thinking about.

She cleared her throat. "How does that thing keep growing?"

And he laughed so hard, he nearly tripped over his own foot as they began to dance.

* * *

Dear Reader: We made it! The Broslin Creek Series is finished. It really is a bittersweet moment for me. If you're looking for your next read, please look at my book list https://danamarton.com/book-list. And if you do go online, would you pretty please leave DEATHTOLL a quick review?

Thank you so much for reading my stories. And for all the wonderful reviews. And for getting in touch via email or on FB. I appreciate your support and friendship beyond words.

Let's hope we meet again soon in another story.

Until then, I wish you all the best,

Dana Marton
Grateful Author

Made in the USA
Middletown, DE
22 December 2023

46592303R00144